Praise for *Four Minutes*

"*Four Minutes* by Nataliya Deleva reminded me that in my childhood I used to hide in a wardrobe, on a tree, in the attic and dreamed of an invisibility cap. In danger, I wanted to put on such a hat on my head, to disappear from the world, to hide in a safe space where no one would find me. Later, I realized that literature and imagination could offer such an invisibility cap. The narrator in *Four Minutes* thinks similarly. She collates excerpts from news articles, listens to her own (internal) voice, to the stories of people she meets on the way, looks into the past, confronts traumas and, pulling the reader out of their comfort zone, asks important questions about our world, about life in exile, about people who are excluded, abandoned, homeless. A beautiful, intricately woven and exciting book."

—Wioletta Greg, author of *Swallowing Mercury*

"*Four Minutes* is a novel about people on the margins of society. Different storylines interlace in order to tell one story: about invisibility. This is a book that grabs you by the throat, a poignant novel."

—Georgi Gospodinov, author of *The Physics of Sorrow*

"[*Four Minutes*] succeeds in making visible both the dignity and the intimate familiarity of lives lived on the fringes of a society that would much rather pretend they do not exist. A strong debut that uses gauzy impression to explore the harsh realities of post-communist Eastern Europe."

—*Kirkus Reviews*

"Deleva's heartrending debut tells the story of a woman scarred by her childhood as an orphan growing up in a group home in p̶̶̶̶communist Bulgaria."

"A difficult, poignant, important, really importar̶

—Marin Bodako̶

Library of Congress Cataloging-in-Publication Data: Available.
ISBN-13: 978-1-948830-37-9 / ISBN-10: 1-948830-37-X

This book has won the Elizabeth Kostova Foundation and Open Letter Books Novel Contest and has been translated with the support of the National Culture Fund-Bulgaria.

**ELIZABETH
KOSTOVA
FOUNDATION**
for creative writing

**National
Culture Fund
Bulgaria**

Printed on acid-free paper in the United States of America.

Cover Design by Eric Wilder
Interior Design by Anthony

Open Letter is the University of Rochester's nonprofit, literary translation press:
Dewey Hall 1-219, Box 278968, Rochester, NY 14627

www.openletterbooks.org

Four Minutes

Nataliya Deleva

Translated from the Bulgarian
by Izidora Angel

OPEN LETTER
LITERARY TRANSLATIONS FROM THE UNIVERSITY OF ROCHESTER

"The pages are still blank, but there is a miraculous feeling of the words being there, written in invisible ink and clamoring to become visible."

—Vladimir Nabokov

"I don't know why people are so keen to put the details of their private life in public; they forget that invisibility is a superpower."

—Banksy

"The world has lost its magic. They have left you."

—Jorge Luis Borges

"The famous curtainless windows of Amsterdam revealed the interior of the houses. These interiors in turn revealed the absence of private life. The sacred right to privacy had been reaffirmed paradoxically: through the sheer absence of it."

—Dubravka Ugresic, *The Ministry of Pain*

"The best refuge if one wishes to remain unseen, is to return to one's hometown."

—Georgi Gospodinov, *The Physics of Sorrow*

INSIDE THE ROOM, damp creeps into the corners, next to the shadows, next to me, as I sit on the cold floor, back pressed against the wall, shivering. We stay close, our bodies huddled next to one another, our breaths like ghosts, our stories—waiting to be heard. We don't occupy the space; we exist in its cracks. It is the absence of us, our abandonment that fills it in. At night, we lie awake invisible to the living, we stalk the mothers who left us behind, we haunt their dreams.

I hear a girl's voice from the next room over. At first she protests, *no, no, no* and her screams pierce the darkness, then the cries turn into weeping and her voice dies slowly in the night. I press my hands tightly to my ears to shut out the sounds but it's too late—the girl's voice is already trapped inside of me.

It's always the voices I recall, never the children's faces or their names, as though their physical existence had been an illusion. It is the echo of their lives, the invisible presence that, years after, still keeps me up at night.

"Mama, can I have some ice cream, please?"

"No, baby, not today."

"Why?"

"Because I said so."

"But I really want some, Mama, please!"

"No more whining, okay? You can't have ice cream every day, you'll get sick."

"*You* get to have ice cream whenever you want."

"I'm a grown-up."

"So?"

"Grown-ups are . . . adults. They know what's best for them and their children."

"Mama?"

"Yes, baby."

"Is it because I'm fat?"

"What?"

"You don't want to get me ice cream because you think I'm fat, right?"

"No, honey, why would you think that?"

"Because. I *am* fat."

"Says who?"

"Everybody."

"Who's everybody?"

4

"Everybody at school, the kids at the playground . . . everybody. They don't want to play with me, they ignore me."

"Don't listen to them, okay? People can be mean sometimes. But you have your friends, right? What about that girl, Megan?"

"You mean Maggie. She's not talking to me right now, either."

"Why not, sweetheart?"

"I told you—because I'm fat. And . . . because I ate her sandwich the other day."

"You did what? Why would you do that, baby?"

"I was hungry. I was worried about the math test and when I worry I get really hungry. And Maggie had left her sandwich sticking out of her backpack. Maybe she did it on purpose, to, you know, trick me. And I . . . I only wanted a bite . . . but then . . . it was so good, and our test was about to start . . . and I was so worried that I just couldn't stop myself. I ate the whole thing. When Maggie found out, she got so mad; she yelled at me in front of the whole class. I apologized to her, but . . . she stopped talking to me."

"Oh, no. Listen to me, sweetheart. We can't just take other people's food without permission, right? That's called stealing, and people who steal get punished."

"I know but . . . Okay, I won't do it again."

"Promise?"

"Promise."

"Mama?"

"Yes, sweetie."

"Why am I fat? I mean . . . you're tall and skinny. Was my father fat?"

"I don't want to talk about your father right now."

"Please?"

"He wasn't fat. Just big-boned. And tall."

"Was he handsome?"

"Can we please talk about something else?"

"Okay . . . But can I see him one day?"

"No, baby, sorry."

"Why not?"

"Because I haven't seen him in a very long time."

"Since you two made that mistake?"

"Don't say things like that!"

"You say things like that. I heard you talking to Aunt Tanche the other day. Was I a mistake, Mama?"

"Listen to me, sweetie. If you were a mistake, it was the most beautiful mistake of my whole life. Got it? I love you so, so much!"

"To the moon and back?"

"Yes, to the moon and back. And to the sun and back. And to every single star and back."

"I love you too, Mama. So can I have ice cream now? Pretty please?"

"Okay, okay. Just one scoop, though. What flavor do you want?"

1

That child was me.

But my mother wasn't there, I made it all up: my mother, the conversation, the ice cream. I wanted nothing more in the world than to walk beside a smiling mother, my little hand squeezed inside hers, happy in the knowledge that no matter what I did or said, or how much I begged her for ice cream, she would love me unconditionally, simply because I was hers. It wasn't even the stupid ice cream that I so desperately craved. I just wanted to walk down the street with my mom, pleading and pestering her for *something*, just as I'd seen all the other kids do.

I ached to leap into this glorified painting in my imagination, filled with whiny little kids always begging their seemingly strict yet inevitably relenting mothers for something, walking along streets that led to parks filled with mountains of ice cream, with yapping little Maltese dogs, their leashes rhythmically tugged by their silver-haired, bouncy-coiffed lady owners, with guys selling colorful Mickey Mouse and Winnie the Pooh helium balloons. I wanted it so badly, all that cotton candy and all those endless rows of park benches filled with young mothers bouncing and rocking their shrieking newborns with a mystifying calm, forcing you to taste their absolute love for the snotty babies tearing up the Saturday afternoon.

But that painting was mounted high up, out of reach; it hung from a rusty old nail, beguiling and unattainable and I was not part of it. So instead, I dreamt her up, imagining her smiling and angry, vibrant and tired, reproachful and soothing. My mother. Summoned by my fragile, seven-year-old imagination. But what I could never quite grasp was how a mother's love, so boundless and unconditional, could exist simply because a child did.

I do have a birth mother, like everyone else. She exists somewhere. She must, I'm sure of it: in some foreign painting that someone else carefully takes down from the wall, along with all that is contained within—all those children and ice cream and permed Maltese and balloons and cotton candy—and they all come alive. Every Saturday afternoon. Or maybe every other. My mother, despite her boundless and unconditional love for me, somehow found it in herself to omit me from that future watercolor. Then she had left. Left me alone inside an incubator, where I took my first breaths, cutting the sterile hospital quiet with my immature lungs and painfully inhaling the abandonment that would come to define me. I somehow sensed, even then, that my mother had vanished as soon as I'd appeared. She'd melted away like ice cream on a hot summer day.

So I imagined her instead.

2

My first conscious memory: I am three, maybe four. I am sitting on the floor of a dark room inside the Home. The room is neither big, nor small, and it reeks of dust and mold. Around me are children my age and some who are older. They pull at each other, shoving and screaming. I crawl into a corner and coil up like a snail, pressing my chin over my knees. I close my eyes and imagine that I disappear, that I become invisible to the others in the room, that I am able to observe the ruckus completely unnoticed. In that moment, I wish for something that, unbeknownst to me, is inevitable. For years afterward, I was certain that I alone willed my life to unfold as it did.

3

Sometimes, new moms arrived to choose one of us. Those were special days. For the moms, and for us. For the Matrons, too. They woke us up at dawn and bathed us, dressed us in clean clothes, changed the diapers of the littlest ones, mopped the floor of our playroom, and carefully arranged the scattered toys. It had the air of a holiday, like an International Children's Day that arrived several times a year. Lucky devils we were.

We strained our necks impatiently toward the director's office where our towering files mounted precariously on her gargantuan desk. But big as it was, the desk still couldn't fit us all.

Then came the moms and dads. They swung open the doors to our dark corner permeated by the smell of mold and soiled diapers, and summer came rushing onto our toys: smiling, dusty, breathless, sticky. When the stale heat settled back, each of us was torn between the urge to run over to a mother and beg her through tears to pick one, any one of us, and the urge to simply stand there, to demonstrate good manners so as to be liked, just as the Matrons taught us. Inevitably, we froze in place like stone crosses in an old cemetery, and waited. Everything slowed. Only a pair of flies buzzing over a child's toilet bowl in the corner embroidered the air.

It was always the mom who stepped forward first; the dad stood against the wall, wringing sweaty hands. The mother. She would choose. The woman unable to bear children of her own had come to take one of us back into her world. It was the law of the *matryoshka*—the Russian nesting doll—out of each, a girl is born; the girl grows up and produces a girl who one day becomes a mother by giving birth to yet another girl who eventually bears one, too. The infinite thread of life renewing the kinfolk. I wondered if the moms came here to save one of us or to find salvation for themselves.

It was always the mother who first braved to meet our pleading eyes and hers always dissolved in water. She approached us cautiously, tiptoeing around each one of us, reaching out to caress someone's disheveled head and with it generating a gust of life that broke the stale air. We got our dose of affection: from a stranger, someone else's mother. And we devoured it like caramel-frosted cake.

Then we looked on as the mother and the director discussed things back in the office, leafing through the dusty binders piled on that titanic desk, and the weight of it fell on us and crushed our heads like hollowed walnuts.

Salim

Salim hustles to the hospital. His mother's been there since last week. Shirtless and barefoot, he strides on the scorching July pavement, and his soles burn. Beads of sweat roll down his brown skin, but he brushes them off with the back of his hand and scurries on. Any other day he'd be walking in the shade, mapping his path underneath the linden trees, but today he cuts straight through the blistering heat.

Salim's not yet seven but he's been roaming the streets for years. For his fifth birthday, his parents cut off his right thumb. His thumbless hand is now the tool of his vocation. He fishes women's purses with it. The thumb may be gone, but on scorching days like these the phantom digit itches. Salim isn't quite sure how such a thing is possible and what's worse, he can't scratch it. "What does he need a thumb for, he won't be holding pens," his mother had said. "We've got enough professors in the world, the boy needs a trade!" And she'd taught him to pickpocket.

Salim's lucky. They cut off his older brother's leg at the knee and now he begs, rain or shine, in the garden by the main street. His *batko* is a beggar, but Salim's a young professional. Stealing is way more lucrative, anyway. Some days he snatched real treasures—that's what he called them—things like pocket mirrors and fancy pens that he didn't show his mother, stashing them under his bed instead.

His father hasn't come by in two years and his mother is raising him and his brother, plus two other girls—three and five—all by herself. There's his grandmother, too. She lives with them because she's too old to steal or sweep the streets, and in this heat can't beg, either. Every Wednesday, his mother mops both stairwells in an apartment building near the Mahala neighborhood, for which she's paid 48 leva in all "so she don't starve." But three days ago, she got ill, so they called a doctor. When the doctor pressed on her belly, she howled like a dying animal. They took her to the hospital, scanned her, poked her with needles, and finally declared she needed an emergency kidney transplant because both of hers had stopped working.

Salim hung at the foot of his mother's sickbed, then left, deep in thought. His mother had done so much for him, turned him into a skilled thief, a pickpocketing master, but she'd somehow failed to teach him how to steal a kidney. Thumb or no thumb, this would be no easy feat. Salim has no idea what a kidney even looks like, let alone where to find one. Five straight nights he can't eat or sleep, tortured over this kidney.

Today he gets up early and goes to wait outside the local grocer, which his mother calls "the garage," although Salim's never seen any cars parked inside. Finally, the saleswoman appears. She reaches to undo the big padlock and throws him a sideways glance.

"What are you sitting here for? Run along."

"*Lelche*, do you have some cardboard?"

"Cardboard? What do you need cardboard for?"

"I need to make a sign. I can't write, but if I tell you what to write, could you, *lelche*?"

"What are you talking about? Get out of here."

"I need a sign that says I'm looking for a kidney. I'll go sit by the mall and if someone has an extra one, maybe they'll give it to me."

The woman eyes him dubiously, decides the little gypsy must be scamming, and responds in jest.

"But why beg for it? Just go to the butcher on the corner of Botev and Zelena Polyana and buy yourself one."

Salim's eyes light up.

"You can buy a kidney at the store?"

"Of course you can."

You could buy a kidney a stone's throw from the Mahala neighborhood, and here he is, sitting around for five days! Salim bolts back home. They live in a shack just across the train tracks, five minutes to and from, if he runs fast enough. He's tucked away a few leva from the wallet he picked the day they put his mom in the hospital. It's gotta be enough for a kidney. He runs like a madman, squeezes the money in his good fist and hightails it back to the butcher. He runs into the shop completely out of breath, opens his sweaty palm and places the crumpled ten leva bill on the counter.

"*Chicho*, I need a kidney for my mother."

The butcher, a large man with beefy forearms, looks down at the little gypsy and stifles a laugh in his beard, but still weighs half a kilo of lamb's kidney, gives him change even.

Now Salim hustles back to the hospital with his kidney wrapped in butcher paper inside a plastic bag. He gets to the building and flies up the stairs two at a time. It's jammed with people but nobody stops him. His mother taught him how to snake through, unnoticed. "Put on your invisible cape and go make some money," she'd say.

He gets up to the third floor and darts into the room. In the same bed his mother had been in yesterday, a nurse takes the blood pressure of an old woman.

4

I was eighteen when I left the Home. I was supposed to feel liberated
and ecstatic, but I felt lost and uncertain. The Home had really been
my home, the only place I knew and where people knew me. Outside
of it, I had no support system. For the second time in my life I was
forced to abandon my place of origin. Only this time it was up to me
where to set out to. One, two, three . . . jump. I opened the door and
the outside world swallowed me.

I wasn't the only one who the institution spit out. Naya and the
twins got sent out too—everyone who'd just turned eighteen. Foreheads full of acne and bouncing thoughts behind them. Eighteen
years in which not a single mother had chosen me for her daughter.
Not a single mother had taken me by the hand and led me back to
her home, decided to secretly shelter me inside the colorful, wooden
nest of her matryoshka. My place in the world had been anonymous
and meek. I'd gone unnoticed by all the mothers in the world. I was
eighteen years old and I was totally, completely invisible.

5

One cold, winter morning, somebody pounded on our door. Naya and I rented an attic room in Reduta, a short walk from the restaurant where we both worked, she as a waitress and I as kitchen staff.

"Identification check!" A male barked from the other side of the door, and the pounding amplified.

I looked at my watch: quarter to five. I threw a long cardigan around my shoulders and cracked the door. Two cops plowed in, knocking me back as they barged forward.

"ID cards!" The male voice scraped the darkness.

I started digging through my bag. Naya finally looked up from her pillow, blinking in bewilderment. She'd only come back from her night shift an hour or so ago. She reached for her jeans, but reconsidered and instead sat up in bed, wrapped up in the bed cover.

One of the cops stared at our IDs like he was attempting to read a foreign language. The other frantically raided the room, pulling all the drawers, flipping and throwing them to the ground.

"What are you doing? Do you even have a search warrant?" Naya finally regained composure.

"Don't you worry about a warrant! Just tell us where you stashed it so we don't have to tear the whole place apart."

"Stashed what? What are you talking about?"

"That's how you want to play it? We were informed that you're in possession of drugs."

"Drugs? Are you out of your mind?" I couldn't keep quiet either. "You're asking ME?"

"Who told you? And how are you so sure it's us? There are tenants in three other attic rooms."

"You're the girls from the orphanage in K., right? Nadezhda Dimitrova, nineteen, eyes hazel, hair brown, height 168 centimeters, National Identity Number . . ."

"Yeah, that's me. But no drugs here. I'm telling you, somebody gave you bad info."

"You're not going to make this easy, are you?"

An hour and a half later, after an endless tirade of cursing and a trashed room, Naya and I took deep drags from our cigarettes by the window, then exhaled. The room was ransacked and of course, no drugs were found. We had no words; there was nothing to say. Our thoughts were singed from what had just happened, still hot to the touch. Below us, the city was waking up in a thick gray smog.

6

Some time ago, a gallery in New York held an opening for an exhibit featuring Lana Newstrom's invisible art. Gallery visitors took in completely blank canvases lit up by projection lights. Throngs of people flocked to the gallery from all corners of the city to catch sight of the invisible, an exhibit of all and nothing: of a blank canvas and of the imagined, created by our own notion of the world. The whole thing turned out to be a PR stunt, a complete hoax, but still, it contained a seed of truth. According to the twenty-seven-year-old artist, "art is imagination." Her goal had been to push people to imagine, to paint their own paintings on the white canvases set in exquisite frames, in a way becoming part of the creation of the art. Stepping outside the contours of reality is only possible through imagination, and it is the substance that injects us with thoughts and feelings.

Lana isn't the first artist to mount an invisible exhibit. Martin Creed and Susan Philipsz have each won the Turner for their empty showrooms: Creed with a light projection, and Philipsz with a folk-song sound installation. In 2012, the Hayward Gallery in London opened a show titled "Invisible: Art About the Unseen, 1957-2012" exhibiting the invisible works of over fifty artists, including screening a movie filmed without film and showing paintings drawn with invisible ink.

According to the gallery director, the show had been dedicated to emptiness: to space, waiting to be filled through imagination. His idea had been inspired by a musical number composed by John Cage, "played" without a single note from a musical instrument. In this conceptual piece, called "4'33'," the unplayed music gives space to the noises inside the hall, creating the feeling of music within the audience. Inspiring them to hear it inside themselves.

7

One day she came. The director summoned me to her office with the gargantuan desk and pointed her out. She stood next to the cracked window, shivering like a dried autumn leaf. She appeared so small and faint, so fragile, I didn't have the courage to run up to her and throw my arms around her. I feared I'd break her with the vibrancy of my nine-year-old body, cause her to collapse like a sandcastle deluged by the sea, turn her into a thousand glistening grains strewn by the wind.

I stood in front of her, captivated by her eyes, drinking in her sorrow, letting it deposit inside of me like black sediment. Did she really see me, I wondered, this small woman, crouched in her own unease? Did she see me standing here in front of her, inhaling her sorrow, forgiving all in that second? I wanted to sink into the warmth of her barely existing body, fall into the dark craters of her tired eyes, disappear into the creases of the wrinkles cutting through her forehead.

She sensed my presence and raised her eyes for a second before burying her face in her hands. I saw her writhing between her slender, bony fingers, her entire body shaken by sobs as she choked on her inability to reach out and hold me. She was atoning for someone else's sins: my mother's. My mother's sister writhed in pain by the window, only a meter away from my uncomprehending eyes brimming with tears. Back then I didn't know my mother was already dead, that she'd died giving birth to my little brother. I wasn't yet privy to the fact that on that day and along with that baby, both of them had vanished. I didn't know this first meeting with my mother's sister would be the last, that it would cause me, for the first time in my life, to weep not for my own abandonment or the fact that I was alone, tossed into this Home like an old Lakta candy wrapper, but for my mother's pain, for the wail that ripped from her like the baby from her womb, the scream that tore her from the living, and that tore her from me, for always.

A Woman in the Park

Today is the Feast of the Annunciation. Lady Day. It is the day the archangel Gabriel visited the Virgin Mary to inform her she was with child and that child would be Jesus. It must be below zero but the cold doesn't bother me. I'm sitting on a park bench in the Borisova Garden, gaping absentmindedly at passersby. There aren't many. It's 10 A.M. on a Wednesday and normal people, with their nine to six workdays, are sitting at their desks. They've gotten up, boarded the city bus or the subway, and pressed their bodies against the others to squeeze intimacy out of their fellow man—in return probably got a choice word from the bus driver or the fat guy by the back door. Normal people then drank their hot coffee at their desks (which took up at least the first half hour of their workday), cigarette in hand, no doubt. So what if smoking indoors was forbidden—wasn't it their office, and their coffee and their cigarette, after all?

I've retreated into my fur coat, holding my steaming mocha up to my face so its velvet aroma can tingle my senses. There's still frost covering the grass but the lazy morning sun winks my way and my mood brightens. The park lanes feel almost deserted, even the usual park crazies wandering around trying to scam a cigarette off you are nowhere to be seen. My mocha is suddenly cold. An hour must have passed, maybe more, because the park has come to life. The coffee shop at the end of the lane has filled up and the temperature feels like it has risen.

A woman draws near. She holds a little girl in braids by the hand and the kid drags a doll behind her. They sit down one bench over. One of the doll's eyes has been gouged out, its hair is bedraggled and protrudes every which way, its cheeks are scribbled over in black pen—a tangle of overlapping circles. I imagine the corporeal damages the doll's pleated dress must be concealing. The mother looks at ease, she's smiling. Doesn't take her beaming eyes off her daughter. From where I'm sitting, she looks quite young, seems fragile, nearly disappears into her morello scarf and coat. I catch her humming a children's song I recognize. *Orange is the sky, orange is the sea, orange are the flowers, and the city's* . . . I'd heard it years ago in the Home. It was one of my favorites. About the brave, eccentric little girl who'd grabbed a brush and painted everything orange, to the dismay of everyone around her. I used to love that song.

I stir. The mother turns toward me and we lock eyes for a moment. She smiles, I smile back. She strokes the child's hair as the child sits on the edge of the bench, kicking her boot heels together and staring off into the distance. The thought "five-year-olds on a rampage" flashes through my mind. A dog walks by. The child yells "Fetch!" and throws the doll at it. The dog grabs hold of the doll and runs off. I imagine the dog's teeth marking the doll's rubber skin. The mother lets out a shriek, her face distorts to unfamiliarity, and she chases after the dog.

I seize the moment to say to the kid:

"Having some fun, huh? I take it you don't like your doll very much."

"Nah."

"Why's that?"

"Only girls play with dolls!"

This reply bewilders me. Again I look at the child's face. Only now do I notice the boyish features, and fingernails bitten down to the skin of hands fiddling with the frayed edge of the wool dress. The child wrinkles its nose and looks indignant, but doesn't take an eye off the dog. The mother is still yelling and waving her arms after it. The dog's owner, a middle-aged man with a beard and checkered jacket, whistles half-heartedly, but it looks like he's having a little fun at the mother's expense, too.

"What a sight!" I say to the kid. "I bet you couldn't get him to come back here."

"I sure can, 'cause we're friends. Check it out. Hrabur, here, boy!"

With only a few jumps, the dog makes its way back over, drops the doll, licks the child's hand, and disappears. The mother runs over panting.

"Martina! Every time, the same thing!"

I don't understand. The name, the doll, the little boy in the dress. I look at the kid then back up at the woman as if I'll find my answers in the cloud of her breath. Only now do I notice that she's really not that young, mid-forties, maybe. Withered face, lips cracked from the cold, jittery eyes above dark circles like mud pits.

I start to walk off, but only take a couple of steps before I stop by their bench. The woman looks up, her eyes invite me to sit. I am uneasy. I can tell she suspects I've discovered her secret, yet she seems to expect me to continue playing along. I'm now something of an accomplice—or at least it's how the whole thing is making me feel. Hesitant, I sit down, barely on the edge of the bench. I don't know what to say or where to look.

"Do you come here often? I haven't seen you before."

"Not really," my response is unsettled. "I work long hours, so . . . what about you?"

Silence. A few beats pass while the woman looks me dead in the eye as if she's calculating just how much she should divulge.

"Me . . . I've come here every year for nine years. Same day, same bench. I just sit and take it in. Nothing changes, really."

Silence. A minute, at least. I'm already regretting this conversation but I sit and wait.

"What happened nine years ago?" I decide social etiquette requires this of me.

"Do you have kids?"

"No." I look down so I can avoid her next question and will myself not to ask her anything about hers.

"That's okay. One day you will and when you do . . . make sure to protect them. Teach them things. Love them. Make sure they know it. Every day. Make sure they know their mother is there and loves them. Unconditionally. Whatever happens, whatever they might get into. My daughter, Martina, was a real troublemaker. You should've seen some of the shenanigans she pulled. She loved traveling, though. All you had to do was sit her in the car and her face would light right up. One spring, exactly nine years on this day, the Feast of the Annunciation, my sister and her husband were headed up to the Trojan Balkan for a few days. Martina was eight, second-grade. They'd just let them out for Easter break and I had no one to watch her, so I asked my sister if they'd take her. I thought why not. A week of fresh air for her, quality time for them with their favorite niece. They came by early morning, picked her up. I tell you, you couldn't wipe the smile from her face. She hadn't slept all night. That's how excited she was. We said our goodbyes and they left. They'd barely gotten on the highway, right over there by the entrance to the park, when a Mercedes going 200 km an hour caused a giant pileup. Somehow, by some miracle, everybody in the pileup made it out alive, minor injuries, mostly. They all lived. All of them, except one. I was at home before my shift, just waiting for my sister to call to tell me they got there safe, when news of the pileup came on the radio. An electric shock went through me. I just knew. Nine years ago to this day. But miracles do happen, don't they? I prayed to God and the Almighty heard my prayers. He sent me my Martina back. She may have a different body, but I know she's still my Martina. Her dad packed his bags and left one day and we haven't seen him since, but we're managing just fine, the two of us girls, right?"

The same tender smile spills over her face. The child again stares into the ground. The doll, smeared in dog drool, lays there, bearing silent witness. I am paralyzed. Words escape me. Eventually, the woman gets up, smoothes the braids, and pulls a wool hat over the child's ears. She takes the small hand and again tugs the kid along. Just before they're out of sight, the little boy turns around and waves goodbye to me.

I look after them for some time then turn around, resolved to wipe away the whole thing from my mind. My gaze slides over the frosted bench and there's the doll, staring me down with one glass eye. I wait a second, maybe two, look around, and quickly shove it in my backpack. I clear my head from all thoughts, I feel light and bright, almost orange . . . *Orange are the mothers, orange are the kids, orange are the guitars, strumming orange songs.*

8

The smell of semolina boiled in milk always takes me back to my first years at the Home. Gooey white semolina that forms a thin, yellowish, chewy crust on top when it cools. With a big spoon, you scoop some out but the crust wraps around it; you try to lick it off, but you can't, it's stuck on there, one with the spoon, so you draw it out with your tongue, nibble at the spoon with your teeth, only to get it stuck to the roof of your mouth, where it stays; and you swallow and swallow and swallow and you haven't even tasted the essence of the dessert yet: the white, fluffy semolina underneath.

I can't say whether I liked it. It was sweet enough to make us all quiet for a second while we shoveled it into our little mouths, dribbling it down our chins and onto our clothes so the Matrons yelled "who's gonna clean you all up now!" and we lowered our lice-infested heads, still greedily eating. I can't say whether I like it, still. I think that despite the saccharine, sticky, fluffy taste, the memory of the Home still settles on top—like a thin, yellow, chewy crust. Memories can be strange sometimes.

9

Memories. I went to bed every night, eyes shut tight under the blanket, yellow circles orbiting each other behind my eyelids, stuck in a spasmodic kiss. I pulled the blanket over my head, breathing heavily and at intervals until I thought I would suffocate from my own hot breath, before finally giving up and taking in fresh air from the other side. It didn't work. Nothing did. Hard as I tried to lose them, the memories didn't go anywhere, they fluttered in my head like moths to a light bulb.

Is there a way to erase my memories?

Is there a way to erase?

Is there a way?

Elina

He knocks on the door and I know I have to open it. If I don't, it will get even worse. I turn the knob and the water from the shower stops. There's no point in wrapping myself with a towel; I trail water behind me—I am wet, barefoot, and shaking.

I stand between the cold wall and his burning body. His fingers move around, sliding down my inner thighs. My heart beats into my temples, into my stomach. The blood gallops in his veins, freezes in mine. A summer breeze sneaks in through the bathroom window and hides inside my hair; I get goose bumps, my entire body is shivering. He pulsates inside of me. The shocks reverberate deep inside my head, childhood memories vibrate inside my thoughts, caught as if in a mousetrap.

The arrogant stench of power and my powerlessness in it crawl down my neck, my shoulders, my too-small breasts. I must find a way to remove myself from the present, to force my thoughts, latched on me like suction cups, like purulent deposits, to exit my body.

Water drips monotonously on the tile, drip, drip, drip, drip . . .

I look out the window. The razor-edged peaks of the mountains have penetrated the sun, tearing it apart; its red bleeds onto the ridge, leaving painful scars. A few minutes stretch on forever. I close my eyes and forget who I am and where I am. I forget everything.

He's finished. He'll be back again tomorrow at sunset, when the dusk is thick and intimate. He'll knock on the bathroom door while I shower. The same thing, over and over and over again, every single day, before she comes back from work. In the shower, secretly, painfully, agonizingly. Again and again, since I was seven. I'm thirteen now. He calls me "sweetheart." I call him "Dad."

10

I didn't end up working the kitchen staff job right away. In those first few months after I aged out of the Home, I slept on a park bench and scrounged for food. I'd find a piece of moldy bread, a half-rotten tomato—the remains of some capricious child's dinner. I'd wolf it all down with my eyes closed, imagining the food was set out on a nice dinner plate atop a crisp white tablecloth, flanked by silverware. There'd be a knife, closest to the plate on the right, a fork on the left, a soup spoon next to the knife and a dessert spoon and fork at the top of the plate; the sweet syrup of an imaginary dessert quick to ooze into my thoughts.

My first job was halfway underground in a basement squat-shop selling liquor and cigarettes. It was called a squat-shop because people had to literally squat down to buy something. Most of our patrons were regulars. I watched their boots approach the small window— leather boots, tall boots, short boots, black boots, brown boots, tattered boots, shiny boots—and the boots shouted orders from the heavens: "A pack of Victory Blue!" "Get me some roasted sunflower seeds!" "A bottle of Atlantic Rum!" Some boots shoved twenties in my face, others dumped handfuls of change on me.

It was the final winter of the twentieth century. Only five months before, the twenty leva bill was worth twenty thousand; the three leva coins—three thousand. When the country scratched the three zeroes, I scratched out my dreams of a real home and a real life. I shivered at the tiny window halfway below the sidewalk, buried alive in the hell of my misery, but I didn't budge. I furiously inhaled the winter chill.

It was one of those bitter winter days just before Christmas, when everyone else was sitting warmly at home in front of the TV. At the end of my shift, I stole a pack of cigarettes. I don't remember the brand, it didn't matter to me. I hid around the corner and sat down on the curb. Some guy whistled my way; I asked for a light, and he took it as an invite to sit down. Our asses were ice and stuck to the ground but we chewed the fat anyway: there was the old year and the new century, the price of gas—which had skyrocketed and taken the price of cigarettes along with it—there was that bar just over there, where, if I was up for it, he could buy me a drink, then maybe go up to his place, just round the corner. Totally up to me, of course. After a while he conceded, maybe because of the cold or the realization nothing was going to happen. He left, perhaps to look for girls more keen on his company and his apartment.

I sat alone on the curb, chain smoking to keep the tiny flame alive. I inhaled the cigarette smoke, closed my eyes, and held it in as long as I could, imagining how my large extended family had gathered for the holidays. My mother, my aunt, and my grandmother all tucked into the kitchen since dawn, cooking the traditional thirteen Christmas Eve dishes, specially prepared without meat or eggs to mark the end of the forty-day Nativity Fast. My mother is simmering the bean stew, and adds a few hot peppers to the pot. My grandmother is drying the boiled barley, grating lemon rind, and milling walnuts to mix into the big glass bowl. She'll then coat all of it with a blizzard of powdered sugar and finally, she'll place a thin taper candle right in the middle. There's my aunt wrapping the *sarmi*, stuffing half into grape leaves and half into cabbage leaves.

Sitting on the curb, I kept lighting cigarette after cigarette so that I wouldn't come out of my daydream, wouldn't lose the vision of the holiday celebration I've never had. There I was on the street like some grown-up Little Match Girl, waiting for the snow.

"Get the fuck out of here!"

An angry male voice ripped me out of my trance, jabbing the tip of his boot into my ribs.

11

Naya and I have been living together since we were born. First in the Home, then in the attic room we shared in the Reduta neighborhood. She was given up for adoption as a three-day-old baby. The story goes that her mother got pregnant at sixteen by some boy she never saw again. To avoid the public indignity of it all, her parents locked her up in their village house on the vineyard, like a prisoner of her own naiveté. Every few days for three months, her mother would come to bring her food and water and to check on her. But nobody was there when her contractions started; no one had imagined she'd go into labor in the seventh month. She would have had little use in banging on the door or screaming—the house was deep off the main road and out of earshot, and since it was right before Christmas, the other villagers were keeping warm inside their houses. Hours passed before her mother found her lying on the floor in a puddle of blood, a sleeping baby swaddled in her lap. They saved the baby's life, but quickly got rid of it.

That's the story of how Naya ended up in the Home. Her mother died a few days later. I picture her obituary reading something like this:

"Rest in peace, our dear child!
Your grief-stricken mother, father, and brother."

Not a word about that other child, the one just barely tasting life but already vanishing in a haze of disremembrance.

Naya came into this world prematurely, unwanted, and marked for life by these events, which the Home's Matrons made sure to recount to every adolescent girl as a cautionary tale. Naya's real name is Nadezhda, meaning hope. It had been her dying mother's attempt to bestow her with good fortune.

One Christmas, a big box of donations arrived for us at the Home. Clothes, toys, and sweets. We were elated, and jumped up and down for two hours. Sure enough, the Matrons ransacked everything. They kept the nicer clothes for their own kids or to give away as Christmas presents to relatives, and what remained they sold to the sales women at the department store, reaffirming that enduring, two-way relationship. Those same saleswomen then sold everything off-register for a percentage of the profit—even the youngest of us at the Home knew this.

To save face, it being Christmas and all, the Matrons allowed us some plain vanilla wafers called "Naya." Our friend, still Nadya then, took such pleasure in devouring the crispy wafers that she insisted we call her Naya, too. We didn't mind. Every time someone called out her name, the sweet taste of the wafers seeped into our consciousness and we munched away our Christmas memories. Na-ya, Na-ya.

One night, the boys broke into our sleeping ward. They were sixteen, seventeen, we were barely twelve. I knew what they wanted to do to us, I'd heard about it from the older girls. There was no point in screaming—even if the only Matron on duty could hear us over her nine o'clock TV show, she wouldn't have done anything about it. The Home was like an aquarium: the big fish ate the little fish, everyone saw it happen through the glass, and no one did anything to stop it. It happened again the following night, and the one after that. I squeezed my eyelids shut underneath the blanket just as I'd done when I was little and I tried to outrun my demons, but they caught up to me over and over again.

Naya turned out to be the savviest of us all. Soon the boys completely stopped bothering her. One day during lunch she whispered to me how she did it. She shat herself. Revolted, they didn't come anywhere near her. At twelve years old, Naya shat herself every single night, of her own volition, and with the outward calm of a Tibetan monk. She told me this in between bites of macaroni and feta. Now it was up to me to choose between these two evils. I chose to follow suit. And I finished my lunch.

12

Sometimes I'm asked what life in the Home had taught me. I used to go for an answer the person asking could actually take; something that rewarded them for caring. But lately, I've gone another way with it.

Stoycho was six when the ambulance took him away and we never saw him again. He had suffered broken ribs, a fractured skull, and a brain hemorrhage. He died a few days later. It all happened when we were making our way back down from the cemetery at the top of the hill. We snuck up there to snatch the food left at the gravestones in memory of the departed, God rest their souls. Usually we found the requisite plastic cups of boiled barley and powdered sugar, but some days we stumbled on plain biscuits and Turkish delight. Anything we came across we were ordered to bring back to the older kids. We weren't allowed so much as a taste from what we salvaged. But we were ravenous, carrying food forbidden to our rumbling bellies, and we found it excruciating to resist. Those of us who secretly tasted the barley with powdered sugar and were lucky enough to get away with it relished the sweetness long into our dreams, but one of the kids saw Stoycho do it and squealed to the older kids. Squealing got you a biscuit. Stoycho was beaten like a dog while the Matrons stared blindly out the window until he was left lying in a puddle of his own blood. Someone did call an ambulance eventually, but at that point it was too late.

Stoycho had been a glutton by nature. Some of the kids said they saw him ducking in the bushes by the street at dusk, waiting for the goats to come home from grazing. They said he suckled one of the does. No one could figure out why the animal had allowed it.

What did life in the Home teach me? The only thing that mattered. Survival.

13

I was twenty-five when I first saw a circus. Even before they'd put up the posters around town, I glimpsed the long line of trucks and caravans stretching like caramel along the street. The anxious honks of horns from the cars came in through the window of my apartment and I imagined how the drivers stuck behind the procession slapped their steering wheels and yelled profanities, but the circus fanfare just kept crawling up the street, contriving a pandemonium that would get people talking ahead of the show.

Just past the Kaufland store, the first truck in line, the one leading the whole procession, took a right onto the lawn—a lawn in a very loose sense; more like an abandoned weed field with shambolic trash lolling around—the rest of the trucks followed him and the line of angry drivers sped ahead. It was dusk. The caravans parked on one side of the field. The circus performers all disembarked, coloring the ground around them, and I remember thinking how ordinary they all looked, except for, I suppose, the dwarf person.

The scent of a complete lack of inhibition and prejudice washed over me like opium. Right away the circus people spread out rugs on the ground, took out food and beer and sat down in a circle around their makeshift table. I couldn't hear their voices, but I could see their smiling faces and I imagined how one of them began telling a story, and everyone else all sat down around listening to it, bursting out laughing or baiting their breaths and chewing their food in symphony. I longed to be there with them too, chewing on bread and frankfurters until night's curtains fell and the circus performers all went back into their caravans.

They started putting up the tent early the next morning and I watched as they raised the canopy. I'd imagined it somehow more majestic. Still, I bought a pair of front row tickets and awaited the date of the show.

Naya had no desire to join me. I vaguely remember her making up some sort of clown phobia as an excuse. I think her actual phobia was of experiencing something new. She was afraid of coming face to face with her childhood dreams now that she was a woman of twenty-five. I couldn't hold it against her. It did require a certain kind of bravery to face the fact that everyone in the audience would be a child accompanied by parents or grandparents and there you'd be, the only half-child, half-adult, sitting alone.

On the day of the show I woke up with a bitter taste in my mouth. I spat into the sink and made myself a nuclear pot of coffee, which only exacerbated the bitter taste. I downed a cup and poured another.

I made my way over to the circus an hour before showtime. The evening was imbued with the laughter of children and the smell of red rooster lollipops and whipped cream. A festive voice came through the megaphone, enticing passersby to join in the fun. The circus performers walked around in their shiny outfits and glazed hair juggling oranges; some were mounted on stilts, walking high up with frozen smiles.

I gave my tickets to a little girl on the street about to pull her mother's arm out had she not agreed to take her to the show. The mother looked at me with a mix of confusion and suspicion. I fabricated a reason for my generosity on the spot, mumbling something about my daughter getting sick at the last minute. The suspicion in the mother's eyes changed to empathy, she thanked me and wished my kid a speedy recovery.

Suddenly, I felt overwhelmed with nausea. I lit a cigarette and promised myself I wouldn't do something so stupid again.

14

One night you vanished. At first I thought you'd gone off with friends after your shift, but as the night pushed on I began to worry. I smoked anxiously by the window—our favorite place, remember? I sat on the window sill and lit cigarette after cigarette. Here, on the ledge, is where I felt most like myself; here, at the threshold of life and our attic, is where we found refuge from our lonesomeness, protection from the incessant buzzing of the outside world. I pursed my reddened lips and blew smoke rings that evaporated into the cool night air. I loved summer nights, when the moon resembled a piece of chocolate wrapped in tinfoil, the last one in the box, just sitting there waiting for the first rays of sunshine to melt it.

I made coffee and poured it into the big yellow mug, looked at the clock for the hundredth time—it was past three thirty. The city beneath had quieted; occasionally a winded cab whizzed by and I prayed it would turn down the street to our building. I took a big swig of coffee and its aroma briefly pushed the smell of mold to the corners. I had to stay awake and wait for you, send out positive thoughts, just like you said I should whenever I worried. I forced myself to think of you brightly, to imagine how you caught that cheerful thread and rolled it into a ball as you walked toward our attic room. Like Hansel and Gretel dropping bread crumbs so they could find their way back home.

But the birds pecked the bread crumbs, the thread got stretched and broken abruptly and my pupils dilated the second I laid eyes on the empty spot by the door where you kept your slippers. I jumped and opened the right side of the wardrobe where you hung your clothes—it stood completely empty save for a lonely spider spinning a web in the corner, spitting its nearly invisible threads in the dark, unperturbed by the panic that now crawled all over me.

The question changed, the letters distorted and regrouped. Only a second ago I asked myself where you could be; now I was numb, feeling nothing but infinite sadness. Why did you leave, Naya?

You shoved your entire miserable existence into that tattered duffel bag you'd bought at the Iliantsi flea market and you disappeared. You left me to smoke alone in the dark. To slap my palm into my forehead, scratch my nails against my numbed scalp and pull my hair, what I do when I feel powerless, then and now.

I took in the warmth of the coffee, watched it transform before me from black liquid into a tiny vapor—light, invisible.

15

One winter night at the Home, she kissed me. Waited until everyone was asleep, slipped inside my bed, and told me she was cold. I didn't ask her to leave. I closed my eyes and she kissed me on the lips. A long, deep kiss. Then she slid her hands in between my thighs. Her skin felt cold against mine, and she shivered slightly. I didn't know what she expected me to do. I held my breath as hers quickened in my ear. Suddenly, a door slammed in the hallway and she jumped out of my bed and back into hers, her eyes flashing in the dark.

The next morning my eyes could barely meet hers. I was afraid I'd made the whole thing up. But I hadn't. She slipped under my covers again the following night and every night after that, for months on end, until we got out of the Home together, and it would be just the two of us. In the little attic room we rented, she could stay in my bed all night without fear of retribution. We were finally free to choose how we lived. At least that's what we thought.

Kaloyan

When he opened his eyes again, she was still there, pressing her naked body against his, showering him with soft, barely-there kisses. It hadn't been a dream after all. He felt electricity shoot up his body, turning him incandescent, and he was in fact certain that if someone had been watching them he'd look like an illuminated lamppost. They were lying beside each other when a bug must have crawled up her thigh because she suddenly flinched, folded herself in two, and slapped her leg.

"Gotcha, little sucker!"

Her voice was soft in the dusk, the blades of grass tickled him and he squeezed her even closer to him. A cricket chirped into his ear and somewhere off in the distance, the muffled sound of traffic crawled on by. Lavender perfumed the air, and he couldn't decide whether the scent rose up from the field that enveloped their bare bodies or if it was just the youthful fragrance of her seventeen-year-old body. He sank into her silken, sun-bleached hair and inhaled; it inebriated him, made the earth flip and the blood erupt in his veins. The thought that she seemed far too experienced for her age flashed somewhere behind his eyes, but what did he know, he'd be twenty-four next week and he'd never even been with a woman before.

The grass imprinted on her skin, stuck to her thighs and tickled her breasts, but she paid no attention to it, sucking on his mouth, his neck, his nipples, sliding down his body, her hair spilling across his stomach. He moaned as her body glided on top of his, teasing him, taking pleasure in his moans, which sounded more like bellowing and ignited her fantasies even more and she chased after his ecstasy only to rein it back in.

Her body fell back next to his. She was out of breath and on her back, her breasts perked up above the grass like mushrooms after rain, her skin damp, velvet, glowing. He felt her shiver slightly as her heart pounded and he reached over to hold her, speaking sweet nothings in his mind, unable to break the silence. Right now, in this silence, was the first time he'd ever felt real happiness; words seemed pitiful and unnecessary.

They lay in the twilight as the sun elongated the shadows in the crevices of her olive-skinned body before licking the hills in the distance and melting behind them. When the last reflections of light skimmed her hips, everything became surreal. He lifted himself up on his elbows and kissed her eyelids then gave her a soft pinch on the bottom; it was time to go. She giggled, bit his lip mischievously, moved a strand of hair from his forehead, and turned on her stomach, up against him. Her eyes fixed on him as she played with his chest hair.

She dressed him, put his pants back on by herself, then tied his shoelaces. She bent over all the way down and swung his arm over herself so she could position him over her back. He weighed at least twice as much as she did, and all her muscles tensed up and she groaned as she unloaded him into the wheelchair. The grass lay flat, outlining where their bodies had just been, the lavender had evaporated and the crickets multiplied, chirping all the way back home. The two of them were silent. When they finally reached his neighborhood on the outskirts of town, she stopped the wheelchair, went around it, and put her beautiful face up within an inch from his:

"I'm coming back tomorrow. You hear me, Kalo? You're gonna wait for me, right?"

She looked him straight in the eye, as though willing him to understand her. He attempted to answer her but the same bellowing wrenched itself from his throat. He went red. She smiled—of course he'd be waiting for her.

She went back to pushing his wheelchair along the path and he heard her singing a tune to herself. He thought how, if someone had been watching them, he'd look like an illuminated lamppost.

16

On March 8, 2014, when women around the world celebrated International Women's Day and got bouquets of flowers from their partners and handmade cards from their children, Malaysia Airlines Flight 370, en route to Beijing, went missing, and with it the two-hundred thirty-nine passengers onboard. It wasn't the first time an airplane had vanished, but a loss of this magnitude was unprecedented. For months on end, there was no sign of the plane, no debris, nothing at all that could aid the investigation. The plane and its passengers had vanished like dust in the wind. The only trace the passengers left were the countless newspaper articles written about them and the black holes in their relative's memories. How can you bury an empty casket?

The news came in as I cut a strawberry cheesecake into slender slices, carefully arranging each one on a petite Jenaer Glas dessert plate. A friend and her daughter had come to visit from Plovdiv for the weekend and I saw the child's face tighten when she heard what happened. I reached to turn off the television but her mother stopped me. "This is life. I can't shelter her from all the bad news in the world."

An hour later the little girl was in her pajamas, a book in her hand. She asked her mother if tonight they could talk first, then read. The mother acquiesced and the two went off to the bedroom to talk and cuddle.

I thought how lovely it must be to fall asleep in your mother's arms after the two of you have been reading from your favorite children's book and you've showered her with all sorts of questions before gently dozing off. The greatest conversations with a child must be the ones that take place in that space between page ten and page fifteen, when the child traces her finger under the words then stops and changes the subject entirely. My friend returned to the dining room after a bit; she looked pensive. "What's wrong?" I asked. Her daughter had wanted to know if there had been children onboard the vanished airplane.

My friend had explained that although the vanished airplane could still be found, there had yes, unfortunately, been children on it. Seven children, the youngest of which was just a year old. Her daughter had grown worried, asking what would happen if they couldn't find them.

"What did you tell her?"

"I didn't know what to tell her," my friend said. "Maybe this conversation wasn't a good idea after all. Or maybe it's me who isn't ready to answer questions like that. How do you explain to an eight-year-old an enormous airplane vanishing, all those souls onboard? How am I supposed to correlate the disappearance with all that death and make it somehow digestible for her little girl's sensibility?

I went silent too. My head was filled with the disturbing faces of the relatives of all those who had vanished—their taut, waxy expressions of fear, desperation and grief forever frozen in time.

My friend's daughter did finally open her book and began reading. The Brothers Grimm's "The Shoes That Were Danced to Pieces." When she got to the part where the old woman gave the poor soldier an invisibility cloak so he could follow the twelve princesses undetected and find out what they were up to each night, my friend's daughter had cried, "Mama, that's it! The kids and all the people on the plane didn't disappear. They just became invisible!"

Invisible, indeed.

I kissed her on the forehead and tucked her in. "We'll continue where we left off tomorrow night."

17

All my mother bestowed me with, all I have to remember her by, is a faded, cream-yellow cotton blanket. It's what she swaddled me in on our first and last day together, and sometimes I imagine how she clung to the sleeping, unsuspecting, pint-sized newborn before giving her up in this blanket soaked with her tears. All these years later it's like the blanket is still imbibed with her sorrow. Like an umbilical cord, it still connects me to her, melds each of my days to the day of my entrance into the world and to my severance from her.

Its edges are frayed and with each new day of my life, I think I see a run further unraveling the fibers, taking me further away from that first and last cuddle. I fear that one day it'll unravel too far, it'll make my bond with her so threadbare, it'll waste away and vanish altogether. And I will forget. I will forget my mother; I will forget that I was ever born. I will forget everything.

Or perhaps I won't.

Maybe I won't forget, and my baby blanket—my legacy and proof of life—won't unravel. It'll remain undamaged and will keep me whole and self-sufficient. Like a mystical, magical cape, with the power to make me invisible, it'll protect me and keep me out of death's way.

Tales of invisible cloaks have been around for ages. Millenia, when you really think about it. Plato writes about invisibility in the second book of the Republic, in the year 359-360 AD. The ring of Gyges turns you invisible, without consequences. Being invisible makes you untouchable, it frees you from all constraints and morality. The idea exists in mythology, too. Zeus gives Perseus Hades's helm of darkness so that he may turn invisible, and by seeing Medusa's reflection in his shield, he's able to approach her and cut off her head. His invisibility makes him invincible, enables him to get so close to danger he conquers it, emerges victorious, unscathed.

In J. K. Rowling's books (and later, films) the cloak of invisibility not only hides Harry Potter from the eyes of mortals, it protects him from danger, evil curses, and bad magic. The cloak, his late father's, is gifted to Harry for Christmas. Harry's father bequeaths the cloak to his son and thus gives life to generations after. The umbilical cord endures.

One day I will give this blanket to my daughter.

Nowadays, capes are made of light-deflecting materials creating the illusion of invisibility; translucent backpacks merge with their wearers; invisible umbrellas keep us dry through streams of air; invisible photography becomes observable for the blind. Even imaginary boyfriends come to life through phone apps designed to simulate relationships, so that you can avoid the prying questions of friends and relatives who wonder why you're still single in your thirties.

***

As a child, I wished to be invisible because there was no cape to protect me from death. I died every day. A hundred times a day. And then I'd make myself get up and start all over.

I wished to go unnoticed in a world where people derived plea-sure from undressing others' lives, sensationalizing them, penetrating them like shameless voyeurs. I was afraid of being seen; I knew that my sorrow and my loneliness were exposed and I was ashamed of my nakedness. I looked for ways to cover myself up, to wrap the blanket of my imaginary mother around me, to feel protected. To pass through life like that.

Each day slipped on by, filled with the inescapable dread that somehow the worst was always about to happen. Every moment of every day was hell. I used to think that being unseen freed you to do whatever you wanted, to make your own choices, to make your own rules. To beat death.

But things don't always turn out how we think they will.

Curled up on the couch, I wrap my favorite wool cardigan around me and turn on the TV.

18

When people and things change, this change is imperceptible to the outside world. Only the distance of time puts everything into perspective, allowing us to ascertain the movement.

How had my life evolved since I was eighteen? Ten? Five?

Suki

"Mind if I sit by you?"

I'd boarded the lunchtime train from Sofia to Bourgas and found an empty compartment, which wasn't difficult. Nobody takes the lunchtime train aside from a couple of mad hatters. Normal people seem to prefer the bus, at least it's got air conditioning.

The train's taken off when she bursts into my compartment. I quickly scan her: short jean cutoffs, a revealing tank sporting some glittery slogan, too-long, too-pink fake nails. She's smacking gum, blowing bubbles that match the hot pink of her nails and filling the compartment with a whiff of strawberry. Her hair's bleached, tied in a side ponytail that contrasts against her tanned skin. There's something enticing, yet off-putting about her.

"I'm Suki. Where you headed?"

"Bourgas." Seems like we're friends already.

"Cool. Last stop, can't miss it, right? Haha. You from there, or?"

"No. Just have something to take care of."

"Nothing wrong with mixing a little business with pleasure. Weekend weather is supposed to be nice and hot, totally cloudless."

"You?"

"Me, what about me?" She blows then pops another pink bubble and it sticks to her upper lip. She deftly unsticks it with her tongue. "I got something to take care of, too."

She takes out a liter and a half bottle of Coke and lifts it to her mouth.

"You want some?" She leans in, lowers her voice and winks at me. "Coke and rum."

"Isn't it a little too . . . hot for rum?" I want to say "early" but decide against moralizing her. I don't know her, she's free to do whatever she wants.

Suki begins theorizing about how the rum can actually raise the body's temperature and therefore alleviate the heat, and all I can think is she has no idea what she's talking about but I bite my tongue. It would be silly to argue over it. Somewhere before Koprivshtitsa I take the offered bottle. Why the hell not.

The sun's almost down by the time we make it to Bourgas. Little old *babichki* dot the platform like seagulls, holding up their "Rooms for rent, 100m from the beach" signs. I go to leave with one of them when Suki tells me that she's got a place to stay and all, but could we meet back up for a beer. I don't really have anywhere to be or anything to do. I'd made the whole thing up earlier so I wouldn't have to explain that the real reason I was on the train was to empty my head, throw all moving thoughts out of it. A spur-of-the moment trip to the seaside seemed like the way to do it, and seeing the sea always recharges me. We decide to meet back up in an hour at the entrance to the Maritime Garden.

Summer's fizz has peaked and thousands of tourists crawl up and down Bogoridi Boulevard like ants from a freshly kicked ant hill. The sticky stench mixes with the aroma of sea salt and fried sprats. When I get back to Suki, she's already waiting and smoking anxiously. She spots me and smiles.

"Hey!" She waves me over and flicks her cigarette. Strangely, it feels like I'm meeting up with an old friend.

"Where should we go?" I ask, but I'm sure she's already picked a place. She seems like someone who likes to have a handle on things, which I don't mind at all so I let her take the lead.

"The Traps, of course! You can't be in Bourgas in summer and not have a beer at the Traps, it's the law."

Suki's a Bourgas native, it turns out, born and bred, but it's the first time she's been back in almost ten years. Her folks kicked her out at sixteen when she started hanging out with a bad crowd. She left for Sofia with some guy she barely knew, and later left the country altogether.

We sit down at a wooden table and I order us two Kamenitsas and a plate of fried sprats. Suki downs half the beer in one go and chats away. I suppose when you're sharing beer and sprats with someone, it's only right that you share your life story with them too. Even if you've only known them for half a day.

Her real name is Petya, but her clients preferred more exotic sounding names so the Dutchman renamed her one night after an encounter with a Japanese woman called Suki. The Dutchman wasn't really Dutch, either. Holland was where his business was based and the pseudonym fixed itself somewhat organically over his bearded face. Suki had been working for him for four years. He found the clients, arranged the pricing, gave her a cut. Made sure she had food and a roof. There were no days off. She worked nights and slept till noon the next day, and when she wasn't bone-tired, she strolled around Amsterdam in the afternoons, sauntered along the streets, crossed over the bridges, and watched the colorful houseboats anchored along the channel bob on the water. Some nights, when she wasn't feeling it at work, she kept her eyes shut and imagined she was inside one of those houses on the water, swathed in plants and perching pigeons. She'd seen two pigeons on a bridge once, she said, watched them "kiss" by knocking their beaks like they were in a fencing match. The female flew away and the male followed and their love game kept on in the air. She'd found it so beautiful and natural, this lovers' play between the pigeons, birds that in just a few minutes would cover the city square with their droppings.

I interrupt her only to order a couple more beers and another plate of sprats. Suki rolls herself a cigarette and goes on with the story. One night, as she stood topless in her brothel window in the Red-Light District, summoning clients, a man stopped in front of her. He just stood and stared. She gestured toward the entrance but he only smiled and dissolved back into the crowd. "Dumb tourist," she thought and continued her window prompts. But an hour later the same man came back flanked by two others. He gestured to Suki that he'd see her on the other side of the window. She went inside and headed to the client room. The Dutchman loved foursomes. Foursomes tripled his profit.

Suki pauses. She lights another cigarette, inhales deeply, and lets it slowly out of her mouth while opening and closing her jaw, exhaling tattered Os.

I'm not interested in the awful details of that night, but Suki's not about to stop now. The sea breeze has made the almost translucent hairs on her forearms stand up. "It's chilly, I need something to warm me up," she says as she gently brushes my hand with hers. It's her turn to order, and she lines up six tequila shots on the table, slices of lime on the side. She wets her wrist with her tongue, pours out some salt then licks it off, makes a vague "cheers" in my direction, knocks it back, and slowly sucks the lime. Her eyes are an invitation to follow suit. The night is going in the wrong direction and I feel like giving in. I lick, salt and down the tequila. Suki winks triumphantly. Time slips away like sand through my fingers.

The three men told Suki to put her clothes on, which struck her as strange, but the Dutchman had taught her not to ask questions, just do as she's told. She began to dress herself slowly, seductively, even tried to wrap herself around one of the men, but he pushed her away and told her to hurry up and get dressed. It was then that, according to Suki, things went south. The three men pulled out guns, signaled for her to keep quiet, and disappeared from the room. Gunshots rang out and total chaos ensued. Suki was frozen with horror as all the other girls ran around, twittering like frightened sparrows. The gunshots stopped. The Dutchman and everyone from security were shot dead, the clients all flew out, running while zipping up their trousers and all the girls continued to flutter. One of the men squeezed her hand, led her outside, pushed three-hundred euro into her palm and told her to run. Police sirens approached and Suki merged with the swarm of people—disheveled and out of her mind with fear. Hours passed before she could process what had happened. The following morning she bought a plane ticket to Sofia and . . . here she was now, drinking tequila on the beach.

"Wow, sounds like a real action movie." I'm really at a loss for what to say to her.

The tequila is splashing inside my head, its waves crashing and then subsiding. I get pulled under and I pop back up above water. One after the other, Suki and I suck down the limes and the tequila and our lips are numb. We are the last ones here now, I can see the boy behind the bar looking at us through a haze.

When I worked in that restaurant kitchen in the months after I left the Home, the longest and most torturous hours were the ones in which we had to wait for the last customers to leave. You're done cleaning and with everything else but you are forced to just sit there, waiting for that table in the corner to finally finish their drinks and leave. But their stupid conversation wouldn't cease, stretching endlessly into the night, their jabber burbling till morning.

I let Suki's thigh carelessly brush against mine and I feel the heat from her skin, smooth as a jellyfish. The fact I will never see her again gives me the courage to go with the flow without reserve or prepossession.

It's almost morning by the time I find myself trying to get the key into the keyhole of the door of my rented room. When I finally manage, I collapse into the bed.

***

My sleep is brief and fretful. I awake from the unbearable heat in the room and the punches coming from inside my head. The tequila is serving her revenge. I go down to the cafe and order a double espresso, black. A local radio station's news reports on politics and murders is ruining the morning.

". . . In the bloody massacre . . . One of the victims is forty-two-year-old Bulgarian citizen Stoyan Nikiforov, also known as the Dutchman, a souteneur, and one of the founders of an Eastern European sex-trafficking ring. Among the suspects in the shooting is one of the sex workers in the ring, P. K. from Bourgas, who is alleged to have hired hit men to kill the Dutchman. The investigation is ongoing."

19

"When will you come back?"

I've been coming to a Sofia-based "family-like placement center for children" for several months now. Every second Sunday of the month I spend my mornings here. It's called "family-like" but I recognize the sorrowed eyes. These are the same abandoned children I grew up with—hesitant, jumpy, dreaming up their parents. I impatiently count the days down to our next meeting, the way you can't wait to arrive someplace beautiful after a long journey. The kids love my being here too, I can tell, their curious demeanors are a dead giveaway. I've brought a giant bag with me that the kids have taken to calling my "magic" bag, and I start pulling out all sorts of goodies: crayons, watercolors, musical instruments, marionettes. I need our playtime just as much as they do. And all the "Naya" wafers we can get our hands on.

We all sit on the ground in a circle, we sing songs and play the instruments and I tell them all sorts of stories in which every kid plays their own part. I plant dreams into their little minds, give them wings to fly over the horrors of their daily lives, so they can believe there's something better out there on the other side of it all. A life that's possible if they only have the strength to believe it. Believe in themselves, believe in the people around them, believe there is some sort of happy ending.

It took me seven years and too many restaurant kitchens before I was honest enough with myself to realize my life would never be any different from how it was in the Home unless I did something to change it. I stumbled around blindly for a long time, looking for the right way, any type of way, to approach my life. I came across an organization that worked with special needs children. They were looking for volunteers for their new marketing campaign, promoting art as therapy. I signed up. They called the next day and I started that same week. I attended the weekly sessions and the rest of the time, I diced onions, eyes red and burning. My work was primarily with children with autism and Down Syndrome. After a year, they offered me a paid position. It wasn't much, but I took it without hesitation. There was now something far more important than money.

I couldn't stop, I had to meet more children whose lives I could impact. It was like a drug then, and it still is now.

I contacted this placement center a few months ago and the director agreed to let me visit on a trial basis twice a month. Twice a month I confront the nightmares of my childhood. In the beginning it was more than I could handle and I had to leave the room to calm myself down. I've adjusted now, the meetings have been therapeutic. In healing someone else's wounds I was somehow healing my own.

20

I'm sitting on a bench in a square in an unfamiliar town. In the center of the square is a fountain with a statue of a naked woman holding an earthen jar from which water spills. It's a sunny morning, the square is empty, and from where I'm sitting I can see a little rainbow just barely over the water. There's the sound of church bells ringing. Everything seems as though it is muted and drawn in pastels. Like a Turner painting.

Suddenly, a shot rings out; the pigeons all scatter and the clap of their wings echoes away somewhere in the back of my mind. I feel a warm, sticky rivulet roll down my face. I slap my hands over it, and press, terrified to let go. A moment passes, my hands are tomato red. I think of the endless crates of tomatoes at the market and go to lick my fingers. Instantly, I see the water in the fountain turn crimson, then everything around it turns crimson with it. The sunlight dissolves, the colors fade, and everything turns pitch black. I'm cold. The world melts and together with the water from the fountain, it drains into the canal.

Gone. My world, vanished.

I wake up and quickly look into the mirror. I am there. Or rather I am "here." I think about the difference between what is here and what is there. What is real and what is made up. Isn't the world merely a projection of our imagination? A mirror image of our thoughts, moods, perceptions. Does the world end when we do? When I do?

21

All I have from my separation with my mother is the cream-yellow baby blanket, which I've carefully folded and buried at the bottom of a drawer. All I have from my split with Naya is *A Hundred Years of Solitude* by Gabriel Garcia Márquez and a single photo. In the photo, Naya and I are standing next to each other, our arms around the other's waist. We are eighteen. It's summer, and we are standing in front of a house in the Rhodope Mountains, where we've gone hiking. We were headed for Trigrad but got lost, and with the sun setting quickly we needed to find a place to sleep. We ended up in some deserted village, no more than five houses in all. Outside one of the houses, on a log laid on its side like a makeshift bench, sat an elderly woman, her back bent by age. The *baba* invited us to spend the night in the empty house next to hers. "All the young people escaped to the cities," she said as she ladled warm bean stew into two bowls and tore hunks of homemade bread, "the elderly all died away. The whole village is just me and two other *babi*." She told us of her children and grandchildren, how they came up once a month to bring her rice and beans and flour and oil, how one of her grandsons recently emigrated to Germany for school. She gathered all the photos from the shelves to show us and I thought how these photos were her only thread to the world outside of these few remaining village houses. We watched her caressing the photographs, delighting in them as though they were not photographs but real people, without registering the emptiness of her act. She held the *memento mori* in her hands, the trapped resemblance of her favorite people inside the photo paper, for whom she was now likely just a burden.

Afterward, she took us to the house next door, brought clean sheets and covers and nimbly made the beds, still bent over in two. In the morning, we awoke to the smell of freshly fried *mekitsi*, set out on the table for us next to a jar of homemade wild strawberry jam. I'd heard about the legendary hospitality of the Rhodope people, but it always seemed like some sort of urban legend passed from person to person. It was all real. As we said goodbye, we asked her to take a picture of us outside her house.

When Naya left, whether intentional or by accident, she left behind the photo at the bottom of one of our drawers. I put it inside a wooden chest, next to my mother's blanket. My treasure chest of goodbyes. I was hoarding items, gestures, words spoken and unspoken—the language memorabilia of other people's farewells. I filled the chest with them so there'd be no room left for my own.

22

Two news items from today:

Young Mother Kills Baby to Keep Job as Priestess of Love

A woman from Cologne, Germany, stabbed her newborn son with scissors minutes after she gave birth to him on the bathroom floor of her apartment. The mother was a sex worker, and, according to her, the baby would have prevented her from being able to continue working. The twenty-one-year-old Helena Zewing had wanted an abortion, but by the time she got to a doctor, she was too far along and the doctor refused to terminate the pregnancy. During questioning, the woman admitted she had been planning the murder for several weeks prior to giving birth. Unable to work while carrying the child, the woman had fallen deep in debt with her pimps, who'd lent her money at an impossible interest rate. The young woman felt she had no choice but to kill her newborn so she could continue working and repay the loan. After stabbing the infant in the chest four times, Zewing wrapped the tiny remains in a black garbage bag, put them inside a tote bag and threw the bag into the Rhine River. An anonymous passerby was the unlucky witness to the event and alerted the authorities.

Following her arrest, the young woman's mother, Joustine, died by suicide. "I cannot take what my daughter has done," she had written in a note before throwing herself in front of a train. (*Nachrichten aus Köln*, July 10, 2014)

Father of Six Strangles Own Twin Toddlers

"It's not my husband who killed our little ones, it was poverty that killed them. We don't even have money for bread. All our welfare checks go for food but the twins were always starving 'cause the older kids got theirs first. It wasn't their father who killed them, they died of hunger." This is the account thirty-eight-year-old Marinka Georgieva, from the village of Boikovo, swears by in the murder charges against her husband, Kiro Georgiev. The eighteen-month-old twins, a boy and a girl, were found by paramedics in extremely grave condition. Both children passed away en route to the hospital.

Forensic expertise showed signs of strangulation. The children had been emaciated, likely left starving for days. Their mother said the children were crying inconsolably and the father had gone to check on them; minutes later they were found unresponsive and the parents called an ambulance. The paramedics called to the scene described a half-dilapidated shed on the north side of the village. An unbearable stench wafted through the room, mold covered the walls. Empty cans rolled around on the floor, surrounded by wafer wrappers. In a matter of days, the remaining four Roma children were expected to be taken by child services. The oldest girl attempted to run away after her father's arrest but was found hiding in a nearby gulch soon after.

The father is accused of negligent manslaughter following premeditated second-degree bodily trauma, prosecutors said; he has been appointed a public defender. If found guilty, Georgiev may face between five- and ten-years' jail time. (*Pazardjik News*, July 10, 2014)

I carefully cut out the news articles and tape them in a notebook; I place the notebook inside my treasure chest of goodbyes.

23

"Will you get off your ass and hand me the clothespins!"

My third-floor neighbor is diligently getting the wrinkles out of the dripping bed sheets weighing down the clothesline wire. Next to her, having his morning coffee and reading the Sunday paper, is her husband, decidedly past his prime with his well-rounded beer belly and thinning hair. Every weekend without fail, he sits contentedly on the rickety wooden bench he built, his ass practically glued to the slats. Even the nippy September morning doesn't seem capable of disrupting this routine. He lazily reaches for the basket of clothespins and hands it to his wife, who's been up since six so she can run the washer at the night rate. I strain to remember their names, try to picture the nametag on their doorbell, their mailbox, but it's as though someone has wiped the blackboard of my memory clean with a wet sponge.

"And I told you not to lean back! You'll get plaster all over your shirt."

There is a different air about this morning, but I'm not sure why. Maybe today is just a composite of every Sunday morning ever and suddenly it feels multifaceted and somehow, different. I prop my elbows on the railing of the balcony and mindlessly gape at my surroundings.

Just below me, on the fourth floor, another neighbor is sitting cross-legged on a plastic chaise lounge. Her multitasking is impressive. She lacquers her nails crimson with the ease of an exquisite painter, chatters away with unabating intensity into her mobile phone, squeezed between her ear and shoulder, and in the short pauses in between, blows and smacks her bubblegum. I spot at least three different men from the apartment building across from ours think up exceptionally important projects on their balconies so they can sneak their ostensibly absentminded glances her way. Their women, meanwhile, are frying up bread in their kitchens, wondering why the quickest way to the heart is no longer through the stomach. No memory of her name either, although I can tell you the name of every single one of her girlfriends.

I see the grandpa from the second floor on his balcony too, cracking walnuts. He pinches them between his leathery, iodine-stained fingers, and "bam!" his fist shatters the shells and the pieces fly everywhere. The grandkid, a nipper of no more than five, runs inside to play with his construction set, then runs back out to the balcony and to his grandpa, mouth wide open for more walnuts. A neighbor told me that up until recently, the old man and his wife lived in a nearby village, but when the old woman died, their daughter moved him into her city apartment to spare him from sitting alone in a house that now bled with emptiness.

"Eat my boy, eat so you can grow big and strong, just like a walnut!"

And the boy hungrily devours the walnuts and grows. What could be more nutritious than a freshly-cracked walnut? The entirety of his grandfather's love is inside of it.

24

Who was I? Nobody had called me by my name often enough to make me feel important. Until this moment, my life was the life of every other child in every other Home for abandoned children.

My universe then and for a very long time had been contained within the four walls of the Home, defined only by what happened inside, by the other children and by the Matrons. And by the wafers, whenever they actually got to us around Christmas. It wasn't until much later that I added new elements to that universe, stitched patches to it, embroidered it with new emotions that were previously mysterious and frightening to me, filled it with new experiences like you'd fill a duvet with feathers, making it fuller and softer.

I had no idea what *chujbina* meant, I only knew the Matrons talked about it a lot. For me, this accumulation of sounds, the sing-song buzzing of *chujjjj-bi-na* carried no importance. Yet somewhere deep inside, I must have felt the meaning: the unfamiliar and therefore shiny and coveted Other. *Chujbina*, this wonderful foreignness, this faraway distant country, the place that was everything my world then wasn't.

The Matrons taught us to read with old newspapers. I always picked the column "From Chujbina," sounding out the names of the foreign countries the news came from, inhaling their foreign lives and their foreign deaths. I scraped pieces of strangers' stories with my nail, layering them onto my all to familiar world like a collection of fantastical mica, studying them with my child's curiosity, inspecting them from all sides until I believed they were mine. I became the star of shocking crimes, gory murders and sexual assaults, of political perversions, of terrorist acts; I turned myself into each one of the twenty children executed with an assault rifle in Newtown, Connecticut.

For a time, the real and the imagined blurred. I didn't look for some connecting thread; each particle existed independently of the rest—like a stream of photos in which I took center stage, strutting the same pose as various panoramas from around the world rotated behind me. My photo album from my travels to Sorrowville.

25

I'm not sure if I'll ever truly leave my childhood behind. A sticky fog seems to have descended around me and it obscures all possible paths. I feel discarded, and the awful memories of those early years press down on me like a sheet-metal lid over a well, all weighed down by an enormous boulder, leaving me with no chance of escape. All my shouting and banging from within feels useless. What's the point? No one can hear me.

It's like I am barely able to tread the water; it rises and soon it will reach the top, to the sheet metal lid. I will begin to gulp down my fear and choke on it until I cease breathing.

Or maybe somehow the water will swell and blow off the lid that holds my life captive and my fears will overflow and then subside, releasing me.

Aksinia Levina

Every morning: she leaves for the store at exactly 9:35 A.M. when the gainfully employed are already in their swivel chairs and the slackers are inside their unaired houses, still asleep or generally not giving a shit. A scant October sun slips a frail ray down the deserted streets and caresses her face. It's been so long since anybody's done that— since she's felt the gentle press of human palms on either side of her face, the warmth of another human, the heat, which as if through an electrical conduit would pour itself from another's body into hers. It's been too long since there's been life injected into her withered face, which now dangles, wrinkly, like the faded winter coat hanging in her hallway, the unfaltering partner to all the winters of her life.

All the stray cats outside her apartment block start meowing with the first scrape of the front door and cluster at her feet as if on cue. They anticipate her morning arrival like manna from the heavens. Missus Levina, Aksinia Levina, has lived here for fifty years and for fifty years the stray cats outside the apartment block have purred expectantly, licking their lips for that first scrape of the entry door. Each morning, at precisely the same time, the barely there body of the elderly woman slips through the crack of that entry door, her grocery bag brimming with food for the neighborhood strays. She's scarcely poured any of it out into the old empty box of biscuits she

74

keeps under the first-floor balcony when the cats hungrily hurl them-selves at the food, purring with contentment. She relishes watching them at this moment—they are calm and almost gracious, perfectly undisturbed. The cats inhale the food at lightning speed and again twist around her still-exquisite ankles, milking her for more as she pretends to shoo them away.

Missus Levina would give anything for these fleeting breaths of affection but she would never admit to as much. Every morning at 9:35 A.M. she inhales them like an almond-flavored aperitif and they briefly warm her palate before evaporating. After the feeding frenzy, she will leave the cats lounging lazily and slowly make her way to the grocery store. She'll buy the usual: bread, potatoes, rice, lokum, and cat food. She'll get a couple of pears, too, but only if they're ripe enough. Hard food is tough on her veneers. After shopping, she'll go straight back to her small but tidy top-floor apartment. She lives there alone, if one doesn't take into account the pigeons, whose beaks knock incessantly against the windowsill. Every now and again, one will wriggle through the cracked window and Missus Levina will have no idea how to catch it and release it back outside.

Word in the neighborhood is that Missus Levina was a ballerina. World class, the story goes. Ticket prices for the ballet performances doubled anytime she was on the bill and people paid it, so hungry were they to see her dance. Like a feather she would glide onto the stage, her feet barely touching the ground, pirouetting in a whirlwind of fervor, and the audience jumped to its feet to applaud her. They say that once, as she danced *Swan Lake*, a zealous fan threw a moun-tainous bouquet of white roses onto the stage mid-performance. Before they could snatch the flowers off the stage, one of the bal-lerina swans landed on the bouquet, something cracked, and the swan swayed and collapsed, wings and all, onto the ground. Mayhem ensued, all the dancers scattered off stage, the curtain dropped, and only the wounded swan remained, curled into a ball of feathers and agony, its right leg protruding unnaturally. That performance, the neighbors whispered, had been her last. Was any of it actually true? No one knows. In any case, Missus Levina's slender frame and her still-poised posture imply at least some of it must be. And if one were to look closely, one would perhaps notice a barely perceptible limp in her right leg.

She ascends the stairs up to her apartment slowly, methodically. Her wrinkled hand isn't so much holding the railing as it's caressed by her arthritis-bent fingers and they glide over its mutilated wooden torso, etched with words and obscenities. She takes a deep breath, one stair, two, three, breathes out, four, five, breathes in again, six, seven, a stream of air whistles out between her lips, eight . . . Her thoughts can barely catch up to her breath.

Fourth floor: four down, four to go. Her heart now gallops uncontrollably and it reminds her of those years, the years when her dreams came easily, when she'd been young and tough, disciplined in each one of her ambitions. She climbs the stairs with the same steadfastness that once enabled her to execute pirouette after pirouette until she would collapse to the ground in exhaustion. Her angular nose and sharp chin are there, it would appear, to reaffirm her resolve. Always and at any cost. Never give up. Sixth floor, two to go. Sweat beads appear in between her silver hair, carefully arranged in a low bun, trailing two rivulets down her long neck, more than once desired by admirers' lips.

She never married. Couldn't stand the sloppiness of some of them. She took them in for a night but was quick to fix the pillows over the impeccably made sheets the instant they left. And to air out the house. She couldn't stand the stench of lust and wallowing. The years came and went, she kept impeccably making the bed until the romantic dates and phone calls thinned out, one day stopping altogether. So it was said. She would live alone on the eighth floor, her only interlocutors the pigeons and the neighborhood stray cats.

Eighth floor. Here's the massive wooden door, scarred by age but holding together like a proud centenarian. Every day it takes her longer to climb up, every day her hands shake ever more uncontrollably as she guides the key into the lock. She enters and the scent of senescence envelops her immediately, but a gentle puff of wind coming through the cracked window quickly dissipates her toxic thoughts. She stands, holding herself against her bookcase, still breathing heavy, white spots dancing before her eyes like beautiful birds. She teeters over to her gramophone and places the needle on the record. Chopin's *Nocturne in F Minor* fills the rooms like a feather duvet. She sits down on the couch, captivated by the music, and lets go of the world around her. The fatigue and the sorrow melt away and soon disappear. Calm comes over her, her breath steadies, her eyelids get heavier, the body lightens. She sees herself flying with grace along the memories of her dancing youth, locked away in a wooden trunk in her bedroom.

The next morning, the neighborhood cats will meow hungrily until dusk before finally giving up and scattering into the streets in search of food, and the wind will play a symphony in F Minor into the gutter.

26

I'm sitting in a coffee shop in the Lozenets neighborhood waiting for my double macchiato. One table over, two women waist-deep into their thirties have crossed their long legs and are drinking their tall white frappes through straws. I eavesdrop as I've got nothing better to do, although it's not like their booming voices give me much of a choice.

"I just don't understand why the kids need to be told about these things, you know? They're what—eight, nine? These are touchy subjects and there will be kids who will take it to heart. It won't just be news to them."

"Absolutely! Today it's honoring the victims of a terrorist act, tomorrow my son's gonna be asking me what happens when the same terrorists come to Bulgaria. You're just scaring them! They'll think they're not safe anywhere."

"Ugh. Honoring. Mila had nightmares all night! She was tossing and turning for hours. Finally, she just came into our bed. She said she dreamt of the murdered kids on those trains, saw the face of each one, she said, wondering what they must have felt. All last week they were teaching them some nonsense about the Syrian refugees. But did they teach them about the diseases those refugees were carrying? No! Mila comes home and tells me, 'Mom, did you know that they killed ten thousand children in Syria? Why was Daddy swearing the other day about Syrians walking down Vitoshka Street? If they're being killed in their own country, why is it wrong for them to come to ours?' Can you believe that? I'm this close to running over there and making that idiot teacher's life a living hell. They're driving my kid crazy."

"Well you ought to file a complaint, Sonche!"

"With who? The principal is the one who bought the TV for the homeroom in the first place. She's the one who told that idiot history teacher to fill their heads with 'news of the day.'"

"Escalate it! History class is for learning history, not to traumatize kids with bloodletting and terrorist acts!"

I think of all the children killed during the first and second world wars, the incinerated Jewish kids during the Holocaust, all the children murdered in Gaza, Iraq, and Afghanistan. I think of the photo of those three thousand three hundred children evacuated from South Vietnam in April, 1975, who crossed the ocean and reached Oakland, California, lying in boxes and tied to airplane seats. I think of the drawing by the Syrian child in a refugee camp: grenades fall from black airplanes over the dismembered corpses of a father and child, their ripped extremities rolling around on the ground as a mother and her boy kneel over the dead bodies, their tears drawn the size of plums . . . I think of the persecuted, the violated, the exiled, the orphaned. Today. The hundreds of thousands of children who aren't in history class. I take a sip from the double macchiato but its taste is suddenly bitter.

27

The new mothers who came in to pick one of us were all different. Different faces, different voices. Some moms' voices were rich and soft like a jar of peanut butter, others' voices sounded effervescent and exuberant, like a glass of freshly squeezed orange juice. But they all had something in common. It was that almost imperceptible scent of a woman about to become a mother.

***

I recently watched a BBC documentary on emotions. The film examined the permanent impact of early childhood experiences on a person. In one of the first scenes, an eight-month-old baby happily plays with a real live chirping mouse. Suddenly, the narrator of the documentary makes a big, loud noise behind the child, scaring her so much that she cries inconsolably for a long time after the fact. In the second scene, the baby is in the same room without the mouse. At the first sight of the mouse, she wails, distraught. According to the psychologists carrying out the experiment, as an adult, the child will be struck with horror anytime she sees a mouse, regardless of how defenseless the animal may be. And she will never realize the underlying reason for this irrational fear.

When I was little, I collected rose petals and pushed them inside a plastic bottle of water. I shook the bottle to create my innocent version of perfume. I dabbed this rose water on my neck and on the insides of my wrists, just as I'd seen the Matrons do. Cocky from my obvious and irrefutable genius, I shoved my wrists under Naya's nose, captivated by the bliss emanating from her half-closed eyes as she inhaled the smell. I wanted her to associate the scent of roses with me; for my touch to bring her the same pleasure that my makeshift perfume did.

The same goes with unsavory smells. I will forever associate the smell of semen with those painfully importunate, feral attempts by the boys in the Home to reach their sacred orgasm while I writhed in hell.

28

Dara quickly made her way over to me anytime I visited the Home for the play-therapy sessions I led. She would sit on my knees or stand in front of me and fasten her eyes on my face. There was something different about her, something special, which I couldn't yet put words to, but to which I gravitated the second I first saw her. I felt the inklings of something new, the zygote of which warmed my entire body. I was careful not to show preference for any one of the children because I knew the terrible effect it would have on the others, including Dara. She'd have a target on her back the moment the other kids felt her status change. The memory of the kids who got singled out like that in the Home was still fresh in my mind. It's when I realized a child's hatred is far more potent than any other: it is unadulterated and pure.

Even so, I couldn't stop thinking about Dara. Increasingly, I associated my visits to the Home with seeing her—being squeezed by her big welcome hug, seeing the tiny flames inside her wide-set, hazel eyes. The color of her eyes on a particular day dictated her mood and I only had to glance at her to know how she was feeling. When she was calm and bright, the green specs shone like a sunny day. When she was angered by something, they took on an orange-yellowish hue, as though they signaled a warning. Her eyes darkened when she was down and in a bad mood.

Dara's story was gruesome and heartbreaking. Her mother had died during childbirth and she was raised by her father and her paternal grandmother. One afternoon, her grandmother took her out to the playground. When they came home, her father was lying in a puddle of blood, stabbed to death on the floor of their kitchen, the bloody knife thrown in with the rest of the dirty dishes in the sink. The television was missing as was her father's wedding ring, ripped off together with the finger. There wouldn't have been anything else to take anyway. Dara and her grandmother waded through the gore and Dara splashed into a puddle with her bright blue shoes, specks of blood marking them forever. She'd been four. She spent the next two years in a psychiatric ward. Her grandmother came to visit her every day. The child stood before her wordless, looking through her as though she were a glass of water. Her grandmother wept quietly and sniffled her grief. Two months before Dara was to be released, her grandmother died and the little girl ended up in the Home.

Five years after her father's murder she continues to draw the same picture over and over again which has, with time, become almost minimalist and yet no less shocking: a little girl with her chest torn open, her heart thrown to the floor beside her. She hasn't uttered a word since the day she saw her father facedown on the ground.

29

The question Naya and I were frequently asked was, "But what will you do when you want to have kids?" We never did anything to hide our relationship and most of our friends knew we were more than friends and roommates. We wished to be free to make our own life choices, including the people we wanted to love. At the same time, we fought to keep the intimacy of our relationship private (as all intimate relationships are, indeed, private) and to protect it from unnecessary demonstration.

We avoided gay clubs because we felt they were exclusionary. They labeled our love as somehow different and forbidden, which to us only served to scream that same-sex couples were abnormal and needed their own clubs, bars, and parades.

I remember once on the tram Naya rested her head on my shoulder and I felt the weight of her day. I kissed her forehead to absorb her fatigue and she smiled and took my hand. At that moment I felt whole. We completed each other and it was as if our love flowed into a fragile porcelain vase and somehow filled the void of the world. I felt the eyes of the man across from us, saw him lick his fat lips and his eyes flash as they crawled all over our bodies. I knew where his thoughts strayed and it made me sick to my stomach. Next to him, a woman snorting from the heat, with sweaty armpits and three overflowing bags of groceries, plus a protruding baguette in tow, waited for her stop before she turned to us and spit out: "You ought to be ashamed! Groping and grabbing and showing off!"

I *was* ashamed. I felt a real, deep, painful shame from the fact that for a split-second I had taken off my invisiblity cloak and had allowed myself to be a normal girl. A girl just like any other. A girl who was allowed to feel love in the tram, and on the street, and in the shop.

Was our love different? Of course. It was as unique and singular as any other love in the world.

30

Four minutes is all it takes to accept a stranger. "Look Beyond Borders" is a 2016 project by Amnesty International Poland. It's based on psychologist Arthur Aron's theory that looking into a stranger's eyes for four minutes is the most powerful way to bring people closer.

The experiment takes place inside an empty warehouse in Berlin. Refugees from Syria and Somalia meet people from Belgium, Italy, Germany, Poland and Great Britain. They sit across from each other and look into each other's eyes. No words, no gestures. Four minutes. A cameraman records the interaction. The results stun. The initial skepticism and mistrust in the eyes of the participants vanish, replaced by friendly smiles and even excitement. After four minutes exactly, the interaction ends. Most of the participants can't hold back and cling onto each other in a deep embrace; some of them cry.

The campaign was launched as a response to the attitudes in several European cities regarding refugee families. According to the organizers, when you stand face to face with someone and look into her eyes, you can no longer see a refugee with no identity, you see a person just like you—someone who loves and suffers and dreams.

At the end of the video, a young woman turns to the camera and says of the man whose eyes she has just finished gazing into: "I hope he asks for my number."

31

Naya and I imagined how one day we'd have kids of our own. We were far too young then, no more than twenty-three or four, so our conversations were only hypothetical. Still, we dreamed about the day we'd be a family. We had decided to adopt our children. Two or maybe even three.

The night Naya left, my dream shriveled like a scorched scrap of leather and the pain of it all was only exacerbated by the complete lack of a goodbye or explanation. I thumbed through all the possible reasons in my mind—from most likely to least likely, from the fatuous to the flagrant, from the timid to the obnoxious and irrefutable—but nothing worked. I became even more convinced that none of them were the actual true reason she left. I blamed her, then myself, untangling our last conversations and searching for hidden meaning in the way she had looked at me, wondering how I'd somehow missed all the ostensibly accidental signs she'd earmarked for me. I went through phases of anger, self-blame, pity, and consummate despair before finally regaining consciousness, licking my wounds and coming to terms with the fact I was alone. I was surrounded by the buzzing of people and their endless chatter and stories, but this only made my loneliness thicker and more impenetrable. I wanted to believe that the world was ours, that it only existed for us, but now I knew it would continue to exist even after her. Even after me.

Years passed before I finally understood why she left. It was one of those days when the memories of the Home burst into my mind like a whirlwind, forcing me to imagine how life had turned out for the rest of the kids there—for the ones who'd found mothers, and for the ones like me, who'd kept on dreaming one up.

Typically these whirlwinds didn't last too long because the awful memories bloated me with anger and nausea. I knew that none of these grown-up children were responsible for my loneliness and it's likely they didn't care to remember me either. Looking back, it comes to light that my trauma wasn't caused by my being in the Home, but by the absence of family. I had never had a real family and this bruised my consciousness, causing me unimaginable pain every time something so much as grazed the wound.

Then it came to me. My proximity to Naya was like a finger digging into those wounds, every day. Every day I'd reminded her of the fact she'd never be her mother's child, that she'd gotten a life sentence with no chance of parole.

Naya. Swallowing the blood from the wound I kept digging into with my presence, the wound that would continue bleeding, scabbing over, then getting infected over and over before finally erupting onto the mirror with puss and guts. Naya had tried to look into that mirror and realized the only way she'd ever be able to see her true reflection was to get the hell away from the mirror and from me. It would be her only chance to heal.

Arine

She wolfs down her food and I sit as still as I can, mesmerized, watching her, afraid that even the slightest move will break the spell. At first she clumsily twirls her fork inside her spaghetti, turns the fork with both hands and smacks her lips as she chews and inhales what she's managed to balance on the utensil. She sucks the pasta down noisily, the ends flick the corners of her mouth and color it red. Soon she tires with the ceremony, throws the fork aside and sticks her entire hand into the bowl. Palpable contentment spills across her face. I wish I too could dig into my meal with my bare hands and savor the food using all my senses.

I watch her patiently. Her dark, flickering eyes look like the black olives on her plate. Her tattered dress barely covers her taut chest. She's no more than nineteen or twenty. Her shiny black hair is gathered into a low ponytail and falls softly down her straightened back. Her bare, dark brown shoulders pull in the sun's rays like a magnet and reflect them back, magnified.

"What's your name?" My question startles her, as though she's completely forgotten I'm sitting across from her.

"Arine," she responds, mouth full, and continues to stuff the pasta in. Now and then I see a glisten of her teeth, white as river rocks.

"How old are your kids?"

"My oldest is going to be three in September, the little one is still a baby, only eight months, God bless them. I'm eating for two right now, as a matter of fact. I'm five months along."

Without thinking I look down to her belly to check. It's what they've always drilled into us: gypsies lie. The table covers her midsection and I can't see. As if reading my thoughts, she jumps out her chair and grabs my hand.

"Feel right here. There it is."

The bump is barely noticeable but my palm feels the unmistakable heat emanating from it.

I only met Arine earlier that day while getting bananas at the supermarket across from Pliska. "Met" isn't exactly the correct way to put it. The whole scene unfolded before my eyes in a matter of seconds. Someone yelled, "Shoplifter, stop her!" when a huge man grabbed a young woman and threw her against the shelves. She collapsed to the ground whimpering like a homeless dog as several packets of rice fell on her, her outstretched hands attempting to protect her head. The man grabbed her again, this time by the shoulders, lifted her up to her feet and started to shake her. Angry splotches like chicken pox broke out on his face.

The store manager appeared from somewhere and elbowed his way through the gawkers. Anger flooded his face the second he spotted the gypsy girl, and without saying a word struck her across the face, the slap sounding like ducks' wings on water.

"Let me go, boss, please don't hit me!" She cried, her hands shaking, still protecting her head.

"Why you stealing, huh?!"

"I'm hungry, boss. I got kids, they're hungry too."

"You're hungry? Guess what, we're all hungry. Where's the food, huh? You'd better give everything back, you dirty klepto." The manager kept screaming and shaking her, as though the stolen food would fall out from under her tattered dress.

The girl reached into the bag hanging from her shoulder and pulled out a loaf of bread and a piece of yellow cheese.

"What else is there?" The man kept screaming and ransacked her bag.

There wasn't anything else. An elderly woman, bent over in two and with her hands shaking went over to the manager and pulled on his sleeve.

"Boy, let the girl go. She tried stealing from you, not good, I agree, but can't you see she's hungry and she's got kids to feed? Let her go. Do good and good will find you."

He growled, "I don't need it from you, Grandma! Let's see if she tries to pull this again." The veins on his neck popped out even worse than before.

All the screaming and yelling must have tired him out because in the end he just let her go, threatening that if she ever stepped foot inside the store again, she'd get the beating that was coming to her. The gawkers scattered. I instinctively grabbed a piece of yellow cheese and a loaf of bread, paid, and ran after the young woman.

She was still there. I saw her shuffling her feet at the top of the stairs by the underpass. I approached her from behind and tapped her on the shoulder. She jumped as if she was stepping on hot sand, her hands spontaneously going up to her head to protect her.

"Don't be scared. I won't hurt you." She looked at me dubiously, ready to flee. "Here, take this."

She reached over slowly at first, then grabbed the bag. We faced each other and I could tell she didn't know what to say. The cars hissed past on the boulevard. Only an arm's reach away, a taxi driver smoked through his car window and glared at us.

"How long since you've eaten?"

"Two days."

"Okay listen, you're coming with me. I'm taking you someplace to eat."

Arine's eyes grew big but were still mistrustful. I started walking. She stood in place for a few seconds but she must have run right up because I could feel her trailing only a step behind. I could smell her. I stopped in front of a pizza restaurant and sat down at one of the empty tables outside. It was highly unlikely they would've let us in. Arine kept standing a meter off to the side.

"Go on, sit down! What are you hungry for?"

"They got spaghetti, sis?"

"Let me see. Yes, they do."

"Spaghetti then. If that's okay. I'm always seeing people twirling this spaghetti around and I don't even know what it tastes like."

The server brings us spaghetti Bolognese, drops the plates onto the table with clear disgust, and hurries off.

"Where are your kids now?"

"I left them with my husband's sister so I could look for food. You got any kids, sis?"

"I don't. But I would very much like to have a child of my own one day too, God willing."

"He will, He will. I know these things. Mark my words."

Arine finishes her lunch, belches melodiously, leans over her skirt and wipes her face in it, then drops the bag with the bread and cheese into hers and gets up. She grins back at me a couple of times as she walks away. Elbows on the glass table, I follow her with my eyes until she disappears. The server's voice startles me.

"Your check, miss."

32

"You told me the exact same thing last time."

"I'm sorry, miss, there's nothing we can do."

"Why? I don't understand."

"It's how the law works. If you can prove you own your residence and have stable income, as well as the fact you intend to marry, it would be a different story. But as it stands, I can't help you."

"I have a job. I have a salary. I get paid every month."

"It's not enough. Your income is too low. Do you have any idea how much it costs to raise a child?"

"Do you have any idea what it is to grow up without parents? Without love or affection?"

"That's not the point. We don't want these kids to grow up without a family any more than you do. But it is our job to select qualified candidates with the necessary skills to raise a child."

"With all due respect, ma'am, your institution will never succeed with its mission if your only qualifying factors are tied to income and marital status."

"You don't even own a home. Where are you planning on raising this child?"

"You're telling me only people who own property have the right to have children? Or to be happy? Families rent all the time!"

"True, but families typically have the support of their close friends and relatives. It's a safety net they can count on if they need to. You have nobody. If, for some reason, you end up on the street, who would help you?"

"I don't need anybody's help. I can take care of myself."

"Even so. Let's look at things realistically. I have no guarantee but your word. How can I take you seriously? We can't risk the life of a child, already traumatized by being orphaned, just because you want to be a mother. Do you know how many couples adopt only to return the child because they just can't handle it? They're not ready. It's not enough to just want to. Notice I'm talking about couples, established families. You're single. That's an added risk. Children need two parents. A single woman like you will have a really hard time raising a child by herself."

"I agree that it will be hard in the beginning. But nothing will stop me. I know what I'm doing. Look, I know Dara. She loves being with me, she trusts me. I would do anything to give her a normal life. Anything."

"Still. As I said, you live alone. I don't want to comment on whom you choose to see, namely other women, but I can tell you that this is not a healthy environment for a young, vulnerable child. Or any child for that matter."

"I don't understand. You believe that same-sex couples are somehow less qualified to raise a child than heterosexual ones?"

"It's the rules, I'm sorry."

"I'm begging you to reconsider!"

"I'm sorry . . ."

33

My treasure chest of things I've never had

Pink silk ribbons
A kaleidoscope
An album of my childhood photos*
Birthday cards from my relatives
Birthdays or relatives
My very own shelf in the bathroom for my toothbrush and my
toothpaste
Kuma Lisa chocolate
Pippi Longstocking, Ian Bibian, Alice in Wonderland, Mary Poppins, Classic Bulgarian Fairy Tales I and *II.* And many others
A red rooster lollipop
A bike for Christmas
Christmas
A locket with my mom's photo
The smell of homemade bread, fresh from the oven
Homemade strawberry jam, stewed on a slow fire for hours by
my grandmother
Homemade Easter buns
Homemade anything
A notebook filled with my mom's recipes**

* The photographs inside the album are black and white. Each one is carefully placed inside its own cardboard frame and below it, in exquisite handwriting, is the date and occasion. The very first photograph, of us on the steps outside the hospital where I was born, is taken on the day my parents brought me home. Underneath the photograph is a piece of notebook paper that reads: "Outside the maternity ward, February 3, 1982." My mother wears a knitted dress, olive green, her coat over her shoulders. Her fatigued eyes are those of a girl who has given birth the day before, a girl still at odds with her new identity. She is gently cradling a baby, a baby so swaddled in a cream-yellow, cotton blanket that its tiny, wrinkly face is barely visible. Next to my mother is my father; one hand clutches a bouquet of red carnations, the other wraps around my mother's shoulder. His wide smile and flickering eyes reveal a late night toasting the health of his firstborn daughter. Or perhaps my dad is just simply over the moon.

I turn the pages of the album. Here's a photo of me asleep, sucking on my thumb; there's me sitting on the potty, reading a book upside down; here I am again on my mother's lap, nursing from her blooming breast; here's me on my first birthday—I look guilty and comical with hands covered in buttercream icing from my two-tier birthday cake; there I am next to my mother, up on my toes and looking at her with wide-eyed curiosity as she breaks an egg over a large glass bowl; there's my dad teaching me to ride a bike; here's me on my first day of school, my backpack bigger than me. I keep flipping pages. I end with the photos from our ski trip to Pamporovo, and from the beach in Kavatsi, and here's me again, slice of watermelon in my hands, its juice dripping down my chin so I'm bending forward to keep it from getting on my swimsuit.

** The notebook with recipes is a day planner from nineteen-eighty-something. The recipes are handwritten and carefully arranged by my mother. They're of my favorite dishes I've never tasted, of cakes, sweets and baklavas, of stuffed grape leaves, moussakas, and creme caramels, of chocolate cakes, of lamb liver with rice for Easter, and bean stew for Christmas, of spinach soup and tarator, of mish-mash and carp with walnuts for St. Nicholas Day, of Bundt cake—the sugar halved, of egg-free almond cake, apple strudel, and semolina cake (Lencheto's recipe), of chicken in béchamel, guyvetch in clay, of stuffed peppers sprinkled with fresh parsley. The planner is divided into different sections, all neatly titled and marked: pastries, hors d'oeuvres, soups, dishes with meat and without, puddings, "economical" recipes (back from when you couldn't find anything at the store—the phantom products sugar and flour and milk). I thumb through the imaginary pages of this cookbook and land on the first page, which is inscribed: *For my daughter. So she may still taste my love when I'm no longer around.*

34

Lately I've become obsessed with spending as much time as I possibly can with Dara. The hope that I can somehow care for her outside the periphery of the Home digs at me like a toothache. I've contacted ministries, government institutions, written letters, even gotten in touch with non-government organizations, but all that I get in response in most cases is an upbraiding for my sexual orientation. Their epithets stick to me like spit, smearing and distorting everything until it becomes grotesque. I feel my right to be a mother is being amputated in cold blood, as though I am lying on an icy, stainless-steel operating table and someone simply reaches over and chops it off.

35

Origami. From the Japanese "ori" (to fold) and "kami" (paper). An ancient art in which figurines are created through the folding of sheets of paper, without using scissors or glue. For a long time, this art was only accessible to members of the upper echelons of society, considered the mark of a good upbringing.

***

I'm devouring a slice of pizza and crumpling the brown paper napkin in my hands. I think about the folds that have guided my life, follow the pre-folded lines as if I'm looking at a square piece of paper, that will, at any moment, assume a distinct shape. I'm not sure what it is yet and I trustfully keep folding on the instruction of an invisible presence, someone I've never met before. The same somebody who has pre-folded my origami and disappeared, like a paper boat down the river.

36

After Naya left me, I continued to live in the attic room for a long time, chewing over the pain of our disintegration like a dried strand of tobacco. Instead of slowly dying, my hope that she would return grew with each passing day like a snowball rolling downhill, gathering snow and momentum until it suddenly crashes into a rock and blows into pieces. I was terrified by my own alienation in that abandoned attic, of the space's desolate other half, the empty half of the wardrobe and the bed, the vanished half of my life. The emptiness felt like a black hole that sucked me in and took away my will to move on. I desperately wanted her to come back, to call, to send a letter, a laconic postcard featuring some kitsch seaside landscape. Anything.

***

The only letter I ever received was from Alex. A jittery scratch marked the recipient's address; the sender was simply "Alex." It was a message for all us girls from the Home, but each one of us took it as though the letter had been written just for her. Likely how Alex intended it anyway. The stamp was stuck on crookedly, again as if in haste, the postal record above it denoted the letter had been mailed two days ago. I sensed her fingers' scent all over the paper. We read the letter out loud.

I'm gonna be straight with you. One day they're gonna kick you out of the Home and spit you out on the street. Don't sweat it, though, there's ways to get through it. Girls, remember these three things:

1. *Get a jacket, good shoes, and a blanket. It's fucking cold outside, especially at night, when you're sleeping on a park bench. You can go without food, but you're lost without a blanket.*
2. *Cops'll beat the shit out of you, bro. You gotta run before they get you. Problem is, by the time you know you gotta run, they've already grabbed you. Sooner or later, you'll get thrashed by the cops.*
3. *When a frog swallows a bee and the bee stings the frog's tongue, the frog's not gonna eat any more bees. Or wasps. Johnny told me this. He got it from Pero, who actually used to go to school. It's the only thing he learned. Now though, he's a big chemist. He's the one who taught Johnny how to cook his own meth. And how to spot pure blow from garbage blow. But blow costs a lotta bones, something like seventy leva for a half gram, which I don't have.*
4. *The best way to make some scratch is to get set up in a strip club. Working the highways is a bad way to go, I'm telling you coz I've been there. Johnny knows most of the club owners and gets us clients every night. But whatever you make, you gotta split it with Johnny. I'm serious. Fifty-fifty and you can't take even a lev over that or he'll beat the shit out of you. Again, been there. Johnny's something of a guardian angel. If a client tries some funny shit, he'll take care of him. He's also a food angel. Once a day, he'll get you a cheese sandwich and some ayran, too.*

If you wanna get set up with Johnny, first you gotta pass the test. What this means is, all the services on the menu first you have to do for Johnny. No two ways about it—one after the other. If you can handle it. If not—there's the door, don't let it hit you on the way out. You're gonna be sleeping on the street again and getting jumped by the cops. Johnny decides whether you pass, and if you do, he'll hire you. He liked me right away. I told him—hey, you gotta know what you're doing and I've been doing this since way back. The nights you're off, you're gonna be with

Johnny. Honestly, he's the best. You learn new things when you're with Johnny. He's been in the business a long time. He, like, taught me how to raise my prices. The client and I agree on one of the more special services and then I'll tell him that he'll also get a bonus. Honestly, the bonus is already included in the price but clients don't know shit. Anyway. Johnny's a real pal, he'll have your back. You ever wanna give him a call, check out his digits below.

Looks like it came out to four things, girls, not three, so that's it from me. In short: You'll figure it all out. Like I said, there's ways

Johnny's mobile:

We read the letter in the bedroom, the same room whose four walls were imbued with moans and the reek of semen. I wiped the telephone number from my brain the second I heard it.

Stamat

"You can't catch me, you can't catch me, lalalala laaaaaa!"

"Get over here right now! I'm going to count to three. Oneeee. . ."

"You can't catch meeeeee!"

"Twooo . . ."

"I can't hear you, lalala lalalala."

"Two and a haaaaalf . . ."

"What are you gonna do if you catch me, huh?"

"I'm gonna pull your ears real good! All you ever do is get into trouble. I swear, I'm calling your parents right this minute. They can come and get you!"

"Yeah but you and I both know they're not gonna. They're in Spain making the moolah, so you and I can afford to eat and pay the bills, like Mom said. You forget already?"

"I might be close to seventy, but you should know that I still remember things quite well. And I don't want any mischief makers in my house, got it? There's no reasoning with you! Either you behave, or they can come get you. Come on, give me back my glasses."

"There!"

"'Here you go,' is what a well-behaved young man tells his baba. Thank you. Good boy. You finally calm now? Look, these are granny glasses. You have young eyes that don't need granny glasses."

"Baboooo . . ."

"Yes, Samatko."

"When will I be big?"

"Why do you need to be big, my child?"

"What do you mean why, babo? If I'm big, I'll be strong. And when the other kids at school make fun of me, I can kick their butts."

"Who talks like that! Why are you going to fight with anybody? Who is making fun of you?"

"Um . . . well, the other kids. Toshko, and Petya, and Hristo. Even little Mimi."

"And what are they making fun of you for?"

"That I always wear the same thing. And that my clothes are old. And that I don't have a phone. Or a PlayStation. Whatever . . . And that I'm eight already and still an only child."

"Oh my dear, dear child. Don't listen to them. Maybe your clothes aren't the latest fashion but they're clean and you're clean. What do you need a cellphone for anyway? So someone can steal it from you?"

"Babo, all the kids have them. Even little Mimi has one and she's only seven. It's just . . ."

"It's just what?"

"It's just that nobody wants to be my friend. They don't talk to me, they don't play with me during recess . . ."

"Listen to me, Samatko. It isn't the man with material things who is truly rich, it's the . . ."

"I know, I know. It's the man with friends who is truly rich. That's what you always say, but I don't have things or friends. So I'm poor times two."

"You will have friends, I promise you. Those who choose to be your friends will do so because of who you are, not because of what you're wearing and because you have a . . . what was that thing you said . . . Pay Station?"

"PlayStation."

"Right. Be patient. And be good. That's it."

"Okay, but who am I gonna play with . . . until the real friends show up?"

"Ah, Samatko. Come on now, do your homework first and we'll figure it all out afterward."

"Figure what out afterward? What will we figure out?"

"Afterward, if you're good and don't steal my glasses, maybe I will show you a game. Once upon a time, when I was your age, it's what my baba and I played."

"What game?"

"No, no, no, homework first."

"Okay, okay. Babooo?"

"What is it?"

"Are you . . . are you my friend?"

"I am your friend."

"A real friend?"

"Well what other kind would I be?"

"Hmmm . . . so that means I'm not that poor, right?"

"No you are not, my child, you are not."

"Babo?"

"What is it, Samatko?"

"You're not poor either, babo. Just so you know."

37

The ground beetle mother eats her young during a deadly game of natural selection and mother's selection. The offspring's hunger is incessant and they wait for her to bring them food. When she appears with it, the stronger and faster of the bunch get theirs, but what is brought is never enough to feed the whole lot, so the weaker are left to starve before being eaten by their mother.

Pandas typically give birth to twins but unable to care for both cubs, they abandon the smaller and weaker one. The healthier the baby panda appears, the bigger its chances are of being selected by its mother.

The hamster mother gives birth to too large a litter, which she is unable to sustain. Her solution? Eat part of the litter and nurse the lucky few remaining pups.

The black eagle mother takes a different approach altogether. She simply doesn't intervene in her newly hatched eaglets' battle for food. Young birds' food rivalry is, in fact, a regularly observed occurrence in the eagle species and nearly always ends in siblicide.

38

The reason my mother abandoned me had been her inability to care for me. She was young and the latest food shortages had devastated the grocery stores and what passed for my parents' savings. They had two older children and my arrival was the "unpleasant surprise" for any family in a time of crisis. There was no cooking oil in the stores, no sugar, no laundry detergent, the expensive imported formula was impossible to get, and my half-starved mother couldn't produce enough breast milk to keep my unrelenting screams at bay. So one night, my mother and my father discussed something, cried tearlessly, sniffled away at their poverty, and made a snap decision. The next morning, a pair of new wrinkles cut across their foreheads like battle scars from that night. They got up while it was still dark, swaddled me in the cream-yellow cotton blanket, put me in a basket like they do in books, and left the basket outside the home of the teacher across the street because—it was common knowledge—she had no children of her own and lived alone. My parents stood at the window with bated breath and bulging eyes like they were watching a horror film, waiting to see what the teacher would do once she found the basket. When she opened the front door on her way out to work, the teacher saw the baby, its tiny hands—*my* tiny hands—frozen from the cold, the face sculpted as if from wax. The child slept with such alarming calm that she had to put her finger under its little nose to check for breath. Pandemonium ensued, all the neighbors came out of their houses and my mother and father watched as I got carried away in the basket to somewhere where they'd never see me again. Like Masha's pierogis, which the Bear carried away on its back in a woven basket.

Or maybe that's not what happened at all. My mother was nineteen, bartending at a nightclub. She walked home late one night after her shift when four men ambushed her, pushed her into a black car and took her to some apartment. All four took turns raping her, one after the other. As one of them snorted on top of her, the others watched, slobbering over the same bottle of vodka. She lay sprawled on the disgusting carpet, her body spent and lifeless, her eyes shut, her brain counting off to a hundred and then starting over again.

She ended up pregnant. By the time she admitted it to herself, it was too late for an abortion. She gave birth one town over and refused to even look at the baby, much less know whether it was a boy or a girl. It hadn't been her baby, it was someone else's. It belonged to those four. To the brutality of that night that had scorched her brain.

Perhaps that's not it, either. Maybe it's an entirely different story. My mother's crazy in love with some boy. They're both second-year economics students in Varna. They've been dating for three months. It's all wild nights on the beach, guitars, the Beatles, bell bottoms, and Sunny Beach cognac. All of life isn't just laid out before them, all of life is happening right now, in this very moment. There might not even be a tomorrow. I'm conceived on one of those wild nights, under a full moon and a gentle sea breeze. Grains of sand stick to their bodies, he traces her name in the shore, the waves wash over the writing and leave nothing but the froth of time. When he learns my mother is pregnant, he makes her get rid of it. Get rid of *me*. He wants to rip me out of her womb to save their love but instead, she attempts to save their love by keeping me. She gives birth, he leaves her. She sobs for days, for weeks, realizes she can't have this baby after all. "This baby" is the love which no longer exists. I am her daily reminder she's been dumped and she decides I should be dumped too.

The domino effect. The first of the dominoes falls, and with it, all the pieces behind it. Each domino's fate is predestined. Am I cursed to abandon everyone in my life? Which is more impossible to live with: to be abandoned or to abandon and live with the guilt of it your entire life? To live with the thought of the person who isn't here and yet still exists, that child who still peeks over the fence of time and asks questions.

I had to figure out how to stop the domino effect. Could any of us alter the course of fate, change how things turn out?

39

Early on in our friendship I gave Dara a doll. She heard and understood everything, but the fact she didn't speak made our communication difficult. I wanted to find a way to know more about her and about how she felt. When I saw that every child in the Home but her had a favorite toy, I decided to do something about it. Attachment to anything or anyone seemed really difficult for her, which meant that even a doll wasn't going to be so simple. I explained I'd found the doll on the street, if she could take it in temporarily, until I found it a forever home. Doesn't she look friendly? I think you might even become good friends, I said.

Dara took the doll in her hands and examined it dubiously. She was rough with it. Lifted up its dress, pulled its hair, prodded its eyes, then threw it to the side and went to the other end of the room. I didn't want to push her; I let things take their own course.

Over several more meetings with Dara, I played with the doll in front of her, showed her how to caress it and how to brush its hair, pretended to be sad and shared stories with the doll, which in the end always somehow understood me and made me smile. Dara observed me from around a corner; secretly, but I always felt her eyes. I knew I had to be very patient.

One day she came over to me, took the doll from my hands, and broke down. I stood over her and soaked up her tears. I was relieved that her sorrow finally poured out of her, like mud water along the runnel. Something changed after that. Our meetings became different. I began to teach her how to write. She caught on quickly and inhaled this new knowledge, never satiated. I felt exceedingly proud and happy. Soon we thought up a game—we left notes for each other everywhere, something like clues the other had to use to find a hidden object. On March 8th, International Women's Day, she gave me a handmade card. I opened it, and inside, large crooked letters spelled out: "Take me with you, Leah!" She stared at me with her giant eyes, expecting a reaction. I stood frozen for a minute, maybe even two. Then I turned and abruptly exited the room.

Iman

She opens her eyes inside the common sleeping room. Still tired, she slowly turns her head and takes in the people around her. Bodies are asleep on the ground. The air is thick, the floor dirty. The day is young but the summer sun presses hard through the tiny window at the end of the room. Iman's gaze arrests on her mother, lying next to her, who has, as always, woken up before dawn. She meets her daughter's eyes and smiles softly. "Come here," she whispers into her child's ear and gently puts her arm around her skeletal body.

Iman is five. She's been on the road with her mother, brothers, and older sister since they left Aleppo the Friday before last. Each morning, she has awoken in a different place. On the night they left everything they knew behind, Iman had overheard her father tell her mother they needed to get out as soon as possible. Unable to sleep because of the incessant shooting in the streets during that night, she had gotten up and taken a couple of apprehensive steps toward her parents' bedroom and put her ear to the door. Through her mother's muffled sobs she understood some men had done something awful to her older sister, Zeyda. She heard the word "rape." She had no idea what rape meant, but she knew it had to be something horrific to make Zeyda refuse to speak or eat for almost a week now.

Zeyda recently turned thirteen. Since that night, the only person she will allow to get near her is her little sister. The two sleep back to back in the same bed, and Iman can feel her sister's wide-open eyes anxiously rove the night. She feels her sister's quick, irregular breath coming from the corner of their bed. It had been Zeyda, the eldest, who'd looked after all the other kids, and now she was the one who needed looking after. But how are you supposed to help someone who is in so much pain and so ashamed that they won't even let anyone come near them?

Only a few hours after Iman overheard her parents' conversation, her mother was packing food and clothing into several small pouches and tying them around her children's shoulders. Quietly, they left their house. The streets, still drenched in darkness, smelled of gunpowder. Her father stayed back in Aleppo to fight. As they said goodbye, he slipped something into Iman's palm and gently wrapped his big hand around hers. He held on for a few moments, his eyes drilling a hole into his little girl's chest. He kissed her forehead. "Go," he said, "catch up to your mom." When they turned the corner and their home disappeared from view, Iman unclenched her fist and looked into her palm. A lucky five-piaster coin gleamed in the dark. She smiled, flipped the coin above her head and deftly caught it. "Heads," she whispered to herself, relieved. "Heads will always bring you good luck," her father had said the first time he gave her a coin and they began their little game.

They headed northwest, crossed the Turkish border on Monday, and a day later arrived at the refugee camp in Kilis, trekking the same route thousands of women and children from Aleppo and other Syrian cities had taken before them. When they finally arrived, they were told the camp was overcrowded and they weren't letting any more people in. They slept outside and in the morning were loaded up on the trucks like chickens and taken off down the dusty road. What little was left of their food was close to gone. They felt exhausted, and yet the sun was merciless, beating down on them while the haze from the scorching heat played tricks with their eyes. The following day, the truck dropped them off in Bulgaria, at a refugee camp set up inside a former army base.

A monotonous male voice on the radio comes through: "In August, over a hundred thousand Syrians fled their country, the most since the beginning of the conflict, which erupted over four and a half years ago." The voice adds that according to international human rights watchdogs, over four hundred thousand have been killed, fifty thousand of whom are children.

Maybe we're lucky, thinks Iman. Lucky that we're still kind of close to Syria, where we left dad; lucky to have found food and shelter in this foreign country only a few days after leaving Syria. There are many other kids in the camp, just like Iman. Some arrived with their mother and their father, others came with no parents and are completely alone. People here say they're helping to look for these kids' parents so they can reunite them, but Iman fears that they might not find them at all. She's lucky she's here with her mother, and with Zeyda, and her brothers. One day they'll return to Aleppo and to her dad and the streets will be free of gunfire and it'll be safe to play with her friends. That's what her mom said. Iman looks at all the other children at the camp and wants to reassure them everything will be alright, but she doesn't know how. The kids all have the same look in their eye—as though an invisible hand has slapped them across the face and they are gritting their teeth to keep from crying.

They ration out three slices of bread and a piece of Bulgarian *sirene* per family. Iman has five brothers and sisters and with her and her mom, it comes to seven people. Iman doesn't yet know how to divide three slices of bread and a piece of white cheese into seven equal parts, but someday soon she'll start school and she'll learn. Her mother tells her there's a school nearby, which makes Iman wonder just how long they'll end up staying here. When he kissed her goodbye, didn't her father promise all of this would quickly pass? . . .

Iman remembers her friends in Aleppo. She thinks of them often. Of their laughter, which was easy and contagious, of their favorite dolls they loved to play with. It was all only a few short weeks ago but now seemed so distant; like a fading dream she'd never have again.

***

Winter arrives before any permission to continue on west does. Word around camp is that a village somewhere in Germany is taking in families like theirs, families whose homes were pulverized by the missiles, forever destroying any hope for a return to life before the war. Each camp family prays they would be the next one called, that theirs would be the family that gets to make its way to a new home. But many months pass and nobody's turn ever comes.

Zeyda still refuses to speak, but every so often she manages a few bites of food. "She'll get better," her mother says with affected optimism, and Iman's heart drops every time. At night, when the two of them sleep in the only bed inside the room and she can hear her sister's quiet sobs, Iman feels the worst kind of fear. Before, Zeyda was her rock, her biggest supporter and protector when their father chided them, and now, she was so desperately frail. The shame of what had been done to her ate through Zeyda's body, which now verged on the point of no return. Iman helplessly watches her sister suffer.

Days pass. Zeyda grows so thin she has almost wasted away. It's now impossible for her to swallow even a bite of food. She lies in bed all day, her forehead burning, her breath belabored. Her soul flutters inside the four walls of the room like a startled butterfly desperate to find an open window.

Zeyda now sleeps on the bed by herself. Iman has moved to the floor with her mother and brothers. Someone brings a doctor, a fellow Syrian. There are no other doctors to speak of. The doctor examines the girl and then has a long conversation with her mother at the other end of the room, while Iman and her brothers wait outside. When the doctor leaves, Iman glimpses her mother's eyes about to well up the second before she wipes them with her skirt.

Just then, something glistens in the mud by Iman's foot. She kneels down. A Syrian coin, a five piaster. Ha! Just like the one her dad had given her when they were leaving. She flips it high over her head, catches it in the air and presses it tightly into her fist.

That night her mother doesn't leave Zeyda's bedside. She holds her hand and every hour puts another rag soaked in cold water on her forehead. Iman stands to the side with her brothers, unable to sleep, wondering how it can be that her sister is burning up and yet it is so cold in the room that she can barely feel her numb, frozen feet. Maybe, Iman thinks, if she were to stand by Zeyda's bed, she could take some of her warmth. Her lips shiver and she presses the lucky coin tightly into her hand.

Dawn is breaking when her mother's wail tears itself from her gut and she shakes in sobs over the body of her child. Iman rises, approaches the bed, takes her sister's hand into hers.

"She's warm," she says more to herself as her mother's cries pierce the silence. Iman slowly opens her fingers and looks into her palm. "Tails," she whispers, then kisses Zeyda's cheek goodbye.

40

I've always detested holidays. Back when I was still in the Home these were sometimes entire days I'd spend locked in some bathroom stall or hiding in a cupboard until someone eventually discovered me. The Matrons went home to their families and we were left practically unsupervised—the only Matron left on duty preferred to lock herself in the director's office to watch another episode of her favorite Brazilian telenovela, *Isaura: The Slave Girl*, and a group of us stood outside the door eavesdropping as she took the main character's fate to heart and sniveled and hiccupped. Oh, poor Isaura!

Outside that door it was complete chaos. Everybody did whatever they wanted. To whomever they wanted to do it to. The littler and the weaker and the sick got it the most. The groans and screams probably echoed all the way to the next village over, but the director's office was like an insular time machine that transported you directly to some magical place impenetrable to the sounds and screams outside it. Probably someplace like Brazil, 1875.

All my friends have their places they go to spend holidays among piles of aunts, cousins, and near centenarian great-grandmothers. To them, these gatherings are like journeys back into childhood. They tear hunks out of the Christmas loaves, dip the hunks into the honey and then they let it drip all over their chins knowing no one will chastise them for it because they're no longer children. They're grown up. Or they'll play the Easter-egg game, cracking their painted eggs against another's, then peel them as they discuss how well each one boiled and whether the dye seeped through, and then they'll sprinkle the eggs with herbes de Balkan and lap it all up with the plaited Easter *kozunak*. Everybody has that place she can go back to. The hometown she left behind when she went away to university or just went away from when lazy afternoons marked by nothing ever happening simply got old.

I left the day I was born and my one-way ticket was nonrefundable and nontransferable—there was never going to be a coming back. In the days before and after the holidays, this void digs holes into my soul that are bigger and wider than anything anyone could ever do or say to fill them.

Anyone except maybe Dara.

41

The most horrifying things took place at night, right here in this room. It still reeks of violation and trauma, of piss and lacerated wombs. I can still see myself in the corner, curled in the fetal position. The dampness has soaked through the floorboards and settled underneath next to our collective horror. My fear drifts low like fog—microscopic drops of it coalesce to form this fathomless feeling inside me. The moans and cries have been walled in and still they twist and throb inside my head.

42

I wonder where Wonderland is. I buy maps of the world, globes, I mine Google Maps, I stare into the most minute delineations, into the cracks of the Earth and yet I fail to find the beguiling, magical place. I'm undeterred, sure that it is there somewhere, tucked behind the knotwork of latitudes and longitudes. I dig back in time with my bare hands, I pick at the scabs of my childhood memories, but again fail to find anything resembling talking rabbits or magic folding fans or tiny bottles of potions that shrink you to the size of a human foot.

Each time I go off on my search, I head someplace different. Ancient fortresses, tiny villages in the middle of nowhere, endless coastlines—it's all mapped out for me and I can go wherever I please. Google Maps is my free ticket to foreign cities and their wondrous fountains, to colorful bazaars with festooned stands and vast squares dotted with pigeons. I climb the vertical cliffs of Mount Hua and ascend to the Lotus Flower Summit, then I sharply shrink the scale of the map, survey the territory like an eagle, and land in Borneo's magnificent rain forests. When the humidity tightens its brace around my chest, I take a deep breath and dive-bomb into the crystal-clear waters of the Andaman Sea, south of Thailand. When I get tired of this too, I go walking barefoot through the tiny villages of Southern France, losing myself in the endless acres of vineyards weighed down by the juicy clusters of grapes, my feet sticky. I gather the whole of summer into handfuls and at night, my head dizzies from the gondoliers' singing in enchanted Venice.

One day, a thought flashes through my head. I get the urge to go back and visit the Home. I enter the coordinates into Google Street View and start marching down the same street, which starts at Village K. and leads straight into my childhood hell. I must feel like recounting all my nightmares to peek back in time with the invisible cloak of the internet. Here's the village, I'm now walking down the street, I pass by the decrepit houses stooped along the road like toothless grandmothers. It's winter, there's not a person in sight, only the sound of snow crunching underfoot. I wrap myself in the same threadbare coat I wore out as a child, the coat that wasn't even second hand, more like third or fourth. The smell of bread, freshly baked, travels out of the village shop and catches up to me. I have no money to buy any. I pick up my pace at the ravine, just a little farther to go and I'll be out of the village, and somewhere over there, where the road ends, will be the Home. Bearded grandpas are playing cards in the pub, sucking down shots of mastika. One of them suddenly looks up through the frosted window, his undereye bags heavy from old age and he locks eyes with me. We look at each other like that for a few beats—him on the inside of the glass, me on the outside. In those few seconds I become old, feel his helplessness. Could this be my grandpa, who in this very moment realizes the weight of his mistake, the fact he did nothing to change my fate? The old man next to him elbows him in the ribs and the eyes of the grandpa, my grandpa, go back to the deck of cards. I'm alone once again and the feeling of being a stray punches me in the gut.

"Where you off to walking alone in the street, girl?" Some woman yells after me from the other side of the frozen river, stick in hand.

I look into her face and think I recognize one of the schoolmarms. I am terrified of her recognizing me and making me go back to that place. Once again I am seven and I am beginning to think that I've been stuck at this age for far too long. Years pass, time goes by for everything and everyone else but me. I take off running and never want to look back but I hear the yells of the woman with the stick. I run faster, fast as I possibly can, without stopping, I press my hands over my ears, my heart's about to jump out of my throat.

I reach the top of the hill and I stop to catch my breath. My lips are ice, I can barely move them. I can see everything from here— the village and everything surrounding it. I rodeo over the roofs of the houses but there is no sign of the Home. It's not there. There's nothing. NOTHING. My panic bubbles up like yeast. I ransack the drawer, I pull out all the maps and globes and run my finder along their glossy surfaces and still don't find it. It's disappeared, melted like a snow-drift. If something isn't on a map, does that mean it doesn't exist? I don't understand . . . Am I here if where I grew up is a phantom place? What's more real: the map or the source of my terror all these years?

I frantically chew over and regurgitate my memories; one of these days a bone is bound to catch on my tooth and break it and it'll be proof that both the bone and the tooth exist. I gag on my own thoughts and vomit everything out. I feel relief and decide to throw out all the maps and globes. First thing tomorrow.

43

When I first laid eyes on her, she reeked like a toilet, a half-dried stream of blood trickling from one of her veins. She was on the ground, rolled up by the entrance to the Sveti Sedmochislenitsi church. Outside the temple, pigeons and autumn leaves touched down on the benches; at this early hour, they appeared to be the only visitors to the square. She'd wrapped herself in a faded sleeping bag and appeared to be asleep, but the way she clutched her tarpaulin backpack seemed to indicate otherwise. It may have been my sharp stare that startled her and she opened her eyes.

"What you looking at! Got nothing else to do?"

"No."

My breathing was heavy—like the time I shoved bits of a newspaper clipping up my nose, an article with statistics, detailing how many children end up in homes every year. A thousand babies. Every year. A long time passed before the Matrons figured out what I'd done. The newspaper had completely disintegrated by then, probably marking the inside of my nostrils with the black numbers.

"Spare some change or get lost!"

"I've got a better idea," I said. She looked at me questioningly, with more skepticism than actual curiosity. "I'll give you food and shelter, and in exchange, you'll tell me your story."

"Huh? What do you need my story for?"

"I need it. Hey! Listen to me. I live by myself, I have an empty bed. You can stay with me for a bit, if you need to."

"What are you, some kind of whack job? Get out of my face."

"Fine. If that's what you want." I began to walk away.

"Hey, hey, crazy, wait up!"

I stopped and turned back. I didn't want to push it but something, something I couldn't quite put my finger on, pulled me toward her like a magnet. I saw myself in her semi-transparent body—I saw my first few months after I left the Home. She eyed me with gall, like a starved stray dog. She wanted retribution, to make me pay for her reprobacy. To her, I was the other. The other who had a home, a family, a job, a future. How far from the truth it all really was.

"I know these streets," I said, "they were my home for a long time. Let me help you."

Her eyes bore into me, probing, like they wanted to tear away my forehead and get to the raw thoughts behind it.

"No joke?"

"None. You coming?"

"Okay. Only for a day," she near-whispered and the wind swallowed the sound.

I helped her to her feet and we strode up Shishman Street, my arm around her waist, propping her up. I crossed the street with the weight of people's condemnation on my back. I didn't ask her name. I didn't tell her mine. It didn't matter. She was me and I was her. I wanted to help myself, to change how my life turned out.

When I woke up the next morning she was gone. She must have tiptoed out and I'd slept right through it. I instinctively grabbed my purse—my wallet was missing. A sharp pain cut through my stomach. The emptiness of the room closed in on me and I ran out and down the stairs. Maybe I really was crazy. I understood that no one could change another's life without the latter's permission. I pushed open the entryway door and inhaled the crisp autumn morning.

44

"You got a long life ahead of you, sis! Five bucks and I'll give you a reading."

It was one of those days caught between spring and summer, when the morning sprinkles you with freshness, but as the day rushes on the heat settles and languishes onto the concrete. The air was sweet with the scent of the linden trees and the aroma blanketed the city in an invisible veil of oblivion. I strode along the boulevard, not a thought in my head. Or at least it's how it felt. I can't imagine how one can possibly think of nothing—there's always some anxious thought waiting to break your Zen.

I probably wouldn't have even heard her had she not grabbed me under the arm with her bony fingers just as a motorcyclist zoomed past right in front of my face.

"Huh?" My oblivion flew off abruptly like a crow.

She'd saved me from getting run over and I felt I owed it to her to stop and let her give me a reading. It was like a sign or a warning—like when you come back to find your home ransacked, only nothing's missing, there's just the aftermath of something that could have happened.

"Sis, give me your palm. I'll read you your fortune."

Before I could muster a response, her brown, furrowed right hand had already taken hold of mine. With her left index finger she began to trace the lines of my palm like a sightless person sweeping a white cane from side to side to clear the path. I flinched. A strange excitement passed through me. For the first time in my life I felt what kismet must feel like; like something was, finally, about to happen.

The gypsy woman lowered her head over my palm, studying it. Slightly hunched and small, with long, clumped hair and a devilish look in her eye, she reminded me of a wood nymph. My very own, benevolent wood nymph.

"Come on, tell me what you see!"

"Not so fast, sis. This is hard work. I'm not one of those charlatans that just takes your money and make everything up. I tell only the truth, see. What I say will be, will be. Let me see here. Aaaaah, look at that! Your life is split in two, sis. See this—this is your life line. Here's where it stops and here's where it starts back up again. Looks like something might befall you, a hardship maybe, something. But you can't let it scare you! It'll pass and then you'll get a new life, y'hear!"

"A better one?"

"Well I can't tell you that. Some things are not written on the palm, sis. They're here," she touched her heart, "and here," she touched her head. "Some things we make happen with how we feel and how we think."

"So why does it have to be a hardship? Couldn't it be something wonderful that happens and jumpstarts my new life?"

"Who pays attention to the good things, sis? Who's got eyes for them? When you get something tough that smacks you on the head, that's when you stop and look around and try to figure out what you're doing. It's only then that you ask yourself, 'Why did this happen?' and, 'Why did this happen to me?' And it's only when you stop and ask yourself these questions that you'll come up with an answer and learn your lesson, as they say. And take off in a new direction. It's like the water in the river—when it comes up against a rock, it turns by, and makes a new path forward. That's it. Okay, give me the five bucks and may God save you!"

She disappeared like fog, just the way she'd appeared. That night I couldn't get to sleep for a long time. I kept thinking of the gypsy woman. I wasn't superstitious but her words filled me with anxiety. What had she really told me? There was nothing concrete or categorical. She could've said the same thing to any one other person walking down the street. But there was something still circling, the haunting of a promise—of a future. I kept thinking about what she said: at least some of the time, we are the deciders of our fate. My beginning was someone else's decision, as was my abandonment. I couldn't stop thinking about something else: did I have the power to alter the lines of someone else's palm?

I greeted the new day with dark circles under my eyes and no answer.

45

I wanted to gift Dara the childhood I never had. I was desperate to adopt her and this desperate desire grew inside me like a malignant tumor. Terminal, asymmetrical, uncontrollable.

We stole moments together, just the two of us. I hung cherries from her ear instead of earrings, made flower crowns from daisies, read her stories, applauded every achievement: the first time she tied her shoes by herself, when she learned to whistle. I wasn't sure who really was helping whom patch up her childhood through these stolen moments.

Although she had refused to speak for five years, I knew she understood everything I said and soaked up every last word and gesture. I sang her songs and sometimes I could swear I heard her hesitantly humming along. It was the only time I actually heard her voice—at once clear and melancholy, yet somehow faraway, like it was coming from my own past life. She was fast on the uptake, swallowed up everything new in big gulps, and when she took too big a sip and got water up her nose, she caught herself for a moment then started right back up. It was intoxicating to watch her, to inject life into her veins. She was changing before my eyes. Healed not by therapy, but by something else entirely.

46

"Zlatko, with the golden curls," she said and her words rolled out her mouth and onto the floor before us. We had surrounded her with our entreating eyes and awaited her verdict. Each one of us had prayed that theirs would be the name she'd call, that theirs would be the timid little hand she'd take into hers and lead away to a new life—where they got their own room and delicious home cooked meals and parents and all the rest of it.

Zlatko, golden boy with the golden curls, froze in place, stared at Ilia for a moment, then ran away and hid under the table. He buried his head between his knees, shaking. Ilia went to him, whispered something in his ear. Zlatko wrapped his arms around Ilia's neck and howled. I'd only heard him wail like that one other time, when the big kids hung his dog from a tree. The dog wasn't exactly his, it was a stray, but Zlatko told everyone he'd adopted it. He saved his bread heels from dinner so he could feed it and at night, he secretly let the dog inside the toilets, curled up next to it on the cement floor and they both slept like that, rolled into a ball.

When they hung the dog, Zlatko scaled the walnut tree next to the fence and wailed at the top of his lungs like an animal until the entire village gathered to see what it was that had happened. But when they saw what it was that had happened, they went right back to their houses and to doing what they'd been doing. Zlatko stayed up in the tree all day and all night, while Ilia stood below trying to soothe him and begging him to climb down.

Ilia was afraid of a lot of things: of the dark, of too many people in one spot, but his fear of heights outweighed all the others. The following morning, we all watched as he slowly and deliberately climbed up the walnut tree, shaking like a leaf. I don't think even Zlatko expected it. When Ilia reached the top, Zlatko was still crying, but quietly, almost whimpering as if to himself. Ilia told him something, we never did find out what, exactly, but he convinced him to come down. Now Ilia was the one who refused to move so they had to call the fire department to bring him down. I envied Zlatko—yeah he'd lost his dog, but he'd gained a brother willing to go to the depths of hell for him.

Now Zlatko was bawling at the top of his lungs again and Ilia again tried to calm him down and get him to come out from under the table. The director awkwardly tried to explain to the woman who'd come to adopt him that it was always like that with brothers and sisters but not to worry, in the end everyone got acclimated to it. The would-be mother again attempted to call Zlatko, the golden boy with the golden hair, over to her but her voice barely reached the middle of the room. We all sat in a bunch on the floor, watching quietly. I think that at this precise moment, each one of us was desperate for a brother or a sister in a way we weren't desperate for a mother.

They tore Zlatko from his brother's arms as he kicked and frantically scratched and they loaded him up into the car waiting out front. Two weeks later they brought him back in the same car. It was the father who drove him in, the mother waited outside. Zlatko had refused to eat; there was nothing in the world capable of making him put a single bite of food into his mouth. Zlatko, the only one of us able to eat the disgusting cabbage soup in pig's fat the rest of us gagged on and threw back up into the bowl, then slurped back up again until we reached the bottom, sticks raining down our shoulders anytime we didn't swallow fast enough.

Zlatko had refused to eat in his new home, the same new home where he'd gotten his own room and delicious homemade meals and parents. When they brought him back, he was barely able to stand on his feet, but he somehow managed to hold himself together and run for his brother. This time it was Ilia who wailed as he squeezed his brother's golden curls in his fists.

47

"If photographs are meant to define a person, I must not exist," wrote Susan Johnson in the *Guardian* recently. Aside from a single photo of her mother pregnant with her, and several photos of her as a baby, there is no documentation of her life. No birthday party photos, no graduation photos. Just nothing. "The only way to preserve my past was through my own memory," Johnson shared.

The article later explains that the reason for the absence of any photographs is that Susan's parents belonged to a cult that forbade its members to collect any material things. When Susan was eleven-years-old, her parents began to withdraw from that way of life, as well as from each other. Their marriage dissolved into the emptiness of their home. Their conversations had dampened the walls like mold. The few valuables that had accumulated over the years—toys, books, records—were quickly sold off or gifted to neighbors. Susan remembers that as they were moving out of their home and into their new rented apartment, she spotted a small pile of family photographs, which ended up at the bottom of some suitcase and were never seen again.

A few years ago, without making the connection between the two, she began to collect other people's old photographs. She scoured flea markets, stands, and sales, and bought up all of them with a fanatical obsessiveness, collecting them in old-fashioned cookie tins. She says the untold stories in the photographs, piqued her interest more than anything else. Without knowing any of the strangers in the photos, their life became part of hers. Or maybe they were a substitute for her own missing history.

Susan is now married with two children. She doesn't have any photographs of them—not from their birthdays, or family vacations, first steps, or the day they learned to ride a bike. It is far easier for her, she has realized, to collect other people's memories. "Our own photographs make us nostalgic, they carry a kind of history, a feeling of something gone and irretrievable," writes Susan. A stranger's past doesn't belong to us and isn't capable of saddening us.

I cut out the article and add it to my treasure chest.

48

Agnes Cakes

250 g unsalted butter

250 g powdered sugar

250 g all-purpose white

5-6 eggs, yolks and whites separated

3 packets vanilla or lemon extract

2 tea cups finely chopped walnuts (about 300 grams)

1 tsp baking soda

Mix the softened butter with half the powdered sugar and the baking soda until smooth, then add the egg whites, the flour, vanilla extract, and walnuts. Mix well, then pour into a baking pan, making sure the batter is about a finger deep. The batter will bake fast. While the batter bakes, beat the egg yolks with remaining powdered sugar, then put to the side. Once the cake has cooled, spread the beaten egg yolks and sugar frosting on top.

From my binder of recipes I've recently started.

Right now the recipes consist of just products and the accompanying instructions on how to prepare them, but one day, they'll be our delicious shared memories. On the first page, I write: *For my daughter. So she may still taste my love when I'm no longer around.*

49

The car horns outside all blend in, screaming like a whistle that rever-
berates in my dream. The pigeons peck the crumbs on the bench
where I'm sitting, beating their wings loudly and scatter in the air. I'm
secretly watching the children on the playground. They're twittering
like little chickens. I'm holding a paper just a couple of centimeters from my face, pretending to read it. But I'm not reading it, I've
pierced a tiny hole in it and am secretly observing Dara playing on
the playground. I spot two of the Matrons, patiently wait until they
get bored with pushing some of the younger kids on the swings and
retire to a corner where they'll sink into their meaningless babble.
"That's right," I think to myself, "keep talking."

I glide my hand over the bulge in my purse to make sure it's in
there. Minutes pass, maybe hours, I am not entirely sure—the passage
of time is a strange concept in dreams.

I let my breath out in little orbs, the cold catches them and swallows them up. I gently peek over my cover and see Dara at the top
of the monkey bars, looking around for how to get down. I feel like
yelling over to her to be careful, I feel like running over to her, helping her get down, or just standing by her, near her, in case she slips
on the icy metal bars, I want to grab her under her arms and lift her
up and kiss her freezing little nose. Instead, I stay put and squeeze
the stupid paper even harder. I feel my fingers crack. Just one wrong
move and the whole thing will fall apart, melt like the tiny snowflakes

touching down on my face. It's so cold that I can barely feel my legs. I knock my boots around.

Seven times I rewrote the course of events, seven times seven, seven hundred times seven . . . Things were taking place before they happened.

That same ringing in my ear.

I stir. It's my phone's alarm, annoyingly persistent. My toes are frozen, I must have kicked my covers off. Five more minutes, I think, hit snooze and doze off.

It's dark, the street lights have come on, lighting the playground. The kids and the schoolmarms have gone off, but Dara is still there, she's looking around her like a scared kitten, hiding in a tunnel. I can see her red coat. I make my way to her, I haven't got time to waste. So she believed me? Decided to listen to me, after all? I get closer. "Dara!" She's curled into a ball, hugging her knees with her arms. I rummage through my purse, pull the blanket out and wrap it around her. The same blanket I kept in the chest for thirty-three years, knitted for mothers to swaddle their kids, which protects from everything like an invisible shield. I throw the blanket around her shoulders and whisper, "You're invisible now. Go!"

She looks at me and I see the trust in her eyes. She grabs my hand and we're off. The dark swallows us. We step softly and slowly like ghosts and we dissipate like two effervescent pills into the air.

50

I wonder whether Dara dreams the same dream that visits me every night. Does she dream of me when she dreams up her mother? Does her mother have my face and my voice?

I startle awake, covered in sweat. I'm crying but there's no sound. The night has begun to lift its veil over the city, the first buses begin their crawl along the boulevard. Maybe today will be the day.

51

"Are we there yet?"

"Almost. Just a little bit further."

"How much further?"

"Half an hour."

"How long is half an hour?"

"Just long enough for one cotton candy. Do you like cotton candy?"

"Mmm . . . I'm not sure."

"Do you want to find out? One for you, one for me."

"Yeah okay, let's do it!"

***

"Leah?"

"Yes?"

"Do you have a mom?"

"Everybody has a mom. It's just that sometimes she's only a memory. Or a dream."

"Where's yours?"

"Mine is . . . up in the sky."

"Ha! Like a balloon, when you've let go of the string."

"Yes, exactly like that."

"Do you think she's met my mommy and daddy?"

"I don't know, maybe she has."

"Leah?"

"Yes?"

"Is it bad that I miss my dad so much?"

"No, the opposite. It's good because it means you really love him. And it's good to love."

"Yes but it hurts here, just above my stomach, when I think of him."

"I know. It always hurts like that when we lose someone important to us. It'll pass, I promise. Maybe the pain won't ever completely disappear, but you'll get used to it. One day it'll fly away just like a balloon and in its place, there'll be nothing but emptiness . . . Do you like the cotton candy?"

"I do, very much! Can I try some of yours?"

"Of course. Just don't eat too much, or you'll get sick from all that sugar."

"Leah?"

"Yes?"

"Do you mind if I don't call you Mom?"

"Of course not. In fact, I would prefer if you just called me Leah."

"You're not going anywhere, right?"

"Never."

"Promise?"

"Promise."

"Are we there yet?"

"Almost. One more block and we'll be home."

"What's 'home'?"

"Home is . . . where everybody loves you. Here it is. Close your eyes!"

Acknowledgements

My treasure chest of people who believed in this book and made the English-language edition possible

1) Chad W. Post, Kaija Straumanis, and Anthony Blake at Open Letter Books. Joining your list of exceptional writers is a dream come true, and I thank you for this opportunity.

2) Izidora Angel who fell in love with the book and took upon the job of translating it into English and became one of the most passionate champions of my work. Thank you, Izidora, none of this would have been possible without you.

3) The book has been accepted for publication after winning the Novel Competition hosted by Open Letter Books and Elizabeth Kostova Foundation. Thank you, Milena Deleva and the team at the Elizabeth Kostova Foundation not only for choosing my book but also for your tireless efforts to promote Bulgarian literature abroad.

4) The National Culture Fund in Bulgaria for the funding they offered for the translation of the book. This is often the chance a book needs to start its journey beyond national borders, so thank you for this support.

5) My Bulgarian editor and mentor Georgi Gospodinov (*The Physics of Sorrow*) who encouraged me to write. Your ongoing support has been invaluable.

6) My family, of course, for giving me the space and confidence to write, and believing in my book when I didn't.

7) People who became the prototypes of some of the stories, care leavers, child adopters – you are all very visible to me.

Even my imaginary treasure box would never be able to fit you all. Thank you!

NATALIYA DELEVA is a Bulgarian-born writer living in London. *Four Minutes* is her debut novel. Originally published in Bulgaria (Janet 45, 2017), the book was awarded Best Debut Novel and was shortlisted for Novel of the Year (2018), and has since been translated into several languages, including German (eta Verlag, 2018) and Polish (Wydawnictwo EZOP, 2021). Nataliya's short fiction, critique, and essays appeared in Words Without Borders, *Fence, Asymptote, Empty Mirror,* and *Granta Bulgaria,* among others. Her second novel, *Arrival*—an English-language original—is forthcoming from The Indigo Press in 2022.

IZIDORA ANGEL is a Bulgarian-born writer, translator, and critic based in Chicago. Her writing has appeared in the *Los Angeles Review*, *Chicago Reader*, *Reading in Translation*, and others; she has been profiled by *Electric Literature*, *Chicago Tribune*, and *Asymptote Journal*. Izidora's work has been supported by English PEN, ART OMI, the Rona Jaffe Foundation, and the Elizabeth Kostova Foundation. She is a co-founder of the Third Coast Translators Collective and *Four Minutes* is her second full-length translation. Izidora is currently translating Yordanka Beleva's short story collection *Keder*.

CONNECTING

THE MENTORING RELATIONSHIPS YOU NEED TO SUCCEED IN LIFE

PAUL D. STANLEY
J. ROBERT CLINTON

NAVPRESS
A MINISTRY OF THE NAVIGATORS
P.O.BOX 35001, COLORADO SPRINGS, COLORADO 80935

The Navigators is an international Christian organization. Our mission is to reach, disciple, and equip people to know Christ and to make Him known through successive generations. We envision multitudes of diverse people in the United States and every other nation who have a passionate love for Christ, live a lifestyle of sharing Christ's love, and multiply spiritual laborers among those without Christ.

NavPress is the publishing ministry of The Navigators. NavPress publications help believers learn biblical truth and apply what they learn to their lives and ministries. Our mission is to stimulate spiritual formation among our readers.

© 1992 by J. Robert Clinton and
     Paul D. Stanley
All rights reserved. No part of this publication may be reproduced in any form without written permission from NavPress, P.O. Box 35001, Colorado Springs, CO 80935. www.navpress.com
Library of Congress Catalog Card Number:
     91-61396
ISBN 08910-96388

Some of the anecdotal illustrations in this book are true to life and are included with the permission of the persons involved. All other illustrations are composites of real situations, and any resemblance to people living or dead is coincidental.

Unless otherwise identified, all Scripture quotations in this publication are from the *Holy Bible: New International Version*® (NIV®). Copyright © 1973, 1978, 1984 by International Bible Society. Used by permission of Zondervan Bible Publishers. Another version used is *The Living Bible* (TLB) © 1971 owned by assignment by the Illinois Regional Bank N.A. (as trustee), used by permission of Tyndale House Publishers, Inc., Wheaton, IL 60189.

Printed in the United States of America

10 11 12 13 14 15 16 17 18 19 20 21 / 01 00

FOR A FREE CATALOG OF
NAVPRESS BOOKS & BIBLE STUDIES,
CALL 1-800-366-7788 (USA)
OR 1-416-499-4615 (CANADA)

CONTENTS

*To those who have
mentored us . . .*

*Joe, King, Lorne
and
Harold, Buck, Denny*

AUTHORS

Paul Stanley has pioneered several Navigator ministries throughout Europe, Eastern Europe, and the United States. He now is the International Vice President of The Navigators. Paul has been involved in the specific area of leadership development for over twenty years. In addition to carrying out his responsibilities directing Navigator ministries in over seventy countries, he also does leadership development consulting for other organizations worldwide. Paul and his wife, Phyllis, have four adult children, and live in Colorado Springs, Colorado.

Dr. Robert (Bobby) Clinton is Associate Professor of Leadership at the School of World Mission, Fuller Theological Seminary. He specializes in leadership studies, including leadership selection, training, theory, and emergence patterns. As background for his contributions in the study of leadership development, he has extensively researched the lives of over 600 past and present leaders. Bobby and his wife currently live in Altadena, California.

ILLUSTRATIONS

TABLES AND FIGURES

PREFACE

Frequently, people ask each of us, "Will you mentor me?" Because of what we have learned, we answer that question much differently now than we would have five years ago. We hope this book will help you both to ask and to answer that question.

My (Bobby's) research on biblical leaders led to a startling conclusion—few leaders finish well. Research on mid-career, contemporary leaders led to another conclusion—other individuals helped most of these men and women in timely situations along the way. We do not yet know if they will finish well, but their relationship to another person significantly enhanced their development. Most case studies listed three to ten significant people who helped shape their lives. And what is true of these leaders is also true of us.

Comparative studies we've done began to unleash information that could be used in a deliberate way to help other leaders go on and finish well. The most helpful overall concept was the definition of mentoring:

Mentoring is a relational experience through which one person empowers another by sharing God-given resources. The resources vary. Mentoring is a positive dynamic that enables people to develop potential.

Since the rash of leadership failures in 1987 that became public and perhaps blown out of proportion, more people recognize the need for accountability in leadership. Adequate mentoring might have prevented most of these failures. Certainly the kind of mentoring described in this book can help prevent failures in leadership and give that needed accountability. Most leaders today want accountability. They want to finish well. They would welcome mentoring if they saw it as an enhancement to their leadership.

Mentoring can reduce the probability of leadership failure, provide needed accountability, and empower a responsive leader. We arrived at this conclusion via different routes. Both of us experienced mentoring in the form of a discipleship relationship. We then passed on these same concepts and techniques to others. Paul was discipled in 1959, Bobby in 1964. As we grew in Christian maturity and in terms of ministry responsibility, we experienced other forms of relationships that empowered us. And we in turn have worked relationally with others to enable them.

The year 1977 was a pivotal one for me (Paul). I began to work deliberately on developing middle- and upper-level leadership for The Navigators in Europe. The following years of experience led me to further discoveries about mentoring, which I have conceptualized in a form that makes it readily transferable to others who want to use it in their own ministries. The balanced Constellation Model introduced in chapter

11 is the result of this conceptualization.

In 1979 I (Bobby) moved to the School of World Mission at Fuller. In 1982 I began to systematically study the development of leaders. Conceptually, the notion of mentoring arose from comparative analysis of six hundred case studies of leaders. My meeting with Paul in 1986 triggered further research into mentoring. Many of the definitions discussed in this book come out of our interaction over what we were learning.

What is unique about what we will present in this book? Four things:

1. How to be mentored even though there aren't enough mentors to go around. We broke the ideal mentor into mentoring functions, and you can almost always find someone who can do one or more of them. The first ten chapters explore these various functions . . . so for those of you who need the big picture first, you might examine the Constellation Model in chapter eleven before you begin.
2. An explanation of what makes mentoring work—we identify three dynamics.
3. A balanced model of mentoring relationships, which will help ensure a healthy perspective on life and ministry.
4. Illustrations and ideas on how mentoring can work for you. We have used many examples of mentoring relationships based on our own experiences, but have changed some names and details to protect confidentiality.

We hope this information will inspire you to connect with those vital mentoring relationships you need for an effective life and ministry . . . finding mentors for your own life and, in turn, mentoring the next generation.

Chapter One

RELATIONSHIPS THAT MAKE A DIFFERENCE

Help in New Surroundings

Sitting in the back row of our new church, I (Paul) could hardly follow the pastor's message. We were recent transplants to the city, far away from family and friends. My mind was spinning with questions . . . personal and professional. I was uncertain and feeling very vulnerable. I faced a new job, adjustment to another culture and neighborhood . . . nothing was familiar. Who could help me? . . . If only I knew someone to talk to! Even if I phoned some old buddies they would not understand my new world, and besides, they'd never been in this situation either.

My train of thought suddenly broke as our four-year-old squirmed in my lap. "I like being with you, Daddy," he whispered, his little arms stretched across my chest. As I drew him close, I knew he was responding to the past week of trauma when I took him to his new school each morning and left him crying and pleading for me not to leave him. I glanced down the row at our three other children. Two were older, in third and fourth grade. I wondered what struggles they were going through. For our new world was Europe, the language was German, and the city was Vienna, Austria.

What I need is someone to talk to who has walked down the path I'm just beginning, I thought. *But who?* As my eyes moved back to the front of the church, the pastor's adult son came into focus. I had just met him, and he had related how his family had come to Vienna from Canada more than fifteen years ago. *That's it!* my mind flashed. *His dad must have gone through what I'm facing; I'll ask him.*

The following week, I called Pastor Abe and we met to talk about our children's adjustment. He related that one of his children cried every day for three months when he took him to kindergarten. "How did it affect him?" I gasped in astonishment. "He can't even remember it, and he went on to love school," he responded. Our conversation that day roamed all through my family's adjustment questions. But it didn't stop there.

Pastor Abe and I continued to meet, both casually and by appointment. He coached me through many awkward cross-cultural situations, and even showed me how to be a better dad. Our young kindergartner survived, and within six weeks was enthusiastically running up the school stairs to his class. Pastor Abe's continual encouragement, prayer, and advice enabled us to "hang in there" and persevere when our emotions were at the bottom and we wanted to give up.

Later, as our relationship grew, Abe's life and commitments began to influence my own attitude and action in ministry. He made time for people and cared for the "sheep of his flock" as a true shepherd. Many of the "wandering and lame" soon found strength and focus for their lives in the Great Shepherd. I was able to reciprocate and work with Abe in developing and leading a discipleship training experience for his rapidly growing flock. Abe became the friend, coach, counselor, and model I desperately needed. His mentorship not only enabled our family to pass through a trying period, but launched us into fruitful ministry and leadership responsibility.

"WOULD YOU MENTOR ME?"

Mentoring is as old as civilization itself. Through this natural relational process, experience and values pass from one generation to another. Mentoring took place among Old Testament prophets (Eli and Samuel, Elijah and Elisha) and leaders (Moses and Joshua), and New Testament leaders (Barnabas and Paul, Paul and Timothy). Throughout human history, mentoring was the primary means of passing on knowledge and skills in every field — from Greek philosophers to sailors — and in every culture. But in the modern age, the learning process shifted. It now relies primarily on computers, classrooms, books, and videos. Thus, today *the relational connection between the knowledge-and-experience giver and the receiver has weakened or is nonexistent.*

Society today is rediscovering that the process of learning and maturing needs time and many kinds of relationships. The "self-made" man or woman is a myth and, though some claim it, few aspire to it. It leaves people relationally deficient and narrow-minded. The resurgence of mentoring in virtually every occupational field and area of life is a response to this discovery. "Please mentor me," is the spoken and unspoken request expressed by so many. What do they mean? How do people get into it? . . . Do it?

Before we answer that, let's look at a few more examples.

Need for Accountability

"Please forgive me, brothers; I've wanted to deal with this for years, but just couldn't," bemoaned a middle-aged Christian leader as he hung his head in repentance. We had just confronted him with a pattern of integrity breaches that went back twenty years. Hadn't others seen his inconsistencies along the way? If so, and many had, why hadn't they shared their concerns honestly with him? These questions and more passed through my mind as I watched a broken brother face his sin and its harsh consequences.

In John's early years of ministry, no one would have doubted his commitment to Christ, the gospel, discipleship, and obedience to God's Word. God continually blessed him with fruit, and John gave himself to not only conserve it but to see it flourish as well. It was exciting to colabor with him.

But subtle pride and manipulation of others began to creep into his ministry. Unknowingly, John drifted away from vital relationships he needed to provide corrective feedback and accountability.

As the years went by, John's drive for ministry and his commitment to be all that he asked others to be deepened. Although commendable in one respect, this was unrealistic. The gap between what John was and what he wanted to be, and in some areas *thought* he was, widened. Not wanting to reveal the gap to anyone, he found himself with "ministry" relationships only. Although his peers and senior colaborers began to observe inconsistencies in John's life, the lack of accountability relationships prevented any honest feedback. He had created an island, and he stood alone on it.

Finally there came a point where intervention was necessary. Others who worked with him were asked to verify certain patterns, which identified more needs, and other men and women acknowledged they had been hurt through many unintentional abuses.

To confront an aloof brother takes more courage than most of us have, particularly when the person is manipulative and defensive. At this point in John's life, intervention and strong discipline were the only recourses, and this was difficult.

At the intervention meeting, John was unaware of the depth and breadth of his sin. "We all fall short," he appealed when confronted with the observed unbiblical patterns. But as we went through the long list of specifics, testimonies, and abuses, the weight of evidence laid heavily upon him . . . and the Spirit broke through. Behind him lay a trail of wounded brothers and sisters, lost opportunities, and ego-driven achievements that would soon fade away.

This situation could have been avoided had he sought out and developed relationships of mutual accountability that would have affected his choices and integrity . . . and lasting contribution to the Kingdom of God. But peers and those who were further along in ministry and life experience were not invited into his inner circle. As a result, habits that could have been headed off while still in embryonic stages built into something that required a major encounter and discipline.

Many fear the transparency in a mentor or peer relationship and feel that their vulnerability could be used against them or is a sign of weakness. However, as John learned too late, mentoring by a spiritual guide, counselor, or peer could have changed his life and ministry. Why did he not initiate accountability and take advantage of guidance and correction, so vital to a young leader? The sad reality of John's

situation is that he wanted a mentoring relationship and mutual accountability earlier but repeatedly postponed it. Life's competing time demands
rendered it unrealistic. He concluded that such a
request would impose on busy potential mentors.
He felt he knew enough about the potential pitfalls to
avoid them. As the years went by, John saw himself
more as being a mentor and less as one who needed
a mentor or peer accountability (co-mentoring).

Who Pastors the Pastor?

He struggled with some fairly normal issues
for a young husband, father, and pastor. At
thirty-two, Bob had moved along well. He met
Christ in college through a student outreach
ministry and colabored with that group as a
student and, later, for three years as full-time
staff. After four years of seminary and an associate pastor role, Bob was two years into his
first pastorate—a small, growing, suburban
church. He was motivated, gifted, and off to a
good start.

Bob wisely found a group of men in the
church who wanted to be part of a discipleship
group, so he had a developing support and
feedback network for his own personal growth.
In addition, he met with an older, godly man in
the congregation who has become a valuable
spiritual guide for him.

As I became acquainted with Bob, I sensed
he was working hard and had high expectations for this new ministry opportunity.
But I also suspected he was under a lot of

pressure from his internal drive and external demands . . . both perceived and real. Couple this with two young toddlers and an eager mate who has high expectations for their family development . . . and we have a pastor with needs.

Having known similar situations and understanding the pressure he was under, I arranged to meet him for breakfast. During the meal, he related his testimony and how God led him into the local church ministry and his current responsibilities. As I listened, the Spirit confirmed some of my earlier concerns. I asked specific questions and commented on the importance of a ministry philosophy to provide the basis for decisions and priority in ministry. Bob fired back some questions that revealed a responsive chord had been touched.

I liked Bob, and we seemed to feel comfortable with one another. We spent a good two hours talking. Just before leaving he shared two prayer needs and asked if we could meet again. I agreed, and continued to pray for Bob.

On the second meeting we jumped right into his schedule and potential conflicts with those church members who seemed to resist some changes he wanted to see happen. My part was to simply listen and ask helpful questions. Then he shared some personal frustrations he experienced as a dad in the midst of competing time demands. That opened up time for me to encourage him, let him know he wasn't alone, and tell him about some of the same difficulties I had experienced.

I related what I had learned as a young father and husband. I also gave a few practical suggestions. Because of his response to what I shared, I proposed that he think through what we discussed and develop a realistic plan for his appropriate involvement with his children and the time he spent praying and sharing with his wife. We set a time for a third meeting to review what effect his plan had.

Bob's commitment and attitude to learn were obvious, but I needed to test his willingness to be held accountable by an older brother before I would commit myself to be his mentor.

In subsequent meetings our conversations became more personal and focused, and I sensed they were important to him. I asked him how he would describe our growing relationship and the most meaningful benefit. His response did not surprise me: "I see you as an older brother with experience in the areas I'm growing in: leadership, being a dad and husband, and bringing about change in older people. Your questions and counsel have been so helpful . . . and have kept me from a few needless conflicts as well."

Then he asked me how I saw our relationship. "You are a very gifted, energetic, young leader who can make a great contribution to the purposes of God. But there is much to learn and the way is not easy. I'd like to walk with you for part of the way. I want to be a brother to you, challenge your thinking and

faith, caution you where appropriate, and
share what I've learned if it can help. Most
of all, I want to pray specifically for you and
with you."

We had a good time talking about some
realistic expectations for our relationship. They
centered around the subjects he wanted to
grow in, how often we would meet, transparency, and accountability. "It is great having
an older brother like you who is outside my
immediate world and with whom I can discuss
anything . . . and who can push me in some
areas and keep me from shooting my foot in
others."

I am also grateful for this relationship,
for Bob will help me keep in touch with the
issues and concerns young leaders face. He
will challenge my thinking. It is a rare privilege
to invest in a young leader in a way that will
help him become godly and effective. I must
pray much and keep tuned to the Holy Spirit's
leading in all of this. Besides, I like Bob and
his wife, and I sense a meaningful friendship
developing.

As shown in this illustration, stepping into a
mentoring relationship can be natural. Just being
aware of the growth needs and challenges that face
any young husband, father, and leader can place you
in a position to listen, ask helpful questions, counsel, and encourage. You don't need to know "all the
answers" or assume a teaching role to be a blessing to
a mentoree. Listening, affirming, suggesting, sharing

experiences, and praying together are invaluable contributions that give a young mentoree confidence, perspective, and practical helps.

Getting a Good Start in Discipleship

It happened in the church hallway. Harold personally challenged me (Bobby) to join a special, six-week-long small group that would explore some basic concepts for Christians who wanted to grow. The invitation appealed to me and yet frightened me. But put on the spot, and not able to think of a reason why I should not join, I agreed.

From a distance I had been attracted to Harold. He was serious about following Christ, and I sensed he knew some things that could help me. I later learned that he had been a believer for only three years. But those years involved steady, solid spiritual growth under the watchful eye of a mature Air Force sergeant. Harold had transferred from Europe to Japan because he had heard the poker was better there. But in Japan, Christ—not cards—dominated his life. He saw some radical Christians who lived out their commitments openly before their fellow servicemen.

In Harold's small group we learned about the basics of discipleship—deepening our personal relationship with Christ, obeying God's truth, studying the Bible, praying, and spending time with other committed disciples who wanted to grow and make their lives count for

Christ. The Holy Spirit used this small group to change my life.

Harold did several things that impressed me. He showed us that he was personally concerned for each person in the group. (There were about six of us, all personally invited.) He challenged us with practical assignments that affected our daily lives—assignments that later we could use with others in the same way he used them with us. He sought to go beyond the time we met as a group and spent personal time with us outside of the small-group setting.

Everything he asked us to do he had done before and continued to do. He systematically memorized Scripture. We learned how to do that. He read his Bible through on a yearly basis. Once he exchanged Bibles with me for a week. I saw in the flyleaf the remark, "Started reading Bible through for the first time," and he gave a date. Then the remark, "Finished reading the Bible through for the first time" and the date was a year later. This was repeated three times. He had been a Christian for only three years. I was challenged. I had been a non-growing Christian for about eighteen years and had never once read entirely through my Bible. So I began to read my Bible through systematically for the first time. His Bible was well-marked—underlined, with notations in the margin. I picked up that habit, too.

One assignment became a "marker event"

for me. Each of us had to read a Christian biography. Harold had a box of books he brought to the small group. We were invited to pick one and read it during the duration of the six weeks we were meeting. I first grabbed for a biography of George Truett, the famous Southern Baptist preacher of whom I had heard. But Harold switched it and said, "Try this one." And he gave me *Hudson Taylor's Spiritual Secret*. Little did I know how that one simple act would affect my whole life. From Taylor I learned of radical obedience. I saw how a person could actually trust God for everyday things and how God answered specific prayers. I saw how vision developed and how God matured a person, gave a destiny, and fulfilled it. In short, I began a lifelong habit of learning from the experiences of others. Taylor became a hero of mine, and other biographies soon followed. Each impacted me — expanded my thoughts, modeled for me various aspects of leadership, and gave me principles for my own life.

Harold invited me to go with him to witness in the home of a couple he had contacted. I watched him use his Bible to answer their questions. The man said two fellows had been in their house that week and told him he had to be baptized in their church if he was to experience salvation. He went on to relate that he had already been baptized twice — once when he was a child and once during the Korean War when he had been afraid that he would die. Did he really have to be baptized again in a certain church for it to count toward salvation?

I remember how Harold went from place to place in the Bible to respond to the couple's questions and help them understand baptism and the importance of a life-transforming experience with Christ. I remember as I walked out that door how I wished I could handle my Bible that way.

During the small-group sessions I began to sense that Harold had more that he could give to me that would aid me in my Christian walk. He invited me to meet with him individually on a regular basis. I responded. I learned much. But most of all, we established a relationship. Though we have since lived in various parts of the United States and the world, God has repeatedly intertwined our lives at crucial decision times. Sometimes our contact was prolonged and we picked up where we had left off. At other times it was momentary and resulted in wise counsel that confirmed or clarified God's guidance. Our relationship is mutually stimulating. I never think of Harold without whispering Philippians 1:3, for I know he was sent by God for that brief interlude that started me on a life of discipleship.

Usually when people are first introduced to mentoring, they think of an ideal mentor — a perfect model who can do almost everything. Few of those exist. Harold contradicts that myth about mentoring and lessens its mystique. He puts mentoring in the practical realm: Anyone can mentor, provided he has learned something from God and is willing to share with others what he has learned.

As a follower of Christ, you can mentor others. Whatever God has given you that has enabled you to grow and deepen your relationship with Him, you can pass on to others. Introducing young followers of Christ to the basics of spiritual growth is part of the process of discipling, which is the first and most basic mentoring type.

Reading about the heroes of the past, or historical models, is another form of mentoring that you can take advantage of any time. Observing the growth, struggles, responses, and decision-making processes of those who have lived before can provide insight, challenge, and often practical help for your own situation.

Occasionally, God may bring a person into your life who makes a timely contribution: a word of counsel, an insight, a question, or encouragement. These "divine contacts" will frequently not know how they are being used in your life, but you can take advantage of them as God-given resources sent along at the right moment.

Long-Distance Mentoring

Jane was in my class. She responded to what I taught about God's ways of developing a person over a lifetime. She was particularly interested in the discipleship aspect of mentoring. She related to me that no one had ever discipled her in that way. Jane was finishing a master's degree and wanted to serve in a church situation. She requested personal time and signed up for an hour on my interview schedule, at which time she shared openly and frankly with me about her past life, her commitment to Christ's lordship, and her spiritual growth.

I listened and occasionally probed with a question. After I'd given what I felt was some sound advice for several issues that seemed critical to her, she said that she would like to keep in contact. She had won a special scholarship that enabled her to study abroad for a year. She would be getting married soon and then would move overseas. I told her I would be glad to keep in contact.

Nearly six months went by before she wrote. It was a long letter and explained her situation in detail. She faced a number of things for the first time. Her ministry internship situation had placed her with a pastor and church staff who were of a more liberal orientation than she. The schooling situation was disappointing and somewhat irrelevant to her needs. There were adjustments in marriage and in the culture, which was close to hers yet different. She experienced the sense of isolation that frequently comes in a new cultural setting. In addition, she struggled with the differing role expectations that frequently plague people in their first ministry assignment.

My letter of response was a long one. I attempted to encourage her by describing others' experiences on their first ministry assignment. I assured her that what she was going through was normal, and she would develop and learn from it. I challenged her to concentrate on her own spiritual or inner-life growth in the midst of the perplexing issues. I gave her some ideas about spiritual disciplines, which I hoped would benefit her.

Jane's response was encouraging. She was relieved to know that her experiences and reactions were quite "normal," and she had taken up the challenge to focus on spiritual growth. This encouraged me, for recognizing God's hand in her circumstances and seeing them as a learning opportunity are major steps for a young, emerging leader and servant of God. Her letter also contained a new set of questions, which I responded to in the same pattern of providing perspective, counsel, encouragement, spiritual insights, and challenges from my life.

The cycle of letters soon included Jane's husband, Jim, who was also in preparation for full-time ministry and had been reading the correspondence between Jane and me. Jim began to add his own letter. He struggled with some doubts about God as he faced new and difficult situations and was concerned about his own walk with God. In addition, Jim faced ordination exams (from a distance) and had questions about both Jane and him being in full-time ministry.

Again, my response was a long one. I sought to encourage Jim about the whole ordination process—I had just witnessed a similar experience with an aspiring pastor over the past six months. Failing ordination exams is not the end of the world but simply a challenge to perseverance and an opportunity to learn lessons about personality and inner attitude that can last a lifetime. I described some patterns of ministry I had seen in married situations and the options that went along with them. In short, Jane and Jim needed perspective and clarification of what God might be teaching in the whole process. I challenged them to respond to God's sovereignty in the situation and assured them of His presence, intimate concern, and ability to lead them.

Face-to-face settings are not the only way for mentoring to happen. Here long-distance mentoring provided the important perspective that Jane and Jim needed. Counseling and teaching can be done via letters or phone.

SO WHAT IS MENTORING?
These mentoring stories shared some common features. They started with someone in need. This person met someone further along in experience who had something to contribute to that need. A relationship was established. The more experienced person shared what he had been through or learned, meeting the needs of the first person. With the acceptance of what was shared, the power to grow through a situation was passed from the mentor to the mentoree. It was not just a sharing/receiving of knowledge; actual transfer and change took place. We refer to this transfer between mentor and mentoree as *empowerment*. This process is the heart of mentoring.

> **Mentoring is a relational experience
> in which one person empowers another
> by sharing God-given resources.**

The person sharing is called the *mentor*. The person being empowered is called the *mentoree*. The God-given resources include wisdom, experiences, patterns, habits of obedience, and principles, as well as a host of other things. Mentors and mentorees frequently share perspectives of many kinds that shed light on a situation. The sharing may take place over a protracted time or over a shorter time. It may occur face-to-face or from a distance. It may be regular, like weekly or bi-weekly or even monthly. Or it may be occasional and irregular. The mentor may initiate the mentoring relationship, or it may be initiated by the mentoree.

SUMMARY
Many different kinds of relationships have potential for empowering a person who desires to learn and grow. These stories illustrated six of the seven mentoring types: Discipler, Spiritual Guide, Coach, Counselor, Teacher, Model, and Sponsor. We will define each of these in more detail as we go along.

We hope you sense something of the potential that mentoring may have for you in unleashing God's power in your life through special relationships with others. Perhaps you are beginning to sense that God may want you to establish relationships with others that will make a difference. Let's explore this more.

Chapter Two

UNDERSTANDING MENTORING

Heart Cry of Many: Will You Mentor Me?

Susan is in her mid-fifties. She had experienced a major setback in her earlier years that would continue to affect her for the rest of her life. But God had wonderfully met her in her struggles and turned defeat to victory. Now she wants to turn her experience into a platform for ministry so that she might help others who face the same problem. How can she go about doing that? After attending a workshop on mentoring, Susan asked, "Where can I find someone to whom I can be accountable and who can help me grow at this stage of my life? Do you know someone who could mentor me?"

Richard is in his mid-forties. He senses God's hand on his life. A successful businessman, he is now interested in developing leaders. His dream is to set up a center where young Christian leaders from around the world can come for short, intensive times of training and be linked up with people and resources for their ongoing development. He has the financial resources and management skills, but he needs to learn more about how to develop others. He read an article on mentoring and realized he himself needs mentoring in order to adequately mentor others. And so he asked, "Will you please mentor me?"

Barry has been a believer for seven years. Successful professionally, he has a good family and has grown steadily in his spiritual life. But Barry, like many others, wonders if he could do more or perhaps do something different. He senses a need to move from success to significance. "Should I change jobs, take on more ministry, or spend more time in prayer and Bible study?" are questions turning in his mind. These are not uncommon questions, but the answer he is looking for is more fundamental and God would be eager to reveal it to him if he would faithfully seek Him for it. "Would you help me do that?" is Barry's request. He needs a mentor.

Mentoring is popular at present.[1] Its popularity attests to its potential usefulness for all kinds of leadership. It also speaks of the tremendous relational vacuum in an individualistic society and its accompanying lack of accountability. In *Habits of the Heart*,[2] the authors see individualism as an American asset turned into a liability. Americans cling to personal independence when they desperately need interdependence. But God did not create people to be self-sufficient and move through life alone. To return to healthy relational living will require recognition of this need and courage to change. In no other area is this change so urgently needed than in leadership development. Acknowledgment of this need is partially responsible for the groundswell toward mentoring. "Will you mentor me?" is being expressed in many ways in every area: business, ministry, family, military, education, and the church. This swelling cry for meaningful relationships can be a springboard to learning and growth.

Your world—business, military, academic, Christian organization, or whatever—will strongly influence your definition of mentoring. For instance, business and military mentoring will focus primarily on coaching, sponsoring, and career guidance. The essence of the mentoring process in business and the military lies in the quality and organizational position of the mentor. In those circles a strong mentor is needed.

In the academic environment, students who know subjects well are being asked to tutor other students. The student mentors don't know everything, but they know something and can provide a personal link to knowledge, experience, and the system. This kind of one-on-one and small-group tutoring will vary in quality depending on how well the whole program is supervised.

Our experience with mentoring and our focus on its use center on empowerment—the increased capacity of the mentoree generated by the mentoring relationship and the resources shared.

> ***Mentoring is a relational experience
> in which one person empowers another
> by sharing God-given resources.***

In our survey of leaders, we found that almost all of them identified three to ten people who made significant contributions to their development.[3] A study of major biblical figures and the biographies of Christian leaders clearly underscored the conclusion that one of the major influences most often used by God to develop a leader is a person or persons who have something to share that the leader needs. These people who influenced others seemed to have some common characteristics:

- ◆ Ability to readily see potential in a person.
- ◆ Tolerance with mistakes, brashness, abrasiveness, and the like in order to see that potential develop.
- ◆ Flexibility in responding to people and circumstances.
- ◆ Patience, knowing that time and experience are needed for development.
- ◆ Perspective, having vision and ability to see down the road and suggest the next steps that a mentoree needs.
- ◆ Gifts and abilities that build up and encourage others.[4]

Barnabas was a people influencer. He saw potential in Saul (later the Apostle Paul) when others kept their distance. Saul's conversion turned this brilliant zealot of orthodox Judaism to a fearless Christian evangelist and apologist. Jews and the disciples alike feared him and were afraid to let him join them. "But Barnabas took him [Saul] and brought him to the apostles" (Acts 9:27). Barnabas was not intimidated by this brash convert, but drew him in and vouched for him. Undoubtedly, he encouraged and taught Saul during those early days and patiently stayed with him, knowing that time and experience would soon temper and mature this gifted young leader.

Later, when the gospel spread to Antioch and "a great number of people believed and turned to the Lord" (Acts 11:21), the apostles sent Barnabas (the Encourager) to the city to verify the phenomenon as genuine. Seeing that the gospel had truly borne fruit and that God's grace was at work, Barnabas knew they would need teaching and growth. So he went to Tarsus to find Saul and bring him back to Antioch to help, as he was a powerful teacher and understood the Greek mind and culture. Barnabas (the mentor) knew the kind of developmental environment and challenge that Saul needed in order to grow, and drew him into it. Thank God for Barnabas and the gift he gave to the Church by taking an interest in young Saul! How many Sauls are in the Church today just waiting for a Barnabas?

Barnabas illustrates a number of the specific ways that mentors help mentorees. Our studies identified several important ones:

1. Mentors give to mentorees:
   ♦ timely advice;

   ◆ letters, articles, books, or other literary
     information that offers perspective;
   ◆ finances;
   ◆ freedom to emerge as a leader even beyond
     the level of the mentor.
2. Mentors risk their own reputation in order to
   sponsor a mentoree.
3. Mentors model various aspects of leadership
   functions so as to challenge mentorees to
   move toward them.
4. Mentors direct mentorees to needed resources
   that will further develop them.
5. Mentors co-minister with mentorees in order
   to increase their confidence, status, and
   credibility.

An expanded version of our definition focuses
more on the empowerment and clarifies the actors
in the mentoring drama.

> *Mentoring is a relational process in which a
> mentor, who knows or has experienced
> something, transfers that something
> (resources of wisdom, information,
> experience, confidence, insight, relationships,
> status, etc.) to a mentoree, at an appropriate
> time and manner, so that it facilitates
> development or empowerment.*

A breakthrough in understanding and therefore
making this definition a personal reality comes when
you see mentoring as a relational exchange between
two people with varying levels of involvement and

degrees of intensity. We found it helpful to understand not only the various levels of involvement, but also the kinds of involvement with different mentoring types or functions. This chart (figure 2-1) shows the three groupings of mentors and places them on a continuum ranging from more deliberate (with more depth and awareness of effort) to less deliberate involvement.

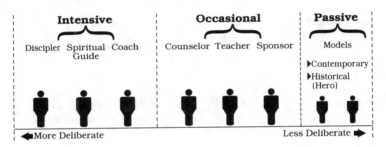

Figure 2-1.
Mentoring Groups and Functions Along a Continuum

Apart from this kind of conceptual breakthrough, a problem exists. *There aren't enough ideal mentors who can do it all.* But lots of people can fulfill one or more of the mentoring functions. All you need to do is identify the specific area of mentoring you need, and that should enable you to answer the question, "Who can mentor me?" Later, we will discuss in more detail each of the mentoring types and functions given on the continuum. For now, to help you with the overall picture, we'll list the central thrust of each type.

Table 2-1. Major Thrusts of Mentoring Types

MENTORING TYPE/FUNCTIONS	CENTRAL THRUST OF EMPOWERMENT
Intensive	
1. Discipler	Enablement in basics of following Christ.
2. Spiritual Guide	Accountability, direction, and insight for questions, commitments, and decisions affecting spirituality and maturity.
3. Coach	Motivation, skills, and application needed to meet a task, challenge.
Occasional	
4. Counselor	Timely advice and correct perspectives on viewing self, others, circumstances, and ministry.
5. Teacher	Knowledge and understanding of a particular subject.
6. Sponsor	Career guidance and protection as leader moves within an organization.
Passive	
7. Model	
Contemporary	A living, personal model for life, ministry, or profession who is not only an example but also inspires emulation.
Historical	A past life that teaches dynamic principles and values for life, ministry, and/or profession.

You may be seeking an ideal mentor who can fulfill the whole range of mentoring functions. You will rarely find one. But if you narrow your mentoring needs to a specific area, you will usually find someone available to mentor you in relation to that need.

Mentoring is an empowering experience that requires a connection between two people . . . the mentor and the mentoree. Factors such as time, proximity, needs, shared values, and goals affect any relationship. But the mentoring relationship needs three additional factors, or dynamics, to bring about empowerment. These dynamics are constantly at play in the context of a mentoring relationship and directly affect the mentoree's progress, change, and level of empowerment.

The following dynamics are vital to the mentoring relationship:

1. *Attraction*—This is the necessary starting point in the mentoring relationship. The mentoree is drawn to the mentor for various reasons: perspective, certain skills, experience, values and commitments modeled, perceived wisdom, position, character, knowledge, and influence. The mentor is attracted to the mentoree's attitude, potential, and opportunity for influence. As attraction increases, trust, confidence, and mentoring subjects develop that will strengthen the mentoring relationship and ensure empowerment.

2. *Responsiveness*—The mentoree must be willing and ready to learn from the mentor. Attitude is crucial for the mentoree. A responsive, receiving spirit on the part of the mentoree and attentiveness on the part of the mentor directly speed up and enhance the empowerment.

3. *Accountability*—Mutual responsibility for one another in the mentoring process ensures progress and closure. Sharing expectations and a periodic review and evaluation will give strength to application and facilitate

empowerment. The mentor should take responsibility for initiating and maintaining accountability with the mentoree.

The more deliberate and intense the mentoring relationship, the more important these dynamics are. Why is this true? Because mutual commitment is necessary for change and growth to take place. These dynamics are the ingredients that produce this commitment.

Think back on the various interactions you have had with knowledgeable and experienced people. A discussion may have centered around a personal need you had, but because there was no mutual commitment you might not have felt safe to fully disclose your situation. Further, the other party to the conversation would not have felt committed to orient his or her response to understand and support your need to the degree that would have specifically helped you. Follow-up on what you discussed would not have taken place, for without commitment the subject is dropped. When commitment is part of a mentoring relationship there is safety, focus, sincerity, and follow-through until growth takes place. We find this to be vital to the Intensive types of mentoring where change and progressive development are the goals.

Occasional and Passive mentoring are not as intense or deliberate. These mentoring roles, for instance, do not necessarily need the dynamics of *accountability* to be effective, whereas the Intensive roles do. *Attraction* and *responsiveness* must be present in all types of mentoring or there will be no empowerment.

Looking at the continuum in figure 2-1, you can visualize a flow of these dynamics (attraction, responsiveness, accountability). On the left end where contact is more frequent, the involvement is more deliberate and intense mutual commitment is strong. But as you move to the right, accountability falls away and attractiveness and responsiveness are more a function of the mentoree's immediate need. We will develop and illustrate this later.

Mentoring is always available if you specify your empowerment need and if you are willing to supply the needed dynamics. Some may not agree with this. Our experience leads us to conclude that many historical models are available to meet a broad range of mentoring needs—that is, if you are willing to search through bookshelves to find them and supply the needed dynamics to bring about empowerment. (We listed a few models in the annotated bibliography to illustrate what is available.) When seeking a mentor, don't look for an ideal person who can do the whole range of mentoring functions. Few of these exist, if any. But if the mentoring needs are specified, someone is usually available who can mentor to that need. We believe that mentors are part of God's development plan for each of His followers. He will provide them as you "ask and seek."

SUMMARY
Mentoring is not just the latest fad or buzzword. For Christians it is rooted in biblical principles. Its current popularity stems from a need arising from Western society's extreme individualism and resulting lack of accountability.

By looking more deeply at the characteristics of the various types of mentoring, you will be more aware of people who could be potential mentors for you in specific areas and at certain times in your life.

It takes commitment to build a mentoring relationship, to allow our lives to be teachable and responsive, and to be willing to be held accountable for our growth. But the resulting empowerment and enrichment to our lives are beyond measure.

FOR FURTHER STUDY (CHAPTERS 1 AND 2)

1. Identify some people who have been important in your own personal development. Using table 2-1, try to identify which mentoring function they fulfilled for you. Can you think of an example of all seven types in your life?

2. List some areas of need you see in your life that a mentor might meet. Be as specific as you can.

3. Structured accountability decreases as you move toward the less deliberate types of mentoring. How would you include the accountability dynamic with a historical hero as your mentor?

4. Do a further study of the life of Barnabas (Acts 4:36 and chapters 11–15), looking for those qualities in his life that made him such a good mentor to those around him.

5. What are the advantages of seeking multiple mentors for your life rather than one all-encompassing "guru"?

Chapter Three

INTENSIVE MENTORING: THE DISCIPLER

Three types comprise the Intensive mentoring group: Discipler, Spiritual Guide, and Coach. They each call for more deliberate and specific interaction and work best when all three dynamics are fully present.

In this group, each dynamic can be more easily analyzed for its degree of presence and effectiveness. In the next three chapters we will examine each of them in detail, beginning here with the Discipler.

THE DISCIPLER

The Discipler is the mentoring type with which the majority of us are probably most familiar. A wealth of books and practical aids on the subject of discipling others has been published over the last two decades. What comes to mind is an individual who helps a new believer grow in the basics of a disciple's life . . . showing him how to pray, study the Bible, and share his faith with others.

> **Discipling is a relational process in which a more experienced follower of Christ shares with a newer believer the commitment, understanding, and basic skills necessary to know and obey Jesus Christ as Lord.**

One amazing fact we see today is the number of older followers of Christ who want discipling. They missed this relationship in their earlier years.

A Late Need for Discipleship

Peter came to Christ early in his life and grew up in a good church situation. He absorbed some basic biblical understanding through the teaching in his youth group and worship services. Though his college schedule was full, he managed to attend church fairly regularly and participated in a group Bible study when he could. Things seemed to go just fine.

Once out of college and into the work world, the group was no longer there for Peter. His job, courtship, and eventual marriage took most of his time, so he didn't realize he was running out of "spiritual fuel." Peter was constantly asked to attend various Bible study groups, but a Sunday service was all he felt he could do now. "Catch me later, when things settle down at work . . . thanks."

Periodically, a sermon or a concerned comment from his wife would stir Peter to evaluate his spiritual growth. This usually made him feel guilty, and he would resolve to "get more involved" . . . but nothing changed . . . until Larry joined his company. Peter was attracted to Larry's life as he observed him sensitively relate to people and handle some business disappointments. At lunch one day Peter learned that Larry was a committed believer and appeared to have an intimate relationship to Christ. His spiritual life had a focus and freshness to it that caused Peter to inquire further as to the reason. "Discipleship . . . learning how to follow Christ through daily time with Him, personal study of the Scriptures, and prayer of all types," was Larry's reply. Praying for people immediately when a need arose was the area of most recent pursuit for Larry, so he invited Peter to join him after work each day.

Praying with Larry opened a whole new understanding of discipleship for Peter. He had never prayed so specifically and completely for people and situations. Prayer led to quiet time together and then to Bible study. Larry had learned most of what he knew from the friend who led him to Christ while in college. Peter asked Larry to teach him how to develop an intimate walk with Christ and was willing to make any personal time adjustment necessary to ensure his availability.

Peter was in his early thirties and had been a follower of Christ for about eighteen years. His early mentoring relationships were basically with Counselors and Contemporary Models, but he had never had an accountable relationship with a mature follower of Christ who discipled him. No one had helped him to learn basic spiritual disciplines that would serve him in his pursuit to know and follow Christ. Within six months of this relationship, Peter was trusting God for more specifics in his life and understanding more of what it means to follow Christ. Their relationship developed into a real friendship and co-laborship as they sought to make Christ known in their workplace.

People in their mid-thirties and forties who have been church members for years are asking for discipling—even full-time Christian workers who never received that personal one-on-one help in their earlier years.

Why is discipleship so appealing today? There are several possibilities. First of all, many people who were socialized in the last three decades suffer from a lack of discipline. These people often long for clarity and practical help in bringing about a stable, consistent growth pattern for their spiritual life. Second, many people who became followers of Christ in recent years are products of dysfunctional family situations due to the turbulent years of the sixties, the "me generation" of the seventies, and the "affluent years" of the eighties. They are willing to go through rigorous and relational discipleship programs if these will bring wholeness at the other end. Third, a well-designed discipleship experience instills a basic Christ-centered spirituality that can provide a foundation for a lifetime of following Christ. The disciplines learned and practiced will strengthen and tune the believer so he or she is quick to sense the Spirit's leading and draw upon God's grace and resources to exploit opportunities and endure hardships. It is similar to a well-trained athlete, who has far greater capacity to fully use all his talents in a challenging situation than a lesser-conditioned one with equal ability. The Apostle Paul and the writer of Hebrews often exhort us in these areas (2 Timothy 2, 1 Corinthians 9, Hebrews 5 and 12). So whatever your age, insights on this type of mentoring may well apply to you or to others to whom you will relate.

A Discipler-mentor teaches and enables a mentoree in the basics of following Christ.

What does this mean?

At the heart of discipleship lies the concept of the centrality and lordship of Christ in believers' lives. Believers usually progress in understanding and appropriating Christ in their lives—Christ as Savior, Christ as Lord, Christ as strength, Christ as life. Early discipleship efforts focus on personally knowing and experiencing Christ.

Flowing from this centrality of Christ there is the recreation of the inner being, which shapes your values, attitudes, motives, and eventually your behavior. Development of your inner being usually requires that you establish some basic spiritual disciplines or habits in your devotional life. This includes reading and studying Scripture for yourself and learning how to pray—both devotional and intercessory.

Establishing right habits is vital to the life of a

disciple. The right habits will provide a consistent means of developing a disciple's relationship with Jesus Christ. Steven Covey in his book, *The Seven Habits of Highly Effective People*, says, "Habits are powerful factors in our lives" (1989: 46). He goes on to comment, "Our character, basically, is a composite of our habits." As the maxim goes, "Sow a thought, reap an action; sow an action, reap a habit; sow a habit, reap a character; sow a character, reap a destiny."

In order to know and follow Christ, a disciple needs to establish habits that will affect his or her character and destiny. Such habits (later we will identify them specifically) are essential to the disciple's life-long pursuit of Christ. Habits do not develop easily; human nature resists change. Covey compares the effort needed to break or establish habits to the great amount of energy initially needed by a rocket to overcome the earth's gravitational pull. Once out of the earth's atmosphere, however, the rocket glides with small amounts of energy (Covey 1989: 46-47).

Habits are developed through a combination of knowledge, skill, and desire (1989:47). Knowledge tells you "what to do." Skill answers the question, "How do I do it?" And desire provides the motive and answers, "Why do it?" The Discipler seeks to provide the answers to all three of these questions so a growing disciple will develop commitment to stay in the habit-forming process and reap the benefit and blessing of intimacy with Christ and co-laboring with Him.

Usually these disciplines or habits focus strongly on the inner life. This then reflects itself outwardly in relationships with others and behavior. Often in the press of external life the new believer begins to hear the Holy Spirit's promptings, probably in the form of convictions for change of behavior and sometimes in terms of guidance in decisions. Meeting with other growing followers of Christ will then support the Spirit's promptings, encouraging and affirming the believer's continued growth.

Giftedness begins to emerge as God's unique working in the individual is recognized. Continued growth brings fruitfulness — both in the believer's life and in ministry to others as he uses his gifts.

Discipling is an intensive mentoring process and all the "dynamics" are fully there and directly affect the empowerment. The following paragraphs describe how they are experienced in discipleship mentoring.

Attraction is similar to other types of mentoring, but rarely does a new believer understand the need for discipling unless he or she has been exposed to it somewhere. A baby simply knows hunger and goes to wherever and whoever can provide it. Therefore, the mentor normally initiates the relationship with a new believer. In the case of an older believer who has never been discipled (as in Peter's situation, pages 48-49), the potential mentoree may exercise more discernment and initiative. In either case, shared circumstances, proximity, maturity (on the mentor's part), and desire (on the mentoree's part) should play a strong role in determining a discipling relationship.

Responsiveness is critical to the success of a discipling relationship. The mentor leads more in this relationship than any other mentoring type, as so much is new for the mentoree. This bears a close similarity to apprenticeship relations as found in the skilled labor fields of masons, electricians, and plumbers. The mentoree (or apprentice) must be willing to be guided and eager to respond to assigned tasks.

Accountability—The deliberateness of the discipling process necessitates accountability. The new believer (or mentoree) will incorporate new things into his or her life and make changes that will demand personal discipline and determination, which most often does not come naturally and needs encouragement. The mentor must be sensitive to this and take the initiative.

WHEN IS DISCIPLESHIP FINISHED?
How long does a discipleship relationship last? A better question would be, "What are the signs that the new believer is becoming a disciple?" What indicates that a new believer is moving from a dependent stage, where external motivation from the mentor basically sustains the development, to a maturing stage, in which the believer is internally motivated to grow and follow Christ?

Christ gave some clear marks of a disciple so you will know one when you see one (even if looking in the mirror).

MARKS OF A DISCIPLE

John 8:31-32	Hold to Christ's teaching . . . obeying His Word in daily living and decisions.
John 13:34-35	Loving others . . . as Christ loved His disciples.
John 15:8,16	Bearing much fruit . . . that glorifies God . . . fruit of the Spirit in you and through your labors.
Luke 14:27	Surrendering to Christ's will and following Him in each area of your life.

Obviously you never graduate from being a disciple, but you make a start and develop some "growth habits" that will *facilitate* your pursuit of Christ as His disciple. While various Disciplers may differ on exactly what are growth habits, in table 3-1 we would like to suggest a set of four areas in which you should establish them. Such habits should lead to the marks of a disciple listed above. When these habits are in place, the mentoree has the basics of discipleship and should be able to grow without direct intervention from the Discipler-mentor.

Table 3-1. Basic Growth Habits

BASIC AREA	IMPORTANT GROWTH HABITS FOR A DISCIPLE
1. Devotions	♦ Sensitive, personal intake of the Scriptures on a regular basis so that the new believer can hear God's voice in the written Word. ♦ Personal, intimate prayer with God on a regular basis so that the believer can respond and draw close to Him.
2. Word Intake	♦ The new believer must learn the Word of God for perspective on life and ministry—both from the teaching of others and personal study. ♦ The new believer needs to apply God's Word in order for spiritual growth to occur. Habits of obedience need to be established. God's Spirit speaks to His children through His Word and the new believer will learn to respond willfully and appropriately.
3. Relationships	♦ The new believer needs to see the value of community and establish the habit of regularly meeting with other followers of Christ who are growing and obediently carrying out Christ's commands. This is necessary for correction, edification, encouragement, worship, and guidance.

4. Ministry
◆ The new believer must feel both a concern that others come to know Christ and an openness to share his or her own relationship to Christ with others. This happens best when a believer faithfully follows Christ in his or her world and loves and prays for those in that world.

◆ The new believer should be established in intercessory prayer for others.

◆ The new believer should share what he or she has learned about following Christ with others.

◆ The new believer needs to be involved in appropriate ministries that encourage the development and use of his or her gifts. In the attempts to do ministry giftedness emerges and fruitfulness is seen.

HINTS FOR DISCIPLESHIP MENTORING

Do *you* need a mentor who can disciple you, or do you need to *be* a mentor who disciples others? Below are some suggestions for those who answer "yes" to either of these questions.

For the Disciple

1. *Select carefully.* A discipleship relationship takes both time and expertise. Your mentor's availability is at least as important as the discipleship expertise he or she may have. Pray for God's choice of a person to disciple you. Ask wise followers of Christ to suggest possible persons who could disciple you. Look for the "Marks of a Disciple" (page 54) being evidenced in the believers and potential mentors around you.

2. *Be faithful.* Do the assignments given. Seek to be responsive to your Discipler. Empowerment is a direct function of a learning posture. Discipline is directly related to the character trait of

faithfulness, which is an esteemed quality in the Kingdom of God.
3. *Spend time with your mentor.* Seek to spend time with your mentor in various situations. Much of what you will learn will come through modeling—seeing your mentor apply principles of following Christ in real life.
4. *Remember, your goal is to get to know and follow Christ,* and to establish certain growth habits that will help you toward this goal. Keep this perspective. Respond to your mentor knowing that he or she is moving you toward that goal.

For the Discipler
1. *Select carefully.* You will usually find more people who need discipling than you can handle. Because discipleship mentoring is relational and time-intensive, you probably should work with no more than one or two at a time. Spend time together before inviting your mentoree to pursue Christ with you. Look for a teachable attitude and common interests and background. Clarify your desire to strengthen your potential mentoree's walk with Christ before you begin.
2. *Establish growth habits* in the areas of devotional life, Word intake, relationships, and ministry (table 3-1).
3. As you guide your mentoree to establish these habits, *discern the uniqueness* of the individual in the area of giftedness (evaluate spiritual gifts, natural abilities, and acquired skills). There are a number of assessment tools on the market you can use, and you should observe the mentoree in

various ministry situations.
4. *Disciple along giftedness lines.* Beyond the common growth habits, you want to give assignments that will develop and bring out the range of giftedness for that particular believer. Be sensitive to the uniqueness of the mentoree. Your purpose is not to simply run him or her through a discipleship program, but rather to lay a foundation and motivation for the lifelong pursuit of Christ and doing His will.
5. When you discover giftedness that you are not equipped to develop, *relate the mentoree to someone else who can.*
6. *Know when to turn loose and allow the disciple to operate on inner motivation and not yours.* Your goal is to bring the mentoree from dependence upon you to independence. There should be a specific time of closure, during which you deliberately release the disciple. From then on your relationship will not be that of a Discipler-mentor. Perhaps it will be one of the other types of mentoring as needed . . . but always a trusted friend.

THE DISCIPLER'S ONGOING MINISTRY
Having a Discipler-mentor is something most believers long for at some time in their Christian life. The Discipler-mentor can have perhaps the deepest and most long-lasting impact of any mentoring type. Whether you are in your late thirties like Peter, a college student, married, or single, if you've never had this type of relationship we encourage you to seek one out.

If you are an older, mature believer we hope you've realized the impact you can have through this type of ministry. Look around and make yourself available to some young believer for intensive mentoring as a Discipler.

Chapter Four

INTENSIVE MENTORING: THE SPIRITUAL GUIDE

Spiritual Checkup

Jordan seemed to be on a spiritual plateau. He had been a believer for a long time and experienced blessing in fifteen years of ministry, both as a layman and full-time. His marriage and family of three children were doing well, so what was the problem? "I'm not sure what it is, but something seems off. I think I'm doing all the right things, but the ol' drive is at 75 percent, and situations bother me that never did before. Maybe I just need to take some time off and reflect on my life."

"What you need is a spiritual checkup," replied his friend. "You know, just like a medical checkup." "Where do you get that?" asked Jordan. "That's just what I need."

"I guess from a mature spiritual brother who has been around a while and knows God, people . . . and probably life," suggested his buddy. So on the way home Jordan reviewed the potential candidates he knew and it "clicked" when he thought of Henry Johnson, a godly brother who listened well and always had a good word to help in a situation.

Henry liked the idea of a spiritual checkup and asked Jordan to give him a week to think about what that meant, as he had never done one before. A week later Jordan sat down in Henry's living room for their first of many meaningful times together.

"When I go to the doctor's office for a checkup, he starts off with the vital signs . . . you know, pulse, blood pressure, temperature, and some recent history on how I'm doing. So I thought we could do the same." With that introduction, Henry began with what he felt was the "pulse" of the believer—intimacy and devotion to Christ. "When you spend time with God, what do you talk to Him about? What is He saying to you? What are you learning about Him?" After an hour or so of working with these questions and referring to the Word periodically, it became obvious to both that Jordan's "pulse" was running low.

"Let's check one more vital sign before you go . . . blood pressure, or how you respond to your daily circumstances like challenges, difficulties, disappointments, and unexpected changes in plans or schedules," suggested Henry. "Let's take a specific situation that occurred this past week which was unexpected and a disappointment."

It didn't take Jordan long to identify one. His partner at work did not fulfill his responsibility for a project and it would take weeks to recover from the failure, including redoing certain aspects and working extra hours. Henry began to ask questions about his response to this development. Aside from the initial emotional letdown (which was normal), Jordan was surprised to hear himself relate how mad he was at his partner and blame other close associates. Although he did not vent his irritation, it did affect his response to them and his mood. "When did you bring God into this situation?" Henry probed. "Not until late that night when I was lying in bed, and then it was more of a confession for my irritation," Jordan replied. They discussed how Jordan could have brought God into this situation immediately. Henry shared some of his own experiences that taught him what it meant to walk with God through circumstances and how Jordan could view and use the "unexpected" as a follower of Christ. It was both encouraging and revealing for Jordan as they pressed a little bit further into some other situations.

Henry diagnosed Jordan's spiritual condition as "low normal" and prescribed a couple of changes for him. He suggested Jordan include ten minutes of worship in the Psalms each day as part of his devotional time and then journal his thoughts in the form of a prayer to God. Then he could take fifteen minutes in the middle of the day to reread and pray his written prayer and discuss with God the events and people he had encountered so far. Henry also gave Jordan a spiritual biography of Hudson Taylor to read. Jordan's assignment was to observe how Taylor dealt with the difficult situations and unexpected changes he faced in his profound ministry as a missionary to China. Next, he was to record his reactions to Taylor's work. They would get back together in two weeks to continue the spiritual checkup.

Over the succeeding months, Jordan and Henry went further into other vital signs of the life of a disciple. Jordan responded to Henry's suggestions and soon found his spiritual vitality returning as he developed new depth and perspective. They struck an agreement to get together every two months for a "mini-checkup" and fellowship. As Henry got to know Jordan better, he put his finger on a couple of potentially dangerous patterns Jordan was unconsciously developing and provided the accountability needed for him to break out of them. Jordan also drew his wife into an "annual marriage checkup" with Henry and his wife to ensure that their marital "basics" (communication, conflict resolution, financial priorities, decisions, intimacy, children, etc.) were developing and some bad habits hadn't crept in through neglect and busyness.

Henry is a Spiritual Guide. His role in Jordan's life is different from that of a Discipler.

> **The primary contributions of a Spiritual Guide are accountability, decisions, and insights concerning questions, commitments, and direction affecting spirituality (inner-life motivations) and maturity (integrating truth with life).**

Simply stated, a Spiritual Guide facilitates spiritual development and maturity at certain critical junctures in a disciple's life.

> **A Spiritual Guide is a godly, mature follower of Christ who shares knowledge, skills, and basic philosophy on what it means to increasingly realize Christlikeness in all areas of life.**

Spiritual Guide-mentors are specialists at assessing spirituality. This differs from Discipler-mentors, who seek to enable others in the basics of following Christ.

You will notice some overlap between this type of mentoring and discipling, which we discussed earlier. Both types of mentoring deal with spiritual growth, but there are specific differences. Discipling, in fact, is a special kind of Spiritual Guide. Discipling deals with the basic issues of commitment—getting a "jump start" on following Jesus Christ. Discipleship normally takes place early in a new believer's experience. It may last a short time and be intensive training. It moves mentorees in a natural progression from dependence on others in following Christ to a certain kind of healthy independence.

You will usually need to be discipled only once in a lifetime (as you start on your journey of following Christ). However, from time to time throughout your growth in Christ you will need a Spiritual Guide. Discipling is *training* intensive. Spiritual Guide-mentoring is *reflective* intensive. A Spiritual Guide will move you on to interdependence, which implies a healthy independence with mutual dependence for greater growth and ministry as a part of the Body of Christ.

An interesting counterpart of the Spiritual Guide is developing in the business world . . . the Executive Coach. As Robert Boynton explains in his article, "Doctor Success" (1989), these Executive Coaches become sounding boards, chaplains, teachers, fans, and coaches in all areas of business, politics, and leadership. They help their clients step back and see the big picture, putting things into perspective. A growing number of top executives are finding they, too, need someone to "just be there" for them and come into their private world to help sort out motives, strengthen values, and encourage right thinking and action. For many executives this type of personal guide is not a frivolous benefit but a necessity. So it is with a Spiritual Guide for all those who desire to strongly follow Christ and finish well.

FUNCTIONS OF A SPIRITUAL GUIDE

Most people need personal guidance on spiritual issues often throughout their lifetime, but not on a fixed time schedule. The functions Spiritual Guides perform help emphasize this need. They:

♦ help believers assess their own development.
♦ point out areas of strength and weakness in spirituality.
♦ help believers identify needs and take initiative for change and growth.
♦ provide perspectives on how to develop growth and depth.
♦ provide accountability for spiritual maturity.

In discussing the value of a Spiritual Guide in his own life, Timothy Jones (1991:43) says he helps him "make sense of everyday life," and "spot God's activity in the mundane . . . by keeping [his] attention focused on [his] life's events, and praying for [his] concerns." A Guide will help you sort out your mixed motives and refocus on Christ when your competing time demands and desire for man's approval blur your priorities.

Even mature followers of Christ need accountability for growth in specific areas. It is easy to see that new or young disciples may need a Spiritual Guide, but less obvious for mature followers of Christ. However, it seems clear that to reach higher levels of maturity in life and ministry requires greater discernment and response to God. As growth occurs, even a mature disciple will experience new situations and issues of inner life growth for which guidance will be helpful. Perspective and direction are always welcome when people face uncertainty. Here a Spiritual Guide can help.

This type of mentoring is not bound by time but is usually need-centered. The length of mentoring varies depending on the issue in focus, the mentoree's perception of need, and the assessment of the Spiritual Guide as to when to bring closure. The time may be as short as a few months and as long as several years. The regularity of meetings will vary — some Spiritual Guides prefer weekly meetings, others prefer monthly.

DISCERNING A NEED FOR A SPIRITUAL GUIDE
The following hints may help you discern whether you need a Spiritual Guide.

1. It is always wise to have a "spiritual checkup," just as from time to time you need a physical checkup.
2. When you sense you've reached a plateau in personal, spiritual, or ministry growth, or you face an obstacle to growth, you probably need the perspective and insight of a Spiritual Guide.
3. When you find that you repeatedly ask questions about growth, or you are being challenged from more than one source for growth, then you probably need a Spiritual Guide. Frequently, others can sense your lack of growth before you can.
4. If you experience a need for an attitude or motivational change, or you begin to experience spiritual things that your present perspectives do not adequately explain, then you probably need the help of a Spiritual Guide.
5. If you are in a place of spiritual influence or authority and have no intimate accountabil-

ity with someone or some group of spiritually mature people, then *you need* a Spiritual Guide. Senior pastors, gifted leaders of denominations or parachurch organizations, and upper-level Christian leaders frequently find that they have little spiritual accountability. Many have fallen for just such a lack of intimate accountability.

Most potential Spiritual Guides hesitate to declare themselves as such. Perhaps there is a vaunted image attached to this type of mentor, but that need not be. Spiritual Guides need to know God and His Word, grow in both, and know life. They do not need to be theologians or psychologists. They should be people who have walked with God and through life enough to understand the challenges and what it takes to persevere in difficulty, be humble in blessing, and pursue His will in the midst of temptation. Godly wisdom is recognized by the fruit of a life.

> Who is wise and understanding among you?
> Let him show it by his good life, by deeds done
> in the humility that comes from wisdom. . . .
> The wisdom that comes from heaven is first of
> all pure; then peace-loving, considerate, sub-
> missive, full of mercy and good fruit, impartial
> and sincere. (James 3:13,17)

A mentoring relationship with a Spiritual Guide is normally initiated by the mentoree, since he or she is the one who is aware of the need. But once the need is expressed and *expectations* from both sides exchanged and clarified, the mentor must assume responsibility for the relationship and work toward meeting the expectations.

An Older Friend

Awareness of my need for a Spiritual Guide came through a series of experiences. First, one of my friends took on a leadership responsibility in a church, and he immediately came under pressure. His response to the pressure was to become irritated, defensive, and place some blame on others. As we talked about this after church one day, I learned he had other pressures at work and home, as well. He felt he couldn't go to the pastor or some of the elders, as they had a vested interest in the outcome and he didn't think they could help with his work and home tensions. I felt frustrated, because I could not be much help to him, and he seemed to be done in. I thought to myself, *Boy, I hope I never get in a situation like that . . . without any help!*

Then I read a book about "plateauing" in a profession. I thought about the chance of plateauing in my spiritual life and ministry. Since the true power to lead and minister comes from the inner life, not techniques and knowledge, I knew the key to staying strong and growing would be to closely monitor my inner life growth. *But it is not easy to always detect how I am doing,* I reflected.

Finally I met a young, gifted pastor at a local conference and shared with him my concern, stemming from my friend's dilemma, about keeping a check on my own spiritual growth. He said he meets with a retired pastor in his area to talk about motives, ideas, plans, etc. This older brother has become a real Spiritual Guide and trusted friend who points him back to God and helps keep his focus on Christ. At the time they were reading *Born Crucified*, by L. E. Maxwell (1945), because his older friend felt the young pastor needed to understand what "being crucified with Christ" really meant for him.

I didn't need any more promptings. I started praying and looking for an "older friend" right away. After sharing my desire with several who seemed to be experienced and spiritual men, one responded and we have met several times already. We've begun by reading *Born Crucified* together and it is proving to be an excellent basis for sharing.

SPIRITUAL GUIDANCE THROUGHOUT A LIFETIME

Spiritual guidance takes time — at least, for the period of time in which there is intensive focus on this relationship. Ideally, the mentor and mentoree spend regular time together. This will vary depending on the mentoree's commitment to the whole process and the Guide's availability. The mentor always seeks to facilitate spiritual growth in response to the perceived spiritual and personal needs of the mentoree. The issues addressed will differ with the maturity of the mentoree and with numerous personal factors in the mentoree's development. Accountability varies in this mentoring relationship. Mentors usually key accountability to the response and felt needs of the mentoree.

Your need for the mentoring function of spiritual guidance will ebb and flow. Regular doses of this kind of mentoring from time to time will ensure your healthy development throughout your lifetime. Probably you need it most in the thirty-five-to-forty-five age bracket, a confusing time when pressures and questions increase and plateauing often begins. Later you need it to ensure that you *finish* your life and ministry well.

Chapter Five

INTENSIVE MENTORING: THE COACH

A coach is particularly important when you step into a new responsibility or try to do something you have never done before. A coach is also helpful when you bog down in a responsibility. Think of some great athletic coaches in our day. What are the marks of a great coach? He knows the basics of his sport. He knows drills that help people learn those basics. He teaches them how to win—and lose. He inspires them.

A coach helps you do more than you think you can do. The general notion of a coach is known to most everybody. But what about the coach as a spiritual mentor?

Let's discuss the idea of a Coach and how one can empower you.

The Coach's central thrust is to provide
motivation and impart skills
and application to meet a task or challenge.

Coaching in Family Matters

Family devotions just weren't going well. Our kids (ages ten, nine, five, and two) seemed to tolerate them, but I (Paul) longed to have them participate. There were no books out on the subject then and few resources. My wife and I were committed to being successful, as we were convinced our family needed to come together around God's Word and prayer.

As I asked other parents about their family devotion times I found plenty of frustrated fathers, and none claimed success . . . most had given up and surrendered to the urgent cry: "Dad, we gotta go!" Then I finally met Allen, who not only had good kids, but whose family had had successful devotions for years. A vanishing breed!

"Allen, what's the secret?" I asked with great anticipation. "Perseverance, participation, and prayer," was his reply. "Could you expand on that?" I pleaded with some hope that there might be more practical ideas behind those words. He went on to elaborate what he meant. He affirmed my commitment and strengthened my resolve by sharing the results in his family of twenty-plus years of coming together to pray and discuss the truths of Scripture on a daily basis.

Allen had learned over the years that consistency and preparation draw the family into the discussion. He explained how he taught his family that the evening meal was secondary—the primary purpose was to be together . . . fellowship. As the father, he felt his responsibility was to lead the family in seeking to understand and apply biblical truth and meaningful prayer time. Boy, I was pumped up to keep going in my efforts, but kept asking, "What practical things have you done?"

It was such a help to me to hear the ways Allen conducted their family times. "Aim at the older kids and the younger ones will come along. Read more of the Old Testament stories, the gospels, and Acts, then have each listen and be prepared to ask each other one question after reading," he recommended. We continued to meet and I reported my successes and flops each time. He would affirm my efforts and suggest changes and modifications. This went on for a couple months until I had it down and my kids were getting involved.

Now our family has experienced twenty years of being in the Word and praying on a daily basis. Our devotions have taken on many different forms as we moved through the years, some good and some not so good. We are all thankful for Allen, my Coach, who strengthened my resolve to keep going and imparted the skills and ideas to make it happen.

Most coaching relationships are initiated by the mentoree as he becomes aware of his need, as happened in the above illustration. However, it is not the exclusive right of the mentoree. Potential coaches who are aware of people who need coaching should feel free to offer, "I've been praying for you, and I wonder if I could be of some help?" Again, clarifying the need area and expectations of the Coach and mentoree are important. One understanding that should be discussed is at what point the coaching relationship is finished. Normally, the termination is in the hands of the mentoree when he declares, "I think I have it now . . . thanks!" The Coach may detect this before the mentoree does and, if so, then he can affirm the mentoree with that conclusion and be "on call" if needed.

> **Coaching is a process of imparting encouragement and skills to succeed in a task through a relationship.**

Empowerment of the mentoree is the result. A key to good coaching is observation (when possible), feedback, and evaluation. An experienced Coach does not try to control the player (or mentoree), but rather he seeks to inspire and equip him with the necessary motivation, perspective, and skills to enable him to excellent performance and effectiveness. A Coach understands that experience is the teaching vehicle, but a wise Coach knows the power of evaluated experience.

Taking on a New Responsibility

"Diane, we would like you to lead a Bible study group this year. Would you pray about that?"

"But I've only been a believer for three years. I'm just not ready to teach others," she replied to Pat. Confidently, Pat nodded. "You

have grown consistently, and your gifts seem to
be in the area of teaching. Besides, we are not
asking you to teach the group, but to lead it . . .
and I would be glad to help you."

By that last sentence, Pat essentially offered
to coach Diane into this new responsibility
and Diane responded eagerly. Pat first gave
her an assignment to review the notes on
"Leading a Bible Study Group with Questions"
and "Creating an Atmosphere in a Group" she
had taken at a group leaders' and assistants'
retreat. She was to be prepared to discuss
them. This tested her readiness and faithfulness and met a relevant need. Diane completed the assignment and set up a time to get
together with Pat. They discussed the application of the various points, since Diane now
viewed them more like a future leader.

Diane was asked to lead a Bible study in
two weeks, so she could practice what she was
learning. Pat arranged to meet with Diane a
few days before the study to review what she
had determined to be the main points of the
passage and what questions and approaches
she had developed to lead the women in discussion in order to enhance their understanding.
Diane's preparation was good, but some of the
questions needed to be adjusted and a few minutes of introduction added.

The Bible study went well, and Pat was
part of it. A few days later, Diane and Pat met to
evaluate the success of the study. Pat brought
up several points of evaluation so that Diane

could be part of the process and evaluate her own experience. Because Diane had prepared well, Pat was able to affirm her through specific feedback and observations. Together they identified the areas that Diane needed to work on and Pat gave her several suggestions that would strengthen her ability to lead well. She also took the opportunity to discuss the "why" behind the skills, so Diane could develop her understanding in discussion-type learning.

Diane tasted success. She realized that she could lead a Bible study group, but that it would take more work and practice to do it well. She asked Pat to stay with her until she felt confident in this new challenge.

As you can see from Pat's example, Coaches impart skills and motivate people to use them well. Coaches usually know the subject they deal with inside and out. They have an overall grasp. They can break good performance down into basic skills that must be learned. They can assess the mentoree's motivation and skill level and adapt appropriately. Most importantly, good Coaches know how to encourage and strengthen mentorees to do what is necessary to develop the skills and attitudes that will lead to excellence.

For many sports such as basketball, baseball, football, and soccer, coaches work with a whole team and are concerned with getting the players to work as a unit, as well as getting individuals to perform well. But some coaches work with individuals. Many sports require special one-on-one coaching. Ice skating, golf, gymnastics, and most track and field events require individual coaching. For the most part, Coaching-mentors in our definition are like the latter. They relate to individuals and help them strengthen performance in personal and ministry responsibilities.

> **Coaching is a relational process in which a mentor, who knows how to do something well, imparts those skills to a mentoree who wants to learn them.**

Coaching-mentors focus on teaching *how to do things*. There is some overlap with the Discipler-mentor and the Teacher-mentor (to be discussed later), but each mentor type has a different emphasis. Discipling focuses on establishing the basics to follow Christ, while teaching seeks to impart knowledge and enhance understanding in a specific area.

THE MENTORING DYNAMICS OF COACHING
Attraction is crucial to effective coaching. Good coaches have an eye for talent. When they spot good talent they also seek to recruit it. So too, with Coaching-mentors. They recognize people whom they can help become better. And they attempt to move toward a relationship that will allow for mentoring. People facing challenges want to do better and search for coaches who can help them reach higher levels of performance. Just as world-class athletes in sports such as gymnastics, ice skating, and tennis make great sacrifices and efforts to be linked to renowned coaches, so it should be with serious disciples who

desire growth in ministry challenges and opportunities. They are attracted to people who do things well and are willing to share what they have learned. Attraction goes both ways. The relationship is particularly important to coaching since it is such an individual matter.

To learn *skills* usually takes discipline. The Coaching-mentor needs to establish some type of agreed *accountability* with the mentoree. This needs to be discussed at the beginning of the relationship when expectations are clarified. Accountability will keep the mentoree working on basic skills until he can perform.

Coaching Through New Challenges

Jerry had observed Doug in several situations and sought his counsel on occasion. He grew to respect Doug as a leader and mature follower of Christ. So when Jerry was given increased responsibility in his parachurch organization, he immediately arranged to get together with Doug to talk about the new challenge he faced.

The organization had grown rapidly, and everyone was so ministry oriented that little thought had been given to long-range planning, staff development, internal communication, and fostering staff relationships. Staff members were beginning to show signs of this neglect, and Jerry's new responsibility placed him in a position to do something about it.

Being a gifted and sensitive leader, Jerry wanted to move in on these urgent needs

immediately. He worked hard to design a plan
to deal with them as soon as possible. As he
shared these plans, Doug suggested he consider the mature and experienced staff and how
they could be drawn into the planning process.
Their participation in the planning process
would affirm them and enhance the plans, as
well as give them ownership and motivation
to carry them out. Jerry wanted to include
the staff in planning, but had never done that
before and asked Doug to help him. Doug
explained several planning procedures, and
Jerry chose one with which he felt most comfortable. They worked together until Jerry felt
he understood the process and material to be
used. Doug identified the critical points in the
process and shared his experiences in leading
a group through a new situation like this one.
They even discussed possible reactions and
resistance from the staff.

Problems developed as Jerry led the staff in
the planning process . . . some anticipated and
some not. But the final result was encouraging.
Doug stayed close to him through phone calls
and meetings as Jerry worked through other
needs. This continued until Jerry felt confident
and was leading well. At that point, Doug continued to pray for Jerry and was available for
counseling when needed.

FUNCTIONS OF THE COACH
What do coaches do that empowers mentorees? They:

1. Impart skills (frequently knowledge is involved also).
2. Impart confidence and understanding in the use of those skills.
3. Motivate people so as to bring out the best in them, usually stretching them beyond what they thought they were capable of.
4. Model the importance of learning the basics of a skill, a process that will prove valuable in all of life.
5. Point the mentorees to other appropriate resources and link them up with them.
6. Observe the mentorees in action.
7. Evaluate the mentorees' experience and give feedback to enhance self-learning and development.

HINTS FOR THE COACH
Coaching-mentors who want to increase their effectiveness in mentoring may want to heed the following suggestions. To be an effective Coach you should:

1. Identify sets of important skills you have. Know your repertoire—*what* you do well and *how* you coach those skills.
2. Recognize the basic pattern that like attracts like in terms of personality, natural abilities, and spiritual gifts. Hence, be on alert for those who are drawn to you and may need your skills.
3. Be open to taking people with you and let them see you when you use your skills, for these are best learned experientially.

4. Model well. This is a powerful motivator, since people who can do things well instill confidence and inspire others.

HINTS FOR THE "PLAYER"
For those who want a Coach, perhaps the following suggestions will help. These points can be especially important when you take on a new responsibility, work, or ministry.

1. Clarify your challenge or task and the skills you need to be effective.
2. Search and pray for a potential Coach who demonstrates good experience in your needed skill areas. You may need to get others to help you identify someone.
3. Once identified, set out to establish a relationship that will lead to mentoring. Remember, most Coaches want responsive people. Be willing to pay the price and be responsive.
4. Set up a growth contract, if you can, that spells out what you want to happen (expectations), what will be done to bring it about, and how long the mentoring should last. If you find a Coach who is more informal and doesn't go for that, at least establish for yourself some growth goals.

Everybody needs Coaches. And everybody ought to be able to coach someone in something. Go for it!

SUMMARY
The Discipler is the most intensive mentoring type, focusing on the basics needed to follow Christ. The

mentoree's early external dependence on the Discipler can be used as a strength to build long-term habits, which will develop reliance upon Christ and move the mentoree to more internal self-motivation in his or her pursuit of Christ. Though usually thought of in the context of young believers, older followers of Christ may also need discipling to internalize basic spiritual habits.

All mature believers will continue at periods throughout life to need Spiritual Guides. In fact, leaders in positions of wide influence have a special need for Spiritual Guides to enhance vital accountability in areas of integrity and to face the temptations that usually accompany such positions.

And the wise will search out Coaches who can help them develop and sharpen their ministry skills and become more effective.

We have labeled these three mentor types as intensive because of the high sense of responsibility that develops between the mentor and mentoree. This intensity is key to the degree of empowerment that will take place. It will take time, commitment, and work for both the mentor and mentoree to build such a relationship.

FOR FURTHER STUDY (CHAPTERS 3, 4, AND 5)
1. Consider the habits listed in table 3-1 (page 55). Which of these habits, if any, do you need?

2. Assess your own experience and skills. In what areas could you pass your experience and skills on to another? (Remember, you don't have to have complete expertise in an area! In fact, one

of the best ways to sharpen your own skill is to teach it to another.)

3. Start a list of younger Christians whom you could mentor. What specific needs do you see in their lives? Pray over those people, asking the Lord to make you available to meet their needs.

4. Seek to establish a closer friendship with those you are praying for on your list. As you take these initial steps, the Lord will direct you as to which ones you might establish a mentoring relationship with.

5. Study 1 Thessalonians 2. What attitude did Paul have as a mentor toward the Thessalonians? List some of the mentor roles he played in their lives. What things did he impart to them?

6. Look at the role of Jehoiada as Spiritual Guide for Joash in 2 Chronicles 24. Note especially verses 2, 17-18. What does this suggest about Spiritual Guides?

Chapter Six

Occasional Mentoring: The Counselor

From time to time God brings across your path people who help you for short periods of time in very specific ways. This is described as Occasional mentoring. Three mentor types comprise this group: Counselor, Teacher, and Sponsor. They don't take the place of the Discipler, Spiritual Guide, or Coach. Instead, *they make special developmental contributions at appropriate times.*

Counselor to a National Leader

Moses was overloaded. He was the leader of Israel, the judge for the people, a dad and husband, and everyone wanted his attention. When his father-in-law, Jethro, visited and observed Moses' limited family life and the frustrated lines of people waiting to have their disputes settled, he took Moses for a little "fatherly walk" and stated the obvious (although apparently not obvious to Moses—which is often our problem, too). "What you are doing is not good!" He then shared with Moses his observations and concerns for him. Moses presumably acknowledged his dilemma and frustration, as Jethro immediately gave his advice.

"You must be the people's representative before God [his priority]. . . . Teach them the decrees and laws, and show them the way to live and the duties they are to perform. But select capable men . . . and appoint them as officials over thousands, hundreds, fifties and tens. Have them serve as judges for the people at all times . . . bring every difficult case to you. . . . That will make your load lighter, because they will share it with you." (Exodus 18:19-22)

Moses was empowered, as he took his father-in-law's advice and applied it immediately (18:24-26). Thank God for wise and timely counsel. Not only was Moses relieved and more effective in his responsibilities, but the people and his family were blessed as well. I'm sure Moses learned to check periodically with his father-in-law . . . hopefully before committing himself to any future action.

We all are responsible to God for our own decisions and to discern His will, but we are foolish to *not* take advantage of the experiences and wisdom of others in the process. The wise King Solomon said, "Make plans by seeking advice; if you wage war, obtain guidance" (Proverbs 20:18).

Perhaps Moses could have avoided the dilemma had he sought counsel early on, but Jethro cared enough to initiate the discussion and offer some advice. "A wise man listens to advice" (Proverbs 12:15), and Moses was a wise man.

What about you? Do you have any "Jethros" in your life? You may not be in a crisis or overwhelmed, but you are always making decisions and planning. Solomon again exhorted, "Plans fail for lack of counsel, but with many advisers they succeed" (Proverbs 15:22). Often we don't see all the factors influencing our lives and decisions or know how to prioritize and interpret them. A trusted Counselor is as valuable as gold . . . not only in crises, but times of reflection and development, as well.

The central thrust of a Counselor is timely advice and impartial perspective on the mentoree's view of self, others, circumstances, and ministry.

Neighborly Counsel

Bill and Marilyn were in their early thirties with a young family of four children, and they were eager to follow God's leading. Sensing that God might be leading them to the mission field, they enrolled in a Bible college to prepare themselves and confirm God's will concerning their future.

As they moved into their little home they discovered that their neighbors, the Joneses, were veteran missionaries of twenty years in Costa Rica. It didn't take long before the families became friends, and Bill and Marilyn communicated their eagerness to serve God as missionaries. Aziel and Marianne (Jones) listened to their many questions and began to share their own experience in determining God's will and their eventual move to Costa Rica. This encouraged Bill and Marilyn since they had similar leading, and it helped them evaluate their own motives. Most of Bill's decisions concerning their future were made on an "open and closed door" basis, but this was a crossroads experience, and he had never faced one before. Almost every week, Bill and Marilyn would bounce their thoughts off the Joneses and pray together with them. It wasn't long before it became clear that they were to head for the mission field.

Now the counseling focus shifted from determining God's will to following it. Bill and Marilyn needed to identify which mission group to join and then the practical and necessary steps to take in order to prepare themselves for a cross-cultural move and effective ministry. They accepted Aziel and Marianne's counsel as guidance from God, and their advice turned out to be crucial and loaded with foresight.

The Joneses became primary Counselor-mentors to Bill and Marilyn at a strategic juncture in their lives. As you probably sensed, they served also as models and periodic Coaches as Bill and Marilyn prepared to meet the challenge before them. Aziel and Marianne did not see themselves as "Counselors" but more as a brother and sister who had some valuable experiences and insight that Bill and Marilyn needed. We wonder how many Aziels and Mariannes out there could share their lives and experiences (good and bad) with the Bills and Marilyns who eagerly desire to follow God's leading. Our goal is to encourage connections between these two groups. The empowering that would take place from such connections could significantly affect the lives and ministries of thousands!

What prevents or hinders this healthy linkup of the experienced with the inexperienced? Perhaps you could think about this further. We find that many are connected horizontally with peers and even share their needs and frustrations, but it is not enough, as experience and perspective are limited. Because we are "outsiders" to groups we speak to or visit, people come and want counsel. This can often be helpful on a one-time shot, but far better would be a Counselor from within their own network, where there is understanding of the context and continuity available. But sadly the reply to our inquiry, "Do you have someone locally to help you work this through?" is often, "No, I don't know of anyone." They need to ask themselves if this is really true or whether they harbor other reasons for not seeking such counsel.

In our experience with many non-American cultures, we find that the generational linkup is quite common and happens naturally . . . it is a value of the culture. Young men and women are not supposed to "know everything" or "make it on their own." Life is seen in the context of multiple generational relationships where there is a constant flow of energy, experience, wisdom, and commitment. But in Western and particularly North American culture, individualism has been lifted up to the point of unhealthy and dangerous independence.

Even church and fellowship groups are structured to cut out the vertical link. If you enter a typical church today you are offered many options for adults, but they are for young marrieds, singles, senior citizens, parents of teenagers, and others. We certainly understand and support the good reasons for affinity groups of professionals, clubs, fraternities, and such, but in these contexts where is the opportunity to sit together, share, and learn from one another in the vertical age and experience spectrum?

Young married couples with both husband and wife working need to expose their lives and struggles to those who have worked through that phase. Conversely, those fifty and older need to understand the new and different tensions and pressures young families experience that were not present when they started out.

Generational Flow of Wisdom

My (Paul's) eighty-five-year-old godly mother is part of a women's Bible study that meets weekly. All the women range from mid-thirties to early fifties, and Mom has questioned her continued participation several times. But the group will not hear of it. Every time Mom speaks, the women lean forward to catch every word and take notes. "Your mom brings into our lives a longed-for voice of wisdom from years of following Christ, weathering the storms of life, and being a mom, grandmom, and great grandmom. Some women come to the study just to be around her," the study leader related.

We are convinced that if more Counselor connections were made, both informally and formally, the Body of Christ would be healthier, wiser, and more powerfully growing and affecting lives than it is today. If you are in a place to influence the generational flow of relationships in your church, fellowship, or organization, then do it. You will be blessed by it.

Alert to an Opportunity

In a small-group session of a meeting for young leaders, Steve related with deep hurt and anger a frustrating conflict with a senior leader in his organization. During a national committee meeting, to save face the superior had blamed Steve for a major project failure. Steve struggled with what to do.

An alert mentor recognized the need for counseling and took the initiative to discuss with Steve how he might handle the situation. A few months later the mentor received a letter from Steve.

He wrote, "I wanted to confront him angrily. Your counsel was rather to approach him humbly, with a teachable spirit, and ask if I had done something wrong. This I did with very good results. Over the next two hours we focused on spiritual integrity, and he confessed that he had blamed me out of desperation, realizing that it would be my head or his. Although many had questioned his integrity behind his back, none had offered help. What a difference. We talked of the necessity of integrity for God to bless a work with power and of the contrast between striving in the flesh to move things politically versus trusting the power of the Spirit to accomplish things.

"It was an amazing and powerful time! I believe that this has helped turn a key leader away from a slippery slope, and that as a result . . . thousands of new disciples will emerge from his work. It is very doubtful that the same results would have been achieved had I run in with guns blazing. Thanks for helping to save a friendship, turn around a leader, and keep an important ministry on track."

Mentors need to be always thinking mentoring and be alert for counseling opportunities where young leaders could easily make serious misjudgments. Informal one-time mentoring encounters can protect young leaders from actions that would have serious consequences.

Counseling can be as simple as a timely word of advice. A proverb underscores that "how good is a timely word!" (Proverbs 15:23). It can also be an extended experience. Counseling can become specialized and lead to an ongoing relationship in which the Counselor-mentor helps the mentoree work through issues that relate to past decisions and experiences. The amount of time spent in the relationship depends on the mentoree's sensed need (attraction) or the mentor's ability to sense a particular need in the mentoree. Intervention is a deliberate initiative by the mentor when he or she senses need and has freedom of access in the relationship. Otherwise it may be infrequent, need-driven, and left to the mentoree's initiative. The amount of time spent together is not an issue in this special relationship . . . appropriateness and timeliness of advice *are.* Empowerment occurs as the advice is applied. Accountability is less of a factor than in Intensive mentoring situations but is important if change and follow-through are needed.[1]

Table 6-1 lists the empowerment functions for Counselor-mentors.

Table 6-1. Eight Major Empowerment Functions of a Counselor-Mentor

TYPE	KIND OF EMPOWERMENT
1. Encouragement	They impart hope and give expectation for further development. They can often point out how God seems to be working in a situation and some of the positive things that can happen in terms of character and perspective from God's processing.
2. Soundboard	Counselors need to listen well. Their listening is focused and they respond to the mentoree with provocative feedback. They can provide objectivity to ideas.
3. Major Evaluation	Counselors can readily point out inconsistency in thought or viewpoint, and test ideas for soundness.
4. Perspective	They give perspective at needy times in a mentoree's life. They relate present happenings to the big picture and hence see positive potential even in negative situations.
5. Specific Advice	They can give specific advice to a specific situation. They are often able to give alternative choices presenting options and possible outcomes, leaving the final decision-making to the mentoree.

6. Linking	They link the mentoree with needed resources. Counselors are often aware of literary resources, people, finances, ideas . . . or whatever a mentoree may need to solve a perceived problem or develop an idea.
7. Major Guidance	Many mentorees are at turning points in their lives and need guidance in order to make major decisions. Counselors are able to view the broader framework of life's various stages and give sound advice and a life perspective.
8. Inner Healing	Specially gifted and trained Counselor-mentors can deal with basic issues in a life that hinder growth.

FINDING A COUNSELOR-MENTOR

There is great wisdom in the Body of Christ. It's probable that you will frequently need one or more of the above Counselor functions. In acknowledging this, you recognize the giftedness and diversity in the Body and move toward healthy interdependence. If you feel you need one or more of the functions listed above, then perhaps the following ideas may help you sort out how to establish a specific and committed Counselor relationship.

1. Using table 6-1, determine the general nature of your need for a Counselor-mentor.
2. Identify potential Counselor-mentors—wise, godly people in the community of which you are a part. In addition to the traits listed below, these potential Counselors should have some one-on-one relational skills. It is not enough that people have wisdom; they must know how to give that wisdom in a timely manner and in such a way as to edify and not weaken—even when

confronting. Frequently, Counselor-mentors
have the following marks of giftedness:

a. *Natural abilities*—analytical, relational, listening, empathetic.

b. *Acquired skills/knowledge*—counseling tech-
nique/perspectives/methodologies, analytical,
synthesis, conceptualization, use of leadership theories, developmental perspectives.

c. *Spiritual gifts*—teaching, exhortation, pastoral, discernment, word of knowledge, word of
wisdom.

d. *Experience*—particularly in the areas of your
development interest or need.

3. Informally seek to establish a relationship that
will allow you to determine if you will be able to
trust the Counselor, if the Counselor can relate
to you, and if the Counselor is willing and able to
help you.

a. This may involve describing the empowerment
function you are seeking.

b. You should have an estimation of your expectations for the duration of the relationship; for
example, one-time advice, ongoing in order to
thoroughly gain perspective and insight, and
ongoing, long-term help dealing with a dysfunctional situation.

4. If in these steps you sense God's confirmation,
then seek to trust the Counselor-mentor and
respond wholeheartedly to his or her advice.

5. Remember, a good Counselor-mentor wants to
help you move from dependence to independence
in terms of your personal decision-making processes. Whatever advice, perspectives, choices, or

assignments are given, you must own them or reject them if you aren't comfortable with them, for you are ultimately responsible for your own choices and decisions. Don't project this responsibility onto a Counselor-mentor. No one else is responsible to determine the will of God for you.

HINTS FOR COUNSELOR-MENTORS
1. Be available to potential mentorees. Be where they are, seek to relate to them as brothers and sisters, and enjoy them.
2. Seek to understand the issues others face and pray for them. Spend time thinking, studying, and praying for wisdom that applies to these issues. Reflect on your own experiences that relate to these or similar issues.
3. Be selective in choosing those whom you mentor on a more ongoing basis.
   a. Ascertain what kind of empowerment the mentoree needs and, if you aren't equipped to help with it, refer him to someone who can. You should identify a network of people, men and women, who function as Counselor-mentors and know their strengths and weaknesses in terms of the eight empowerment functions.
   b. See if there is a real attraction and responsiveness and if you will be able to establish accountability.
4. Ascertain the expectations of a potential mentoree in terms of need and duration.
5. Don't predetermine solutions. Frequently Counselor-mentors have a "pet solution" that they

attempt to use like a computer program. Listen to the mentoree to understand, and listen to God in terms of the individual's situation. Be prepared for God to break through with new ideas that you have not seen in the past.

6. Seek to bring closure to the relationship in such a way as to move the mentoree further along from dependence toward independence or interdependence.

Chapter Seven

OCCASIONAL MENTORING: THE TEACHER

Where would we be without good teachers? Most of us have experienced bad teachers, average teachers, and a few good ones. Usually the good ones stand out to us. What do teachers do in general, and how can we transfer that over into a developmental relationship that does not have to be in a classroom?

> **The central thrust of a Teacher-mentor is to impart knowledge and understanding of a particular subject.**

And we would add . . . to motivate the mentoree (learner) to use it.

In this era information is abundant (almost too abundant), and the challenge "to know about things" is always at hand. It is difficult to keep up with the new discoveries and developments. We can become intimidated if we allow these "learn-more voices" to overwhelm us. On the other hand, as disciples of

Christ, by definition we are to be "learners" . . . learners of Christ and His Word primarily, but also of our world and what influences our lives, jobs, and family. Each of us has various gifts, callings (service to Him), professional demands, and capacities, so we must determine before God (perhaps with the help of good mentors) what learning needs we may have. One of the best learning resources is the Teacher-mentor.

A Need to Know

Having grown up in a traditional, conservative church environment, David's view of the charismatic movement with all its unfamiliar manifestations evoked immediate resistance and later rejection. Then he met several charismatics in a Bible study at work, and he was thrown into confusion as he got to know them and appreciate their commitment to Christ and His Word. David bought a book on the issue, but that seemed too one-sided. It came to a head when he was teaching through the book of Acts in his adult class at church.

"What about the gifts of the Holy Spirit and all these manifestations we see in Acts? Should we expect all of this today?" asked one woman. "Let's put that discussion off until the end of the study and then we'll take that on as a separate topic," David responded. It was a good idea to delay the discussion, perhaps, but now David needed to know some answers. He prayed and went to his pastor and shared his learning need. He asked his pastor if he would help him develop a good grasp of the subject of the Holy Spirit, and the gifts and manifestations from the Scriptures. He wanted to understand the present views and interpretations that various groups in the Body have. They only had two months to do it!

The pastor was eager to mentor David in this and sensed his motivation was sufficient to realistically pursue it—at least to a point where he could lead his class in a profitable discussion and learning experience. They arranged an appointment for the next Saturday morning. The pastor warned David that he would have homework to do.

Over the next two months, the pastor gave David Bible passages to study and asked him to write summaries of the teaching. Their discussions were intense, loaded with questions as David searched the Scriptures for answers. Traditional thinking was challenged and only what the Bible said counted. David had to read several books by authors representing various points of view and report their positions. The two men analyzed each viewpoint from what they concluded was the biblical teaching. This process strengthened some conclusions and changed others.

In the end, David made a decision to not try to conclude the Acts study with a short session on the Holy Spirit and His manifestations, but rather treat the subject more fully in a three-month class. Needless to say, the class was packed and was often visited by the pastor, who sat in the back, never making a comment . . . only smiling with delight as he watched his mentoree lead the class into new understanding and appreciation for the ministry of the Holy Spirit.

No matter what the subject, someone will always know more than you do and may be eager to pass it on. We've been mentored by Teachers in areas like leadership, group dynamics, language learning, womanhood, child development, problem resolution in groups, woodworking (with some Coaching added), and handling the dynamics of change. Learning with a mentor is more focused and personal—and, therefore, faster and often deeper. Try it . . . you'll love it.

A mentoring relationship with a Teacher can range from the very informal to formal. The illustration of David and his pastor was more formal in that there was a specific focus, commitment, and duration. David (the mentoree) was eager for knowledge and understanding and was willing to respond to the pastor to get it. He saw that the pastor possessed the knowledge he desired and had the experience and skills needed to pass it on to him. On the other side, the pastor recognized David's need and motivation and felt he could provide what David wanted and needed. The commitment to accountability was never formally expressed, but was inherent in the pastor's comment as they parted after the initial meeting—that there would be homework. David agreed and demonstrated his commitment by fulfilling all his assignments. We would encourage a clearer expression of expectations and accountability at the front end. This strengthens the learning process and ensures empowerment. Also, the more the mentoree learns and responds, the more the mentor is motivated to teach. Mutual stimulation has an extraordinary effect on learning.

The informal teaching relationship needs some clarification and exchange of expectations simply to alleviate the frustration of unfulfilled expectations. People have expectations in any relationship, particularly a mentoring one, so it is better to express, clarify, and agree on them at the front end. This gives more freedom in the relationship and a sense of purpose and progress — as well as helping to avoid disappointment.

Teacher Extraordinaire

I (Bobby) have a special T-shirt that I wear proudly. On it in green is the facsimile of a hundred-dollar bill. Above the bill in big letters it says, "The Buck stopped here." On the bill in large, dark green print are the words *James M. Hatch, 39 years of service*. Below the bill is the logo: *Columbia Graduate School of Bible and Missions*. Mr. Hatch, nicknamed "Buck," truly did stop there effectively for thirty-nine years. He was one of the reasons I went to Columbia Bible College.

He impacted me, of course, via his content and concepts. But in terms of mentoring me as a Teacher he imparted three things and motivated me to make them my own. First, he always had an overall perspective on a whole subject. He taught the framework and then oriented every smaller item into that framework . . . so we saw *where* it fit, *why* it fit, and *what it meant* in terms of the whole. He was a master at that. The first five minutes of every class were spent in reorienting us to the broad picture and the progress made to date on it. Reviewing previous material and placing new material in context—two key insights gained from this powerful classroom Teacher.

A second thing Mr. Hatch taught me was the importance of always staying fresh in the material. Many times I heard him say, "Last night for the first time as I was going through this I saw . . ." and out would come some new and fresh truth from his treasure box. That has become a goal of mine. Each time I teach a subject again, I always seek to go further into it myself. I always assign myself a growth project that will make me personally expand myself with regard to the course. No matter how many times I teach a course, that is my goal. That habitual attitude came from Mr. Hatch.

A third thing I learned from Mr. Hatch was the concept of "being faithful to who you are, your giftedness." Mr. Hatch stayed within his competence. He never grasped for fame, publicity, or exposure through media. He was a good teacher. The classroom was his forte. And thirty-nine years' worth of students all over the world can attest to his effectiveness.

Mr. Hatch mentored me without ever

establishing accountability between us or even a personal relationship. He remains part of my ministry today. I studied under him for three years and took more than half a dozen courses. Those intense times of learning were life-changing in knowledge, motivation, and skills. He was a Teacher who mentored another Teacher by demonstrating how to do it.

This illustration shows that mentoring can be found in formal training or classroom modes if the mentoree will supply the effort to initiate the dynamics needed: responsiveness and accountability. Character, teaching methodology, and faithfulness to imparting the basics of whatever subject he taught were Mr. Hatch's major contributions. Teacher-mentors differ . . . some impart knowledge, some organize, some motivate. But the basis of their mentoring is the relevant knowledge they have amassed through experience in ministry.

Informal Co-Teaching

It was one of the finest teaching/learning experiences for us both. It was stimulating, personal, and open—reflective, with no holds barred on questions. And it happened almost by chance. Paul desired to learn about leadership developmental theory—Bobby's specialty. Paul is involved in so many decisions that affect leaders' careers that he wanted to know as much about an overall perspective on what happens to them as he could. His schedule never allowed him to attend Bobby's formal course. Finally four days were set aside for Bobby to go to Colorado to meet personally with Paul and his wife, Phyllis.

It was agreed that the four days would be intensive, without interruptions. Bobby would take Paul and Phyllis through his self-study manual, *Leadership Emergence Theory.* They would do some work before his arrival and an assignment afterward. Bobby, in turn, wanted Paul to share with him his insights on mentoring—Paul's specialty.

There was a sense that God had divinely appointed those four days. The Stanley dining room table became the center of the exchange. Manuals and materials were spread all over it. We spent time interacting over ideas, getting into God's Word, and praying together. It was an intense time (with frozen yoghurt breaks and one Air Force football game).

The Teacher-mentor role reversed back and forth. The concepts that one put forth, the other would expand upon, so there was mutual learning. Bobby brought to the session the ability to conceptualize and Paul supplied the illustrations and insights from his experience. At that teaching session, we both sensed God might have us work together to produce a book on mentoring.

Our experience suggests that teaching can be an individual thing. It does not have to be a formal classroom setting. What is needed? Just three things.

♦ You need someone who knows something worthwhile to teach and is willing to teach it.

♦ You need someone who wants to learn it and is willing to spend the time to do so.

♦ You need a deliberate decision to get together and pursue the learning experience.

The time can be short. The subject matter can be large or small. In this case we have an example of *co-mentoring*. Both of us were mentors and mentorees.

Specific Need-Centered Mentoring

I (Paul) was given a special assignment about five years ago—to survey our leadership across the globe (at that time about sixty-seven countries). I was asked to take a look at where we were in our leadership development, particularly with reference to middle- and upper-level leaders. I had been trained for military leadership and been a leader for a number of years. But it is one thing to lead and quite another to understand what you do conceptually and be able to evaluate it across a wide spectrum of roles and functions.

I had been out of circulation on what was happening in leadership in the States for about eleven years (my time overseas). I didn't know where things were in that field of study. So I thought, *Where can I go to get up to date on what's happening in leadership?* A professor I'd known for a number of years came to mind. I knew that he was in tune with leadership. He'd worked on it, spoken on it, and was a tremendous influencer in that area. I asked him, "Would you be a Teacher-mentor for me for about six months? The task would be to bring me up to speed on the latest thinking about leadership." And then I threw out a flood of questions: What issues did I need to know about? Who are the people I needed to read? How could I get into the subject in a six-month period? Were there seminars or courses that would help?

He listened. Finally he said, "Great, Paul, I would love to do that." And he sent me a list of books to read, subjects to think about, and people to contact. From time to time we would talk about some of the issues I saw and what I learned in my reading. In six months he had me into the whole subject of leadership so that I could begin to identify and understand trends, issues, and influences. At our last meeting we went over these and I realized how much I still had to learn, but I had a revitalized framework and a sense of where to go with it.

Notice in this case that I, the mentoree, took the initiative. I knew I had a need and was able to specify that need. I did not wait around for someone to come along that could help me. I approached someone I thought could meet the specific need. A prior relationship allowed me to make the request.

The words "up to speed" connote an important function of Teacher-mentors. They can organize information and present it in such a way that the mentoree covers ground rapidly—much more than would be the case if it just happened over long periods of time. The duration of this mentoring relationship was six months. My Teacher had a fairly minimal role: organize the learning, link me to the resources for learning, and debrief from time to time.

This kind of mentoring ought to be going on all the time with middle- and upper-level leaders. Notice the pattern: a challenging assignment, recognizing a need for knowledge and understanding, specifying which mentor function was needed (in this case a Teacher), identifying a mentor who could meet that need, and receiving empowerment through the mentoring process.

Teachers are special kinds of mentors. They usually have knowledge in some needed subject area, the ability to organize that knowledge, and the desire to impart that information so as to enhance a mentoree's understanding and application of that knowledge. They do so not in a sterile way that transfers information from one notebook to another, but in a way that makes the material vibrate with relevance and cry out for use in life.

One thing all these illustrations depict is that Teacher-mentors are always available. You simply have to look for them. And the prerequisite for finding them is to recognize a specific need.

FUNCTIONS OF THE TEACHER-MENTOR

Teachers empower mentorees in the following ways. They:

1. Know what resources are needed and available or who to approach in order to find out.

2. Link mentorees to resources.
3. Organize and impart knowledge to mentorees.
4. Show relevance of knowledge to mentorees' situations.
5. Show how to use perspective from which to assess.
6. Motivate mentorees to continue learning.

Normally we think of teachers as those who present knowledge, but a Teacher functioning as a mentor has a much broader influence.

NEED A TEACHER?
Most people probably need Teachers; they just don't know that they do. What about you? The following suggestions begin with the assumption that you have a need. What do you do then?

1. First, identify the area of knowledge you need (e.g., perspective on child-rearing, interpersonal relationships, biblical knowledge on aspects of leadership or ministry philosophy, discipline in family, discipline in the church, knowledge of the Bible and its relevance to modern life, etc.).
2. Then identify who can meet that need. You may need some advice on this from other followers of Christ who have access to resource networks.
3. Ask yourself: Can it be done in a normal group context—such as a course, church-sponsored program, small group, or Sunday school class? Or must it be more personal?

Must I find some individual who can help me
with it?
4. If it is available in a group context, then go
for it. If it is to be uniquely done, then begin
to establish a relationship with someone
who can do it and make your request when
the relationship allows it.
5. You will find that the more you can specifically identify your need the easier it will be
for a mentor to link you to resources that
can meet that need.

TURN YOUR TEACHING INTO MENTORING
Perhaps you are a teacher, but you've never thought
about using it to mentor others. Here are some suggestions about becoming an effective teacher who
can mentor:

1. Catalog the major subjects that you can
teach so you are ready to share them.
2. Recognize how you would tailor them to
work with an individual.
3. Make it known that you have resources
available to help others in the areas of your
knowledge.
4. Use Gregory's teacher laws and the Laws of
the Learner to help you become a more effective teacher. [1]
5. As you teach to impart knowledge, illustrate
also the dynamics of the teaching/learning
process. This motivates learners and suggests to them how and why they, too, can
use the knowledge with others.

6. Revise the knowledge base to fit your mentoree's situation. Do not overkill. Teach what is needed.
7. Challenge your mentoree to use it. You do this best by demonstrating its usefulness in your own life and by showing relevancy to the mentoree's situation.
8. If you teach in a group context, be on the lookout for those who should be mentored individually. You may want to invite those who respond well into a special relationship that will allow them to move more rapidly.
9. Be open to unique teaching sessions where needed. When requests come for teaching that do not fit your normal patterns, think of the possibility of empowerment for the individuals concerned. That is, be open to mentoring via teaching.

Teachers who are open to deliberate mentoring and establishing personal relationships with people in order to empower them through teaching are greatly needed. Perhaps God is challenging you toward this important kind of mentoring. Now let's look at our last specific occasional mentoring type—the Sponsor-mentor.

Chapter Eight

OCCASIONAL MENTORING: THE SPONSOR

The Manager Who Put Others' Careers First

Robert Greenleaf gives an intriguing illustration of a Sponsor in his booklet *The Servant as Religious Leader*. It is a good resource to inspire potential mentors. Greenleaf was an AT&T officer involved in career training and development of leadership. In his job he frequently did research on upper-level leaders. Once he studied the twelve executives who made up the top leadership of the organization. He found them able but not exceptional people, so he sought to find out what it was that had moved them upward in their careers. He discovered that each reported there was one early boss who greatly accelerated their progress as managers.

But most surprising was the fact that *four of the twelve had their early formative experience under one mid-level manager*. His level of management included nine hundred managers. He had no more access to up-and-coming leaders than anyone else at his level. Yet during his career with the company he not only accounted for one-third of the top-level management, he had people all over the business in middle- and upper-level positions who had their early formative experience under him. Greenleaf says that he was probably the most influential manager of his generation—significantly influencing the course of AT&T as a whole by his development of people.

He cites several characteristics that made this unknown person a good mentor. He had a passionate interest in seeing young people grow, which he maintained through thick and thin during his whole career. He was a good intuitive judge of potential. He carefully selected those he would mentor, spending time only with those who would respond well. He made sure his mentorees had challenging jobs. He believed that people learn significantly through negative situations, and he took advantage of those or even contrived them in order to use them as opportunities for growth. He knew the importance to young people of crucial formative experiences; major values can be instilled that guide them through life. He was available for debriefing, giving perspective, and interaction of all kinds. He was concerned for the progress of those he mentored and communicated his concern to them.

This man was what we call a Sponsor-mentor. The Sponsor's central thrust is providing career guidance and protection as a leader moves within an organization. This is a special type of mentoring. Initially, we see it taking place in the context of organizations whether they be secular, ministry, or local church. But our research shows them active in informal networks (infrastructures) and communities as well.

A significant fact about the AT&T Sponsor was that he had relatively little positional influence in the organization. Most Sponsors are usually in senior roles or have a widespread reputation that gives them credibility in the organization with upper-level decision makers. This Sponsor was not such a person, yet he creatively developed and enabled potential leaders to be promoted within the organization so that the end result was the same as if he had been in a more influential position.

He also illustrates a reverse mentoring dynamic that seems to be common with Sponsor-mentoring. In other mentor types the attraction dominantly flows upward from the mentoree to the mentor. In this type, usually the mentor is first attracted to the mentoree because of potential seen there. The mentor senses some innate drive to help the up-and-coming person cultivate that potential.

The AT&T mentor selected potential persons whom he felt he could develop and who would respond to his mentoring relationship. He encouraged them. Simply by selecting them as people to work with him, he boosted their confidence in themselves. He imparted skills. He was a competent manager, knew the basics of supervisory skills, and passed them on to the rising young leaders. While he was limited in resources to develop them, he stretched what he had to the limit in order to develop his mentorees. He gave perspective on organizational life. He knew the organization, had networks of relationships, and understood career tracks. He inspired the mentorees he worked with. These Sponsor functions are general and do not necessitate a high position.

We surmise that he also did some functions associated with influential roles, such as opening opportunities or maybe even suggesting to his supervisors career tracks that would benefit his mentorees. Certainly he did what he could to help them along. The amazing thing was that he found his niche. He did not have to be promoted himself. He was comfortable where he was and understood that he fulfilled a role that was uniquely his.

Influence Networks

Recently I (Bobby) listened to a tape by David L. Emenhiser on identifying those who exert strong influence in a community. He illustrated his topic from a particular city in the Midwest. He described his research method for identifying the influence networks. What struck me was the fact that there *are* influence networks, and people know who are in them and who are not.

As he shared the characteristics of those who were among the influential in that city, I made a second important observation. Even among the rich and powerful, one striking thing was that almost all of them had at least one mentor who had helped them develop and rise to their place of influence in the network. Sponsoring does not take place just in organizations.

Sponsors aren't limited to organizations alone. They expand empowerment beyond organizational boundaries. Networks of people provide a major resource. Sponsors help mentorees tap into them. Sometimes within an organization a mentoree's opportunities are limited. A wise Sponsor recognizes this and can frequently bridge a mentoree into a career track elsewhere that will ultimately be more beneficial. Sponsors are people who are usually "in" and mentorees are not yet "in." Bridging mentorees "in" is a major function of Sponsors, whether within or without the organization.

A Resource Linker

In 1980 I (Bobby) was in a time of transition. I knew that God was moving me on from my previous missionary role to something new, but what? Chuck was the link. I was studying for a doctorate in missiology. He was my mentor. He saw potential in me and invited me to teach on the faculty. Then he went out of his way to stand up for me before the new dean, other faculty members, and even the Provost, who was not so keen on the idea. Like Barnabas in Acts 9:27, he championed my cause. The faculty invited me to a three-year probational position. It was God's open door for me.

Chuck continued to watch over and cham-

pion me as I advanced in the institutional setting. Afterward, I found out that what Chuck
had done for me he had done for several others.
He was a Sponsor and resource link. He could
see potential and convince both the potential
leader and the needy faculty of the fit. He was a
special kind of Sponsor-mentor, one who could
match the development needs of an individual
with the needs of the organization.

Sponsors are not self-seeking, at least in their
role as mentors. They maintain a balance between
the tension of what is good for the organization and
what is good for the individual. Chuck could intui-
tively spot people and situations in the organization
and match them up. He had enough credibility with
his peers and supervisory leaders to get his innovative ideas accepted. He opened doors. In fact, he
created them.

A Timely Sponsor

Dean was part of a worldwide mission organization that has a large outreach in the United
States and overseas. His early ministry success
in the United States led to a missionary assignment in Scandinavia. After working in campus
ministry for some years and getting into his
mid-thirties, Dean began to lose his motivation
for this type of ministry. Unfortunately, there was
not a "fit" for his new interests and apparent gift
of teaching and administration. The Scandina-
vians were taking over in those areas, so Dean
and his family returned to the States to minister.

Several ministry opportunities were given to Dean, but more on the basis of organizational need rather than his gifts and desires. As Dean had a commitment to serve and was loyal to the organization, he willingly took these assignments.

It so happened that Dean joined the same local church as Stan, one of the senior leaders of his organization, and began teaching an adult class. Stan and his wife joined the adult class, too, and it wasn't long before a friendship developed between Dean and Stan. The class grew as Dean's gift of teaching blossomed. Stan looked into the responsibilities that Dean was carrying and talked to Dean about them. He also learned of the tension between Dean and his supervisor. Dean was about to be transferred. He was a man who read widely, spoke his mind, and asked a lot of questions. This bothered his boss. Being a man who liked to take action and influence others, Dean was not fitting into a group that was more long-term growth oriented.

Stan saw great gifts and potential in Dean that both he and the organization needed to develop. Stan used his authority to extract Dean from the team he was in and had him reassigned to a team that needed his gifts and style of operating. Because there was an unwarranted and negative reputation surrounding Dean, Stan quietly met with some of the key supervisors to affirm Dean and let them know how highly he regarded him. Dean just needed the right assignment and the space and support to demonstrate his gifts and abilities. "He has great value to the ministry if you just give him a chance."

Although Stan was not a prophet, his prediction of Dean's contribution and value proved right and a new reputation grew. He has moved to an even better opportunity in the last year and is flourishing.

Stan was able to spot fundamental leadership characteristics and budding gifts in Dean even though Dean did not fit the responsibilities and opportunities he had in the organization. Further, he was willing to commit himself and his reputation to Dean's development and proper placement, even though others could not see that same potential. Stan illustrates organizational loyalty to members . . . something unusual in many organizations, which often see loyalty only one way — up. He also illustrates the *protection function* of a sponsor. At one critical point Dean's future with the organization was on the line. Stan stepped in and virtually created a new career path for Dean. This illustrates the more altruistic of the empowerment functions of a Sponsor. He inspired and created a sense of destiny within Dean. He protected. He opened doors. He opened up the possibility of a new career track and guided Dean into that.

Many Christian organizations have a big back door. Some of their finest potential leaders frequently leave an organization before they develop into effective leaders. They do so for many reasons. Perhaps they:

◆ do not fit the patterns,
◆ have ideas that are beyond the present vision
of the organization,
◆ have rough edges that cover up their good
leadership qualities and potential,
◆ do not want to be overused and under-
developed,
◆ are placed in non-challenging roles, or
◆ in general do not have connections to the
decision makers of the organization.

Those leaving organizations may do any number of things. They may:

◆ quit the ministry altogether,
◆ found their own organization in order to do
what they want,
◆ become effective leaders and contribute to
some other organization, or
◆ perhaps fail to develop.

In any case, they do not benefit the organization they left. Can this back door be closed somewhat? Mentors who can sponsor are desperately needed in organizations in order to prevent the loss of potential leaders.

Sponsors are strategic people in an organization, for they benefit both younger leaders and the organization. Organizations need to identify, reward, and release those mentors who are good at sponsorship functions. Usually this type of mentoring is done informally, on the backstroke, and is never recognized by the organization. This ought not to be.

Let's conceptualize the definition of the Sponsor-mentor that we have illustrated. Here is a fuller definition:

> **Sponsorship is a relational process in which a mentor having credibility and positional or spiritual authority within an organization or network relates to a mentoree not having those resources so as to enable development of the mentoree and the mentoree's influence in the organization.**

Table 8-1. Sponsor Functions and Empowerment

FUNCTION	EMPOWERMENT	EXPLANATION
1. Selection	Confidence building, expectation, sense of uniqueness	They select potential leaders and build in them a sense of confidence and uniqueness—that they will bring a significant contribution to the organization.
2. Encouragement	Perseverance	They believe in their mentorees and encourage them to believe they will make it and will accomplish things.
3. Impart Skills	Some leadership, some influence skills	They impart relational skills—how to use networking, the proper use of authority, and other direct leadership skills.
4. Linking to Resources	The resources	They link the mentorees to needed development resources including education, training, finances, and people.

5. Perspective	Analytical skill	Sponsors have an overall picture of the organization, its structures, its networks, its long-range purposes, etc. These provide a framework for decision making not usually accessible to lower-level positions.
6. Inspiration	Sense of destiny	Sponsors usually begin with the end in mind. They see what the mentorees are capable of being and achieving and can inspire them to become that.

PRACTICAL HINTS ON SPONSOR-MENTORING

Sponsor-mentoring is a type of Occasional mentoring. It is not always available to the mentoree nor can the mentoree usually establish such a relationship, since it is most often mentor-initiated. This can prove frustrating to the potential leader waiting to be discovered. There are, however, some general suggestions for those who desire this kind of mentoring.

For the Mentoree

1. In career decision making, where you have the choice, choose an organization to work for that believes in mentoring as a concept and practices it.
2. Concentrate on developing yourself toward the potential you know is within you.
3. Demonstrate a healthy loyalty (not "blind" loyalty) to the organization and the leadership above you. Loyalty is a trait that mentors look for.

4. Remember, promotion is a byproduct, not a goal. It is God who ultimately moves a person to positions of influence. Set your heart on pleasing God and using what He has given you for His purposes.
5. Ask God to give you relationships with those who can best develop you. Trust Him to do that—to open doors, make new career paths, and guide you toward accomplishments. Ultimately your trust must be in God and not in any Sponsor.

Those of us in organizational positions of influence should be aware of the importance of mentoring as Sponsors. Here are some suggestions for those who should be Sponsors.

For the Sponsor
1. Credibility, a function of integrity and competence, is crucial. Model consistently and with a view toward establishing a godly testimony.
2. Position influence must be used. The fact that you are in an influential role carries with it a special responsibility to use your influence well. Mentoring is just one of those ways to use it responsibly.
3. Develop networks. They are important. They will give you access to resources that you do not have. They will enable you to get cross-training for mentorees and exposure to other philosophies—a cross-pollination effect that can be important to the balanced development of a mentoree.
4. The best development track may be outside the

organization. Seek to give the mentoree a jump start. Use networking for this.

5. Sponsor-mentoring is a downward mentoring function that should be part of the responsibility of a leader.[1] Among those we supervise there ought to be people with potential who especially need our help. We need to seek them out. First, we pray to God to give us leaders. Then we watch. Leadership selection and development are major functions of effective leaders.

6. Often a number of potential mentorees in an organization are leaders who have plateaued. Sponsors should be on the lookout for these needy people. Sponsors can infuse new enthusiasm for leadership by coming alongside and encouraging, giving need-oriented training that will upgrade those who have plateaued, and opening up new job opportunities. This latter opportunity, a new, challenging kind of job, frequently will renew a plateaued leader. Sponsors have the resources to revitalize plateaued leaders. What they lack is perspective on how valuable these leaders could be, the discernment to spot them, diagnostic skills that will help assess what is needed, and the motivation to recover these leaders.

7. Avoid the pitfalls of nepotism. Nepotism is privilege shown to some because of a special relationship and not because they deserve it based on merit. Sponsoring is a developmental process that confers special privilege on those whom we think God wants to develop.

8. Utilize the Barnabas leader-switch principle.[2]

Leaders you sponsor may have potential to develop well beyond you. Be prepared to elevate them above yourself if that is the next step needed to expand their potential.

9. Keep the organization as a whole in mind. Sponsoring is not developing the individual for the individual's sake but for the good of the organization and the individual.

GOOD NEWS AND BAD NEWS

Occasional mentoring (Counselor, Teacher, Sponsor) contrasts with Intensive mentoring (Discipler, Spiritual Guide, Coach). Whereas Intensive mentoring occurs to the left of the mentoring continuum and requires deliberate effort, Occasional mentoring involves less deliberate effort.

Two implications of this contrast should be pointed out. Fewer mentors will be available for Intensive mentoring than Occasional mentoring due to the deliberateness of the process and its time-intensive nature. Occasional mentoring, with its lessening of dynamic factors and deliberateness, broadens the number of mentors available. That more mentors are available is good news, but there is a down side also: empowerment may be weakened due to the lesser effect of personal relationships and accountability.

SUMMARY

Though Occasional mentors are less intense, that does not make them less valuable to our lives.

Business people frequently pay a retainer to lawyers or business consultants to have them available whether or not they actually use them. So, too, we ought to have already established relationships with Counselor-mentors to whom we can go for help.

Not all teachers are mentors, and one does not have to be in the teaching profession to be a Teacher-mentor. Teacher-mentors go beyond the transfer of knowledge. They combine their ability to communicate knowledge with inspiration, encouragement, and modeling to effect empowerment in the mentoree's life.

And without a Sponsor, many potential leaders are lost in the corner or through the back door of organizations. This mentoring type, even more than others, requires a spirit of humility on the part of the mentor . . . to seek out and identify the potential in others, develop it, and put the mentoree's (and the organization's) best interest ahead of his own. The more a Sponsor focuses on helping others grow, the more he or she will grow, as well.

FOR FURTHER STUDY (CHAPTERS 6, 7, AND 8)
1. Perhaps the most famous Counselors in the Bible are Job's. Yet they were ineffective, and empowerment certainly did not take place for Job through them. They seemed to cover all eight functions listed in table 6-1. What was missing? What lesson do you see in this example about seeking or being a Counselor?

2. Moses walked with the Lord (talked face to face with Him!) and was a great leader of Israel. Yet he, too, needed mentors in his life. Look at Exodus 18, where his father-in-law, Jethro, visits him.

a. How did Jethro serve as a mentor in Moses' life? What was Jethro's attitude as a mentor? And how did Moses respond as a mentoree?

b. How did the dynamics of attraction, responsiveness, and accountability come into play? Did empowerment take place?

3. What factors made Jethro's counseling effective? What do you notice in Moses' relationship with Jethro and his response to Jethro's advice that enhanced the counseling experience?

4. Using a concordance, dig into Joshua's early life. How might you infer that Moses acted as a Teacher-mentor for Joshua? In Numbers 27 you see this mentoring culminated in Moses' sponsorship of Joshua.

5. To better grasp the six types of mentors we have discussed so far, interview some older believers. Articulate to them your understanding of the various types and ask them for examples of mentors in their own lives. As you add to the illustrations that we have given, you will expand the mentoring concept for your own life.

Chapter Nine

PASSIVE MENTORING: THE CONTEMPORARY MODEL

Where have all the models gone today? Are any heroes still out there? Many of those considered to be positive models and heroes seem to have fallen. The pressures of public life, the irresistible forces of power, wealth, and sex, and the cynical spirit in today's media and society have caused many would-be models to fall, fade, or simply retreat. Into this vacuum have stepped many confused and ego-driven stars of the rock music, sports, and business worlds. Even though there are exceptions to the trend, the idea of modeling has taken a beating in American culture. One professional job and placement interviewer told us he had been forced to change his interview question, "Who are your heroes and models? Tell me about why they are." Very few of his job candidates had any heroes and would simply shrug their shoulders.

Are there no models or heroes, or are they just "lying low" for fear of attack? Or is it that Americans have become skeptical of anyone who seems to "have it together" and forgotten that a model is not one who is perfect, but simply progressing in living out the values we hold personally? We believe that plenty of models and heroes are all around. They need to be sought out and allowed to impact our lives. But how?

WHEN THERE SEEM TO BE NO MENTORS

At least three major problems exist with the six models we have listed thus far.

1. The six mentor types *may not be available* to you in your present situation. Either you can find no competent mentors of the type you need, or they don't have time for you.
2. Even if one is available you *may not be able to establish a working relationship* that will allow mentoring and empowerment.
3. Competent people may be around, but they *have neither the inclination nor the skills* to mentor you.

What do you do in situations where these problems exist? Convincing you that you need mentoring and then motivating you to find it when it is not available is more than frustrating—it may even be cruel! In fact, it may do more harm than good, as it could discourage you from ever finding a mentor. How can we avoid this negative situation? By recognizing another form of mentoring. You can gain the advantages and empowerment of mentoring from indirect relationships with unavailable mentors. There are two kinds of passive mentors—the *Contemporary Model*, a living person who can mentor you even without a deliberate effort on his or her part, and the *Historical Model*, who has passed on yet can mentor you via input from biographical or autobiographical sources. These "model mentors" are always available, but mentorees must make an effort to find them.[1]

The Model-mentor is primarily Passive. There is less deliberateness in the relationship in contrast to the Intensive and Occasional types of mentoring. Essentially this means that the mentoree must supply the three mentoring dynamics (attraction, responsiveness, accountability). The Model-mentor probably will not even know the role he or she plays in the life of another. But empowerment can take place if the mentoree will provide what is needed to make it happen.

Modeling is certainly a biblical concept. The Scriptures validate Paul, Peter and Christ as Models and encourage modeling as a means of empowering others.[2] Consider Paul's use of modeling as a means for empowering Timothy. In 1 Corinthians 4:16-18, Paul talks about modeling as he challenges the Corinthians,

> I urge you to imitate me. For this reason I am sending to you Timothy, my son whom I love, who is faithful in the Lord. He will remind you of my way of life in Christ Jesus, which agrees with what I teach everywhere in every church.

What a powerful statement! "Go ahead, Timothy, imitate me. I'll model for you. No, I'm not perfect. But I'm trying to embody every truth I teach. And if you go back to those churches where I've been, they'll tell you that what I taught, I also lived out."

In 2 Timothy 3:10-11 we see the extent to which Paul was transparent in his modeling with Timothy.

> You [Timothy], however, know all about my teaching, my way of life, my purpose, faith, patience, love, endurance, persecutions, sufferings — what kinds of things happened to me in Antioch, Iconium and Lystra, the persecutions I endured. Yet the Lord rescued me from all of them.

But it wasn't just with Timothy that Paul empowered through modeling. It was his approach to ministry in general. In Philippians 4:9 he gives a general exhortation to the entire church at Philippi.

> Whatever you have learned or received or heard from me, or seen in me — put it into practice. And the God of peace will be with you.

In Hebrews 13:7-8, the author extends the idea of modeling and empowerment in a leadership mandate:

> Remember your leaders, who spoke the word of God to you. Consider the outcome of their way of life and imitate their faith. Jesus Christ is the same yesterday and today and forever.

This command exhorts us to follow the example of those who lived their commitments out before us. It encourages us with the promise that Jesus, who is ever-living, was the source of their lives and can reproduce in ours those same good qualities.

Don't get sidetracked looking for perfect models. You won't find them apart from the Lord Jesus. But be concerned to look for people who progress in modeling certain values that you aspire to. That is the key.

Contemporary Models may be any people you can observe today. They live out the values you hold important. You are able to watch them, learn from them, and in some cases, get to know them. They normally "pop up" through a circumstance that causes them to reveal their values and their commitment to them.

Walking in the Steps of a Model

I (Paul) was a high school senior when I read about Peter Dawkins, who was in his last year at West Point. He had just been awarded the Heisman Trophy, given to the most outstanding college football player in the United States. He was also an all-American, top-ranking cadet in the whole Corps of Cadets (equivalent to student body president) and seventh in his class academically. What really challenged me was his perseverance in difficulty and high commitment to excellence. He had overcome the effects of polio as a boy and had been too small to be seriously recruited as a high school football player.

Once Peter entered the U.S. Military Academy, he quietly began to go to work. He lifted weights to gain muscle, ran to build up his speed, and applied all that his coaches told him. His classmates could depend upon him to complete a task. Peter was never content with anything less than his best effort. In the midst of this highly competitive environment, he often put the needs of others ahead of his own. He made time to help his classmates and be a friend. I learned some of this from the many articles written about him and more later as I followed in his steps by entering West Point and talking to his friends.

Although I met Pete only once, his life served as an inspiration to me during the early difficulties of adjusting to the rigors of West Point. My own athletic ability was not sufficient to reach Pete's level, but I could persevere to be my best . . . lift weights, run, and work hard at applying what the coaches said. I never was great and probably went further than my raw abilities should have allowed, but the first game at which I was introduced as the starting halfback brought tears to my eyes. I thought, *I've made it . . . not by superior talent, but by perseverance and commitment to excellence.* My coach once commented to my parents in my presence, "This young man can be depended upon. We can ask him to do anything, even beyond his ability, and he'll get it done—no doubt about it!" Thanks, Pete!

Needless to say, the values I saw and aspired to in Pete Dawkins have continued to affect my life and how I approach most challenges. Recently at a special Hundredth Anniversary of Army Football, several hundred former graduates and football lettermen gathered to celebrate the occasion. Pete was there and, of course, was the center of attention. He has continued to persevere and maintain a standard of excellence for his life (I've followed his career). With all the autograph seekers and old friends around him, I could not presume to take any of his time. But I did walk up to him at a slow moment and pat him on the shoulder and say, "Thanks, Pete, you're doing a great job!" He nodded and smiled, not realizing all that I meant behind that statement. Someday I'll get to tell him.

In this illustration, Pete Dawkins was never aware of the impact he had on me, the mentoree. We did not even have a direct relationship, only an indirect one that went one way—from me. I was *attracted* to Pete, not just through his good reputation, but through shared values and common experiences and pursuits. There was no agreed-upon *accountability* as in Intensive mentoring, but I *responded* to Pete and experienced empowerment by applying what I observed.

Modeling can impact you in practical areas as well. And in some cases the mentoree is not initially aware of the mentor's influence. We call this *Subliminal Modeling*. A Model can influence a mentoree in attitude and values simply by association and working together. A child's attitude toward money and people is often adopted from his parents long before that child consciously responds to their instruction. You probably find yourself taking on desirable traits and habits from others you respect for various personal reasons, and you may not be consciously aware of it. What we encourage here is that you be more conscious as an adult mentoree to pursue mentoring from Models (even though they may be unaware of it).

Modeling by Doing It Together

Todd was always uncertain when it came to evangelism. But Bud seemed to do it quite naturally. One day Todd and Bud got into a conversation about relating to the lost people around them, and Todd was really stimulated. He was fascinated to learn that Bud did not have much of an agenda in mind when relating to people but simply tuned into them, and his interest often resulted in them doing things together. Unlike Todd, Bud spent most of his time among nonChristians and felt comfortable with them. Bud invited Todd and his wife to join his family the next Saturday when they were going to have several neighbors (nonChristian) over for a barbecue. "I'd like you to meet them . . . they are my friends."

For Todd, the barbecue was a tremendous learning experience just watching Bud respond to his friends. They obviously enjoyed being with him and Bud worked at loving these neighbors in practical ways.

Todd returned home that night with a whole new understanding of the process of evangelism and with new excitement and release. He continued to pump Bud with questions and soon launched his own efforts to relate to his neighbors and love them in natural ways.

Bud and Todd became friends and began praying together for their friends. Bud shrugged off any effort Todd made to credit him with helping and teaching Todd through modeling. To Bud, Todd simply joined in the adventure of reaching the lost around them. But to Todd, the seminar on evangelism he attended and the books he read did not help him until he saw someone doing it . . . "up close and personal."

There may be practical areas in your life that you long to develop, but you just need to be around someone who is doing it. From getting things done in the kitchen to conducting family devotions, our word of encouragement is that you find someone who is doing it, or trying to do it, and get around them. You supply the empowering dynamics.

Perhaps this is the time to introduce an important exception to the normally passive Model-mentor. Up to now we have said that the initiative and proactivity come from the mentorees . . . they provide the three dynamics of attraction, responsiveness, and account-ability. But there are occasions when mature follow-ers of Christ understand the power of modeling and know that they can be Models (albeit imperfect) in certain areas. In such cases, these mentors may take the initiative and invite mentorees into a relationship or opportunity to observe them in action—consider the Apostle Paul's invitation to Timothy to join him in his missionary journey (Acts 16:1-3) and the Lord Jesus' choosing the twelve disciples to "be with him" (Mark 3:14).

Exposure to Models is one of the most effective tools in leadership development. Mentors may not always be the Models, but they may choose another Model more appropriate to the developmental need of a mentoree. The point is that Model-mentoring may not always be mentoree-driven. Both of us have invited emerging leaders to join us in a ministry experience or trip. They often pick up different things than we had in mind, but that is the value of such exposures. The Holy Spirit is faithful to touch the "real" needs of mentorees. Also, the interaction provides valuable feedback for mentors to learn as well. And the relationships grow in such a context.

Learning opportunities can be enhanced when the Teacher also becomes a Model for a mentoree.

Teaching Plus Modeling

Pastor Tom was an unusual man. He did more than teach the Bible. He believed that people learn to minister by doing ministry, and he knew how to launch people into ministry. He would share his pulpit and leadership in home Bible studies with up-and-coming leaders. He believed in cross-exposure to other Bible teachers for his people so they would be more well-rounded, and he constantly invited good Bible expositors to teach.

Just to be around and involved with Pastor Tom would be a developmental experience for anyone, but Dale wanted more. In his heart Dale longed to affect peoples' lives like Pastor Tom did and lift them up to a higher standard of ministry and leadership. In order to get beyond what Pastor Tom was doing with the young leaders in his broad ministry, Dale made himself available to be with him more often. He also determined to find out what passions and values drove him, and then make application along the way.

Sitting in on some of his small-group Bible studies and traveling and praying with him soon revealed some lifelong challenges. Pastor Tom was a consummate learner and constantly sought to know more of the Bible—a lifetime goal. He studied, read, and talked about the truths of Scripture. Anyone around him caught his enthusiasm and was soon part of the venture. He knew if believers got into the Word they would love it, and it would change and empower their lives.

Dale learned Bible study and group leading skills simply by watching. He saw "average" believers get involved in ministry and come alive through the loving and confident "urging" of Pastor Tom. Dale's zeal for discipleship was dealt a blow one time when he challenged his group, and they did not respond in the manner he desired. In a fatherly way Pastor Tom commented, "If just *one* responds, that's all you need." Tom backed that up by his focus on the "ones" who did seem to want more.

But Dale also learned another lesson from a flaw in Pastor Tom's style of relating. Pastor Tom would go for the "ones" enthusiastically at the outset of the relationship, but he would only stick with them for some months and then go on to others. In the meantime, the expectations of the people would be lifted too high to be suddenly left hanging in space. Dale reversed this trend, ensuring he clarified expectations up front and gradually increasing them—and then sticking with his commitments.

As Dale looks back to his few years with Pastor Tom, he is amazed by how many of Tom's passions, habits, and ways he has incorporated into his own life and ministry. He will be forever grateful.

Contemporary Models perform three major functions: *They embody values, provide role models, and often demonstrate how to carry out commitments.* In addition, depending on the amount of time mentorees have, Contemporary Models may fulfill some functions of the other six mentoring types. Though Contemporary Models may not challenge mentorees directly through a defined relationship, they do so indirectly, by example. But the end result can be the same if mentorees take advantage of the modeling.

The power of a consistent, value-led life is always a refreshing challenge . . . seeing someone faithfully living out his convictions in a way that does not purposely draw attention to himself. Exposure to such models is a gift that you need to acknowledge and draw from.

The Quiet Model

After much searching and a series of divinely led events, a disillusioned Asian businessman became a believer in Jesus Christ. Mr. Wong's cynicism had made the process a long one, and it continued to make him hold off any attempts by Western missionaries to help him grow in his newfound faith.

But there was one Westerner who lived in the next building in a simple room with only the basic furnishings. Mr. Wong could look from his window down into the window of this man. He observed his lifestyle—both in the privacy of his own room and out on the street among the throngs of people. He saw his generosity to others when he had very little to eat himself. He watched as the man spent hours on his knees in prayer and lived out his faith on a day-to-day basis. He saw the genuineness of that faith.

Eventually a discipleship relationship developed between the two men. But the impact and empowerment had already begun as that missionary had modeled Christ in his life. Today Mr. Wong has a worldwide ministry of his own. Though he acknowledges he learned many practical aspects of discipleship from this Western missionary, after forty years what he most frequently recalls is that life he watched from his window.

> **The Contemporary Model is a living person whose life or ministry is used as an example to indirectly impart skills, principles, and values that empower another person.**

The essential empowerment of this indirect mentoring relationship is the embodiment of values in such a way as to challenge observant mentorees into emulation of these values. Usually little time is spent in any kind of deliberate development of a relationship between mentors and mentorees. Mentorees observe the mentors in action and absorb ideas, values, content, and skills or at least the desire to have these personally. Not only do mentors embody important values, but they also inspire others toward those values by successfully and relentlessly living them out. Goodwin's expectation principle is the dominant means of stimulating empowerment.[3] His principle is an observed social dynamic, which says, "A potential leader tends to rise to the level of genuine expectancy of a leader he or she respects." In other words, the more mentors expect of their charges, the higher the mentorees will rise.

Empowerment in this indirect relational mentoring can be enhanced if mentorees understand the major means of influence. Contemporary Models essentially do three things that require a response from mentorees. Table 9-1 points out the suggestions for mentorees to enhance empowerment.

Table 9-1. Suggestions to Enhance Empowerment via Contemporary Models

WHAT THE MENTOR DOES	WHAT THE MENTOREE SHOULD DO
1. Embodies values.	a. Feel the impact of the values being modeled.
	b. Identify the values and clarify those worthy of emulation.
	c. Where possible, determine which steps or experiences led the mentor to live out these values.
	d. Determine to have those values before God. Trust Him to bring them about.

2. Demonstrates the possibility and reality of these values in a life.

"Remember your leaders, who spoke the word of God to you. Consider the outcome of their way of life and imitate their faith. Jesus is the same yesterday and today and forever" (Hebrews 13:7-8).

a. Accept the command of the leadership mandate of Hebrews 13:7-8 as something for you to personally obey. Imitate your godly leaders.

b. Believe the promise of the leadership mandate of Hebrews 13:7-8. Jesus Christ is the same today and can inspire the same sort of leadership in you.

c. Believe that God is in this process and is using this model personally with you.

3. Motivates by example.

a. Spend as much time as you can in various ministry and relational situations (if possible) to observe the mentor in a variety of experiences.

b. Remember your task: to identify the positive values and seek to emulate them. No Contemporary Model is perfect. Don't fail to desire a good value because your model has other poor values. Frequently, emerging leaders become disheartened when they see faults in those they respect.

Chapter Ten

PASSIVE MENTORING: THE HISTORICAL MODEL

Historical Models provide a gold mine of virtually untapped mentoring resources.[1] Essentially, Historical Models do what Contemporary Models do, but they do it through the pages of a book rather than a live demonstration.

> **The Historical Model refers to a person
> now dead whose life or ministry
> is written in a(n) (auto)biographical form
> and is used as an example to indirectly
> impart values, principles, and skills
> that empower another person.**

Mentoring Across the Centuries

Historical Models are those who can mentor us through their biographies and autobiographies. I (Paul) have a number of them. I reread them often. I find that on a first run-through of a biography I pick up certain values. But on a reread I pick up other values and insights.

For instance, George Mueller is one particular Historical Model who has mentored me. One of my goals is to reread him on a yearly basis, though I don't always make it. I wish you could see my copy of *George Mueller of Bristol* (Pierson, 1899). It's marked all over. Each time I reread it I add more notes. Those notes are values, principles, insights into situations, or suggested applications to things I am now facing. George Mueller lived over one hundred years ago. But as I reread his biography and review his commitments and decisions, his life continues to mentor me.

In his early life as a pastor, Mueller was led to trust God for his financial needs without letting anyone know of those needs but Him. He placed a wooden box in the vestibule of the church for the small congregation's gifts and offerings, but did not call attention to it. Often weeks went by and barely enough would come in to meet his and his wife's needs.

They quietly and faithfully brought their special needs to the Lord. Then they would find a large gift in the box—with a note that designated it for another need. George would sometimes go for weeks struggling with the idea of letting someone know of their need, but on his knees he was strengthened to continue to trust God and remain silent. God honored their faith and consistently met their needs, often in miraculous ways. This laid the foundation of faith for the great steps they were yet to take.

On many occasions in my life I have been led to trust God for His provision. In a recent situation time was running out, and I contemplated alternative methods of meeting the need my way instead of waiting on God. Mueller's life mentored me as I went back to read the portion of his biography where he struggled, yet kept the faith. I remembered the empty box in the back of the church. I thought of the months he barely had enough, yet as people gave him money for other purposes he would faithfully pass it on. I was encouraged to keep trusting, waiting, and expecting. George had stepped alongside and mentored me.

I was also impressed with George Mueller's approach to decision making. He had principles. He never made a decision until he had prayed through it and heard from God. That principle inspired me. In the midst of major decision making today, I follow George's example. It has become a habit.

George Mueller has reached across the centuries to empower me in many areas . . . including faith and its testing, and the importance of prayer and waiting upon God in decision making. The mentoring continues as these values become habits and I read and reread his story.

An important characteristic of Historical Models is their availability for extended learning. They continue to inspire, convict, and challenge as new situations arise in which to apply the lessons they impart.

A Cloud of Witnesses

Among the many biographies I (Bobby) have read, eight historical mentors continue to have input into my life. All eight finished well— something of a rarity among leaders.

I reread their biographies, trying each time to explore a different aspect of their lives. I write in all the books and underline. Second and third readings often stimulate new insights for me. As I get older and experience more of life and ministry, I can see new things on rereadings that I didn't discover before. Experience gives more perspective from which to view these historical mentors. My current situation often forces me to see different things as I read with a new question or purpose—to find some insights for today. I am refreshed as I review my past notations and insights.

The list that follows indicates my eight historical mentors in order of my discovery of them (approximate dates) and their major empowerment for me the first time I read them.

In my rereading, many other values have become mine. Taylor's entry into deeper spiritual life, which he calls "The Exchanged Life," showed me the necessity of that experience as a value for myself. Fraser's life of prayer illustrated for me the cycle of prayer—the divine initiative, asking, receiving, praising. In particular, I saw how God moves one through the crisis of faith (from believing to receiving). He also showed me the necessity of having a circle of intercessors behind my ministry. Carmichael and Nee showed me how God develops the inner life through isolation. Their responses to this deep experience brought them closer to God and gave them a deeper spirituality, which resulted in spiritual authority in their ministries. Elliot's journals reinforced for me the value of transparency in the inner life with God. Goforth and Brengle are sterling examples of finishing well in all three aspects of life: ongoing learning posture, a vibrant, personal relationship with God, and leaving behind a legacy. I could go on and on.

These mentors stay with me today and continue to look over my shoulder, whispering applications of their principles when I encounter situations that bring them to mind. I am thankful to the people who took the time and effort to chronicle their journeys.

Table 10-1. Eight Historical Mentors

YEAR	MENTOR	FIRST IMPORTANT VALUE
1964	Hudson Taylor	Vision—trusting God in and for ministry
1965	J. O. Fraser	An effective prayer life that changes ministry
1966	Jonathan Goforth	Lifetime mastery of the Word of God
1966	Jim Elliot	Zeal for relationship with God, purity of heart, and desire to count for God
1967	Amy Carmichael	Intimate walk with God; deeper life model
1969	Adoniram Judson	Perseverance to complete a task
1975	Watchman Nee	Saturation in the Word of God; lessons on spiritual authority
1989	Samuel Logan Brengle	Spirituality—finishing well

These illustrations focus on repeated readings of biography. It does not tell the vast number of other mentors who came at a given moment, did something, and then were not reread. These are the more powerful ones that somehow indelibly imprinted upon me their continual worth. Notice that the majority of these came within a five-year span. This happened to be the time in my life when I was transitioning into leadership—an impressionable time, when the learning curve is high. After that period of time the mentors that I picked up were more in response to present needs. Nee came at an important crisis time in which I was learning spiritual authority. Brengle came at a time when I was studying the latter phases of leadership development and had a strong desire to learn about finishing life well.

People often tell us, "I never had anyone to mentor me." When they say that, we know they have not discovered the power and availability of Contemporary and Historical Models. They have much to learn in terms of vicarious learning. Let's close this section on modeling with a word of exhortation from one who learned to be mentored via historical Bible Models.

Advice from a Godly Old-Timer

Samuel Logan Brengle wrote this in the latter part of his life. He lived single for the last twenty-one years of his life after his wife died when he was fifty-two. Listen to Brengle:

I am a lonely man, and yet I am not lonely. With my open Bible I live with prophets, priests and kings. I walk and hold communion with apostles, saints and martyrs, and with Jesus, and mine eyes see the King in His beauty and the land that is afar off. . . . My daily reading has brought me into company with the great prophets—Isaiah, Jeremiah, Ezekiel, Hosea, Micah, Malachi, and others—and I live again with them in the midst of the throbbing, tumultuous, teeming life of old Jerusalem, Samaria, Egypt and Babylon. These prophets are old friends of mine. . . . They have blessed me a thousand times, kindled in me some of their flaming zeal for righteousness, their scorn of meanness, duplicity, pride and worldliness, their jealousy for the living God; their fear for those who forget God and live as though He were not; their pity for the ignorant, the erring, the penitent; their anxiety for the future of their people; their courage in denouncing sin and calling men back to the old paths of righteousness. (Hall 1933:182-183)

This is the heart of historical modeling.

We need heroes! Abundant newspaper, journal, and magazine articles detail the lack of traditional heroes for our young people today. Extensive media coverage makes it difficult for today's heroes (even historical ones) to maintain their image as character flaws are discovered.

No one chooses to become a Model-mentor, but all of us model and others are watching. Integrity becomes the key for Models—that their lives reflect the values and principles they expound. It is not whether they fall short of those standards, but how they respond to the failures in their lives. We are not looking for perfect people as Models, but for those who are progressing.

SUMMARY
You do not have to be disappointed if you cannot find mentors who are available or capable of mentoring you. You can be mentored by observing contemporary modeling in the lives of mature Christians around you. Contemporary Models usually embody values that are first caught and later learned. And should you feel Contemporary Models are scarce, you still have the wealth of biographies of those who have gone before — Historical Models. Both types can challenge, motivate, and give you hope by their example that indeed some ideals can actually be attained.

Though these Passive mentors do not offer the same relationships of the other mentoring types, their constant availability makes them a priceless resource.

FOR FURTHER STUDY (CHAPTERS 9 AND 10)
1. Who have been the Models in your life (both Contemporary and Historical)? Why? How have they impacted your life to make you a different person today?

2. If someone were to look to you as an example to follow, what are some things you would want them to see?

3. Ask some mature followers of Christ to list the five most important biographies they have read

and what major lessons they learned. This will provide a future reading list for you. (But remember, just because a biography is important to another person may not make it so for you. Don't be disappointed if some of the "hot" books for others don't do much for you. A lot of dynamics are involved in why a book appeals to someone.)

4. Look through our annotated bibliography of biographies and select a Historical mentor you would like to get to know, locate the book . . . and get started!

   You might also check at a Christian bookstore to find out what biographies sell the best . . . but don't be daunted by looking at some of the older classics.

5. Consider Jesus' life in the gospels. List ways that He modeled what He was teaching. Especially note ways in which His actions spoke more powerfully than mere teaching.

Chapter Eleven

THE CONSTELLATION MODEL: A RANGE OF NEEDED MENTORING

Each year brings its new rash of fallen leaders in the political world. Not defeated by their political views, they fell because of some moral indiscretion . . . a misuse of money, sex, or power. And though Christians know their spiritual leaders have the same human natures, they continue to be shocked to see that their leaders are not exempt from such temptations.

Local pastors are forced to leave their pulpits, big-name evangelists ruin their own lives and hurt the name of Christ, Christian authors fail in the very areas they write about. The world looks on with glee, eagerly searching for the next tidbit, and the Christian community is embarrassed.

It breaks our hearts to realize how much potential for the Kingdom is wasted and destroyed—many times through just one act. When we see it happen to those we considered "spiritual giants," then it brings it home that it could happen to anyone. You and I are not immune.

Misuse of money, sex, power, or whatever may not destroy us or our ministry as it does those in the spotlight, but it can make us ineffective or much less effective as leaders. Remember our account of John (his need for accountability) in chapter one? He had become a relational "island." He still was able to minister to people, but his ministry had become crippled. The tragedy was to realize how much more powerful his ministry could have been. He will probably finish but perhaps not well. Only eternity will reveal to us which portions of our service for Him are "wood, hay or straw" and which are like "gold, silver, costly stones" (1 Corinthians 3:12).

Are there any safeguards? How can we protect ourselves? Dr. Ronald B. Allen (1988) has observed:

> Sex, money and power are not evil in themselves. They are gifts of God, designed by Him to be used for good pleasure and God's glory. But so easily they corrupt, so profoundly they destroy.
>
> It appears to me that the only escape for those in leadership positions is to do what the rest of us have to do and that is be responsible to others. Leaders—and their people—need to surround themselves with a circle of accountability. Leaders—and their people—need to expect of themselves the same moral, ethical and personal standards of behavior which they demand of others.

The solution . . . a circle of accountability. This leads us to an important aspect of mentoring.

> **A *growing leader* needs a relational network that embraces mentors, peers, and emerging leaders in order to ensure development and a healthy perspective on his or her life and ministry.**

A network of vertical (mentors) and horizontal (peers or co-mentors) relationships is not an option for a believer who desires to grow, minister effectively and continuously, and finish well. It is imperative! In our studies of leaders, we can clearly conclude with few exceptions that those who experienced anointed ministry and finished well had a significant network of meaningful relationships that inspired, challenged, listened, pursued, developed, and held one another accountable. Those that failed to reach full maturity and finish well did not have it, or cut all or part of it off at some point. We have personally determined that we will develop and maintain an active relational network for ourselves and pay whatever cost is necessary to do it. And it is alive and growing for us both.

Other than Jesus Christ, the Apostle Paul is probably the most powerful leader of the New Testament. Yet even with limited biblical narrative, we can see part of his network: Gamaliel and Barnabas as mentors; Timothy, Titus, and others as mentorees; and numerous "partners in the gospel" as co-mentors. With most of these, Paul enjoyed and grew from a mutual sense of responsibility for one another and an "iron sharpening iron" (Proverbs 27:17) effect. We imagine that his relational network was dynamic, with some people closer and more involved during certain circumstances and others more involved at other times. But until the very end he kept the network alive through letters, visits, ministry, and living together. He needed each one, and they needed him.

Unfortunately, most leaders (emerging, growing, established, or whatever) fail to recognize their need for a network of significant relationships until something happens that reveals their aloneness and vulnerability. Our burden is to "blow the whistle" before the game is lost so as to alert believers and growing leaders to this urgent need and encourage them to do something about it.

A Network Safeguard

I was meeting with a very gifted forty-year-old pastor of a growing church and his staff. It was exciting to hear all that God was doing in their midst. My internal "Relational Network Meter" was beginning to signal as he and his staff discussed their schedules and plans. "Overload! Who's involved in their lives?" the network meter was calling out. So I decided to ask some questions.

"Who is committed to your growth and keeping you strong in Christ?" They looked at each other and the pastor said, "We are to each other," and they all nodded. But as we discussed the specifics of how Jesse was pursuing his relationship with Christ, it became obvious that Bill was unaware of Jesse's struggles. Both their schedules were full, and demands were growing. "What do you think will happen if Jesse continues to follow the schedule he now has?" I asked Bill. He unhesitatingly blurted out, "He'll crash or barely survive!" and again they all nodded with concern. "But have you talked that through . . . together?" Their silence answered the question.

"Who are the resource people [mentors] in your life . . . those committed to help you develop in your need areas and give you periodic input on how you are doing?" Some named a few, mostly in other parts of the country, whom they hadn't seen for a considerable length of time. "If I were to call these mentors and ask them about their commitment to you and what they were helping you grow in, what would they say?" "Not much," admitted the youth pastor.

"Do you brothers realize how alone you are . . . how vulnerable . . . and without valuable development input at a very important phase in your lives?" They all agreed and we spent some hours discussing in specific terms how they could change this. An interesting postlude to this conversation was that the pastor broke down in tears in a worship service a week later from pressures that some knew about, but nobody had access to or realized how they were affecting him. He has upgraded the priority to develop a network.

Take a look at a model that we call a constellation of mentoring relationships. It shows how you can organize the range of relationships that you need over your lifetime. This range includes *upward mentoring*, which means establishing mentoring relationships with mature followers of Christ who have resources and experiences to offer that you need. The previous chapters identified these types of mentors and discussed what they mean. The constellation also brings in *lateral relationships*, which we call "co-mentoring" with peers. Finally, it involves *downward mentoring*, which places you in the role of a mentor with younger followers of Christ. You need all dimensions, but they are dynamic in nature and require deliberate effort to develop and keep current. We'll talk about this later.

Figure11-1.
A Constellation Model of Mentoring Relationships

Each category of mentoring relationships involves development and a degree of accountability. Each offers some kind of empowerment. Each does something unique that the others do not. Let's take a closer look at the categories.

UPWARD MENTORING

Every leader needs upward mentoring from someone who has gone before and can give direction and perspective. Our main hope in describing the seven mentoring types has been to urge you to find those with experience and God-given resources who can mentor you in various areas of your life.

The need for upward mentoring is most obvious in the early and middle stages of a leader's development, but it is also needed for a lifetime. Even those well-established in their ministries should still have a learning posture and continue to seek out the occasional mentor in times of decision or transition . . . or just for the periodic spiritual checkup and insights gained from a broader perspective.

During the early stages of ministry, discipling, coaching, and teaching mentors are needed as young believers and leaders establish foundations in their lives, discover their gifts, and find appropriate ministry. As leaders move to the middle stages of leadership and ministry and experience more responsibility and effective use of gifts, they need the periodic empowerment of Spiritual Guides, Counselors and (if in an organization) Sponsors. Plateauing in one's career, ministry, and spiritual life often takes place in the middle stage and beyond. In such situations, Spiritual Guides and Counselors are important. In transitional or new ministry times, Coaches are invaluable. Of course, Models are needed and appropriate at any stage.

The upward mentor provides perspective, accountability, and the stimulus to persevere. You need these three ingredients to finish well. The important thing to see about upward mentoring is that you need some kind of mentoring throughout your lifetime in order to ensure continual development.

DOWNWARD MENTORING
To complete the vertical dimension of the constellation model, look at downward mentoring. All of us need to be concerned for those who are coming up behind us . . . no matter what our age. Downward mentoring is a primary means for helping develop the capacity, commitment, and values that will enable the next generation to serve God faithfully.

We said earlier that you probably won't find an ideal mentor, one who can do it all. In the same way, if you try to *be* a multi-purpose mentor for another person, you won't be able to—no one can. That is why each of us needs several mentors. And you can be one of those special mentors for others. But you must begin in a small way. If God has taught you something and it has helped you (empowered you in some way), then you have a potential resource to share with someone else. Start small and be specific.

Many people involved in ministry have never really used mentoring as a means of developing people. For these folks, we have paraphrased Hebrews 5:11-12. "We have much to say about this, but it is hard to explain because you have not been doing mentoring. In fact, though by this time you ought to be competent mentors, you need someone to teach you the elementary concepts of mentoring types."

So get started! Make the most of the experience you already have and use your time now to begin mentoring. Usually the best motivation for taking those early steps in mentoring comes from first being helped by someone else. A needy person who has been empowered by another, even in some small way, is a real candidate to help some other needy person. From being helped to helping—that's the basic conviction that will lead you into the first stages of mentoring.

There is mutual blessing in mentoring others. Both the mentor and mentoree are developed through the experience. The mentoree is empowered in the many ways described in chapters three through ten. But challenges and blessings will come to the mentor that enhance his or her own life, ministry, and leadership.

Over the years, our mentorees have:

- ◆ *Challenged our thinking* by their fresh ideas and different mind set.
- ◆ *Tested our flexibility* in developing approaches to familiar problems.
- ◆ *Forced a special kind of accountability* that checks our consistency and integrity. A mentoree can quickly spot an inconsistency in a mentor. What we suggest must be real in our lives.
- ◆ *Inspired ideals.* Younger mentors are usually refreshingly idealistic. Experience has not yet turned their ideals to cynicism. We've often been renewed and challenged to return to certain ideals.

The mentor's attitude is the key that will guide his or her approach in developing a mentoree. A mentor must be mentoree-oriented; that is, the mentoree's needs, goals, and desires determine the pace, content, style, and approach.[1] The mentoree's progress is primary. As we listed above, the mentor will experience reciprocal benefit in the process, but this is a byproduct of the relationship and pursuit.

PEER CO-MENTORING

Our peers are our friends, those with whom we naturally relate because we have so many things in common: age, families, circumstances. Peer relationships are the vital lateral dimension of the Constellation Model. A great source of mutual encouragement and protection lies within them. You might have experienced some degree of this empowerment already.

We see peers as mentors of one another, so we call them co-mentors. Since mentoring is a relational experience in which empowerment takes place through the sharing of God-given resources, peer relationships can become a mentoring experience. Unfortunately, most of us do not tap into this tremendous resource to the degree that we could.

Unlike the vertical dimension mentors, peers are the same age and share more common experiences. This allows them to be more relaxed, relevant, and open with one another. It is precisely these qualities in the relationship that enable peers to stimulate, interact, and hold one another accountable at a more personal level. They can and will shoot straight with us as well as empathize with our concerns and challenges, as they undoubtedly face the same ones. We can share confidential matters that may not be appropriate for upward mentors. We can also expect understanding and support.

In comparing notes with others concerned about the relational emptiness among male adults, and after taking some informal surveys of the state of man-to-man relationships, we are deeply concerned about this area. Two out of ten males seem to have a meaningful, open, and safe relationship where both parties share a trust and commitment to mutual responsibility for one another. Six out of ten women have this. Yet every man and woman needs at least one peer relationship (other than a spouse) like this where there is continuity and proximity in relating to one another. We will go into this more thoroughly in chapter twelve and also explore the various types of peer relationships and the strengths of each.

SUMMARY
A circle of accountability . . . the safeguard for finishing well. Western individualism makes for exciting adventure stories, but the "lone-ranger" approach leads to spiritual ill-health. We need a balance of

- *Upward mentors* . . . who have gone before and can show the way.
- *Downward mentorees* . . . who shake our complacency, renew our convictions, refreshingly keep us on our toes, and multiply our ministry for His Kingdom.
- *Peer co-mentors* . . . who know us, identify with us and provide mutual stimulation and personal accountability.

The Constellation Model is ideal, with mentor-mentoree and co-mentor relationships empowering the person in the center with specific and necessary contributions. This dynamic model will constantly experience change, growth, and shift of emphasis as those in the relational network develop and circumstances alter. But it is also a model to reach for and is worth your every effort if you desire to be strong in the inner life, effective in your roles and ministry, and finish well.

FOR FURTHER STUDY (CHAPTER 11)

1. Using the Constellation Model diagram, place names of the mentor/mentoree/co-mentor relationships you have in your life in the corresponding category.

2. Evaluate each relationship you noted in question one and determine the degree of empowerment you experience and how current (mutually updated) the relationship is.

3. How can you strengthen the relationships identified above to ensure that a greater influence and sense of accountability take place? Do you lack the mentor/mentoree/co-mentor relationships you need in your constellation of relationships? Where? Are there possibilities?

Chapter Twelve
PEER CO-MENTORING

Peers . . . the most available source of relational empowerment, but the least developed. "I guess I just took them [peers] for granted. They were all around. We'd talk, laugh, do things together. But when you asked us to identify the peer relationships that encourage and strengthen us—the ones [peers] with whom we share common commitments and a sense of mutual responsibility for one another—where you feel safe to be honest and transparent about yourself, I couldn't name one!" related Bill after a seminar on "A Leaders' Relational Network." It wasn't that Bill did not have friends and even some important peer relationships, but he had never thought about developing some of them to a point of significant mutual benefit.

Unfortunately, Bill's situation is typical . . . many peers but few, if any, who are developed to the point of shared commitment and trust. Our research agrees with sociologist Daniel Yankelovich that seven of ten

Americans sense a void in their lives as they confess to many acquaintances but very few close friends (Jones 1991).

Bill underscored this reality several months later when he began to experience some times of difficulty in his life and job and no one was close enough to pick up on it. It took several weeks more before he felt free to share his struggle with one friend, and even that was done partially and cautiously. Vulnerability often elicits a positive response and causes two people to draw together. This is what happened with Bill and his friend.

Peer relationships complete the circle of important relationships we described in the Constellation Model in chapter eleven. They are vital to all of us. There are unique aspects to peer relationships. Peers are at the same stage of life—in development, age, and situational pressures—and face many of the same decisions and challenges. These shared realities allow for a natural flow of conversation and a sense of being understood and accepted. This fosters an openness and honesty that can lead to mutual encouragement, stimulation, protection, accountability, and empowerment. But this will not "just happen." It takes time, priority, and commitment.

David and Jonathan—Co-Mentors

It was an unlikely mix, but a powerful one. Jonathan was the heir to the throne of his father, King Saul. He was also a proven warrior and turned the tide of a battle with an individual heroic act (1 Samuel 14:6-23). He was a leader. David, on the other hand, came from a shepherd's family, but like Jonathan was a warrior and hero. He became extremely popular after killing Goliath and then going on to lead Israel in one military success after another. Crowds cheered him and sung his praises (1 Samuel 18:5-7). "All Israel and Judah loved David" (1 Samuel 18:16). He, too, was a leader.

Jonathan and David were about the same age, young leaders with great futures. Under normal circumstances, one would expect that they would be competitors and resent one another, but the opposite was true. Unlike Jesus' disciples, who seemed to always vie for the best place and elbow one another in the process, David and Jonathan constantly sought each other's best (1 Samuel 20)—even at the risk of their own lives.

PEER CO-MENTORING

A friendship or peer relationship like David and Jonathan had is worth praying for and pursuing. Let's look at this relationship in 1 Samuel a bit more closely and see what made it so meaningful and mutually empowering.

1. They shared: "Jonathan became one in spirit with David" (18:1).
   - ◆ A heart to follow God and do His will (14:6, 17:45-47).
   - ◆ Interests and skills of war (background).
   - ◆ The same environment in the house and army of Saul.

2. They committed: "We have sworn friendship with each other in the name of the LORD" (20:42).
   - ◆ To God (chapter 14).
   - ◆ To each other's best — "Jonathan made a covenant with David because he loved him as himself" (18:3).
   "Whatever you want me to do, I'll do for you" (20:4).
   - ◆ To each others' future and family (20:12-17,42).
3. They experienced:
   - ◆ Protection by watching out for each other (chapter 20).
   - ◆ Openness and trust — they could share anything (20:3).
   - ◆ Friendship and fellowship (20:42, and generally implied throughout their story).
   - ◆ Strength and encouragement in times of difficulty — "Jonathan went to David at Horesh and helped him find strength in God" (23:16).
   - ◆ Love that was committed to the other's best, even if it meant personal sacrifice — "Don't be afraid. . . . My father Saul will not lay a hand on you. You will be king . . . I will be second to you" (23:17).
   - ◆ Sharpening and challenge to follow God.

It is easy to look at a relationship like Jonathan and David experienced and conclude that such would be wonderful and desirable for ourselves. Yet most would believe it unrealistic in today's Western world.

However, we have experienced it and met others who know this kind of relationship and its benefits. It is reachable! We believe everyone needs it. But where does one start?

We have broken peer relationships into three general types. They vary in terms of openness, trust, and commitment, as well as accountability and empowerment. Let's observe them on a continuum in figure 12-1.

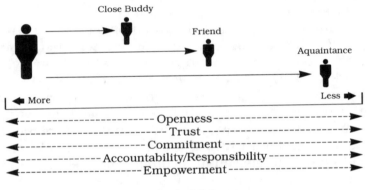

Figure 12-1.
Types of Peer Relationships

We need all three types of peer relationships in our lives. Each makes a contribution to our lives, our work and our world. Peers provide information, feedback, affirmation, and meaning to our pursuits and being.

Because of who they are, you will tend to more naturally relate to them. But each type has its limitations and strengths . . . and that is why you need all of them.

THE ACQUAINTANCE

The acquaintance is on the far right of the continuum (figure 12-1) and would seem unimportant, but is quite the contrary. Acquaintances are everywhere. You meet them in almost every sphere of activity. They come in every size, shape, color, and personality. Some you see once in a while, others daily, and still others only at specific events. They come to you as neighbors, colleagues, relatives, teammates, fellow church members, and numerous other sources . . . they are all over.

You exchange basic information with acquaintances. They are information sources who help you learn about your shared world in which you live, work, and play. They help you understand situations by passing on facts, observations, and experiences. You rarely know more about each other than what you see and pick up through casual conversation. As noted in figure 12-1, there is a low degree of commitment and trust in an acquaintance relationship because of the unknowns about one another. Yet this is where most relationships begin. Some will go deeper, but most will stay at this level.

THE FRIEND

The friend is the next level of peer relationship. You know much more about people in this category. You begin to reveal more about yourself—interests, thinking and feeling about things, concerns, likes and dislikes (and why) and your past—the more your sphere of involvement or traffic pattern overlaps with them. Because you have more time with one another, this relationship can deepen with trust, openness, and commitment. But personal effort and time must be invested for you to experience this.

At this level of relationship (friend) you begin to realize significant empowerment as you experience "one anothering." It is worth listing these (table 12-1) just to see what awaits if you are willing to open yourself to others and risk being vulnerable. Faith frees you to practice "one anothering" and expect God to work in and through you as you do.

Table 12-1. The "One Anothers"

Love one another— as Christ loved His disciples.	John 13:34-35, 1 John 3:11
Restore one another . . . *carry* each other's burdens.	Galatians 6:1-2
Bear with and *forgive* one another.	Colossians 3:13
Build up one another.	1 Thessalonians 5:11
Encourage to believe . . . *protect* from sin's deceitfulness.	Hebrews 3:12-14
Stir one another to love and good works . . . *encourage* to hope.	Hebrews 10:24-25
Confess sin to one another . . . *pray for* one another.	James 5:16

On a recent flight I (Paul) became engaged in a fascinating conversation with a psychologist who had a counseling practice to a wide social spectrum. As he related his concerns for the unprecedented rise in the number of people needing counseling, I detected compassion and frustration. He saw no solution to turn this trend around. At that point, I suggested that there is a solution . . . reconciliation of man to God through Jesus Christ. He confessed that he came from a Christian home and church, but left them both as it appeared the gospel had little effect on those who embraced it. "I would say that more than two-thirds of my clients are practicing Christians!" he added. Then he paused and said something profound. "Do you know the one anothers in the New Testament?" he questioned. I nodded, and he went on, "I am thoroughly convinced that if Christians practiced them to any degree at all, 90 percent of my Christian clients would not need me." Then he added, "And all the others—Christian or non-Christian—would flock to the church where it was happening."

Why is "one anothering" missing from Christian fellowships? It's missing for a number of reasons, including self-centeredness and fear of being vulnerable when reaching out to another person. This attitude is not readily manifested among "acquaintances." But at the "friend" level, among those meaningful peer relationships, "one anothering" can really go into action . . . and that is the level we find missing in many fellowships.

Why do so many followers of Christ have so few friends? Can we lay the blame on individualism, which tells us that we must make it on our own and that seeking another's help is a sign of weakness? How about mobility? Most families move every three to four years. Time-oriented societies like America believe that "time is money" so relationships become subordinate to time. These all may affect our relationship building, but each one can be overcome if the commitment is present.

The real barriers that hinder our relational intimacy come from within . . . *fear* and *pride*. Being vulnerable to another person is to most a frightening experience. To expose their inner life would reveal that they do not "have it all together." Many think they would be the only ones who did not. Also, those who lead in churches are perceived as "having it together," and little is done to correct that false perception. So many people go around just giving calculated and filtered "peeks" at their inner life. They then stiffen their resolve to go it alone in the strength of Christ . . . just like the Apostle Paul! However, while Christ and His grace are sufficient, we were not created to walk through life alone. Paul never did either. We need each other!

> Let us consider how we may spur one another on toward love and good deeds. Let us not give up meeting together . . . let us encourage one another—all the more as you see the Day approaching. (Hebrews 10:24-25)

> Two are better than one, because they have a good return for their work: If one falls down, his friend can help him up. But pity the man who falls and has no one to help him up! Also, if two lie down together, they will keep warm. But how can one keep warm alone? (Ecclesiastes 4:9-11)

Where do you meet peers who could become *friends*? You find them in the pool of acquaintances God has placed around you in all your spheres of involvement. A natural place to start, then, is in those spheres of involvement most important to you. Doing things together that hold common interests creates a shared context that allows friendships to grow. Continual exposure in this context will provide you with ample opportunity to get to know others, but you need one-on-one time to discover compatibility.

Moving from Acquaintance to Friend

Ruth was one of those with many acquaintances. Her life was full with her husband and two young children, a part-time job, a women's Bible study, and the social activities of a new neighborhood. More acquaintances were not her need, but meaningful relationships were. She discovered this when she received a letter from her mom telling about her parents' plans to divorce.

At the Bible study she shared the divorce news as a prayer request, but did not relate how she felt and the struggles she had in determining how to respond. "My faith should carry me through this. Why am I handling this so poorly?" she blurted out through tears as she drove home from the study.

Sherry was in the Bible study and had gone through her parents' divorce several years before. She knew how hard it could be. She got home and picked up the phone to call Ruth, then hesitated, thinking, *Am I intruding? What if she doesn't want to talk about it?* But remembering how much a friend meant to her in her time of struggle, she went ahead and called.

Ruth was surprised to receive Sherry's call and appreciated her concern. Knowing that Sherry had gone through what she was facing did encourage her, but she still was a bit guarded in her response to Sherry's questions. *Why am I afraid to let someone know how hard this is for me?* she wondered, and determined to set up an appointment with her pastor.

The next day Ruth called her mom, but there seemed to be no hope for reconciliation. Out of desperation she called the church and found that the pastor was out and would not be back all day. She called her husband at work. He was understanding, as he had been all the way, but she could tell he struggled with how to relate to her inability to accept this. *Maybe I should call Sherry,* she thought. *But she is so strong, I'm sure she handled this problem much differently. I'm so weak and disappointed in myself.*

Finally, after working through her morning routines in robot fashion, Ruth called Sherry and arranged to take a walk after lunch. It took all the courage she could muster to confess to Sherry how hard the week had been and that she was just not coping. With great empathy Sherry said, "I know just how you feel. I felt so alone and disappointed with my lack of faith." With that, Ruth poured out her heart and struggles to a very understanding friend. Knowing that Sherry understood and that her reactions and feelings were not abnormal brought great relief to Ruth.

The relationship between Ruth and Sherry continued to grow through walks, telephone conversations, and times of prayer. Opening her life to Sherry gave Ruth courage to reveal more of herself and her needs to the women in her Bible study. Her sharing drew others to her and she found great encouragement in their concern and prayer. It was not long before Ruth and Sherry were walking and talking on a regular basis and even invited another to join them. Going deeper in one relationship and experiencing the effect of the "one anothers" led to a new openness and trust in other relationships.

Opening yourself to another is a step of faith that's well worth the risk. You do not need to share only your struggles; you can reveal personal pursuits or goals. We have found that the barest expression of a desire to grow and experience the strength of another brother or sister in an area often is enough to launch a friendship. Once a "friend" relationship has begun, you may find it helpful to discuss and agree upon some expectations for the relationship in order to go deeper and stimulate one another in areas of desired growth.

THE CLOSE BUDDY

The third type of peer relationship is a special gift from God. We call it the "close buddy." To have a close buddy in your relational network brings tremendous blessing and strength not found in any other relationship. This relationship is characterized by unrestricted openness, trust, commitment, and a high sense of mutual accountability or sense of responsibility for one another. The close buddy relationship is epitomized by Jonathan and David, whom we discussed at the beginning of this chapter. You may want to review that or read about it in 1 Samuel 16–23.

Obviously, in any relationship beyond acquaintance each person has a need for chemistry or compatibility, but that is not often obvious until the people get to know one another and pursue a friendship. In the close buddy relationship, a mutual appreciation and respect emerges. Close buddies don't see differences as problems, but rather as complementing strengths in the relationship. As friends discover and affirm common goals and values, and openness and trust grow, the opportunity to move the relationship to a close buddy emerges. What moves people from friends to close buddies is a mutual commitment to the pursuit of a deeply meaningful goal. Out of this will grow a sense of responsibility for one another that will lift each buddy to new levels that would not be reached alone. It also provides accountability for integrity and inner-life growth, which is vital for those who desire to finish well.

A Close Buddy Can Correct in Love

Ted and I (Paul) got to know each other through a men's breakfast. Casual conversation revealed some common interests and backgrounds.

We began playing racquetball and doing some things together as families. Ted's earnest pursuit of Christ was refreshing and attractive. I had been a believer for many years, but was just breaking out of a plateau in my spiritual life. We decided to meet together once a week for study and prayer.

During lunch one day, Ted expressed some frustration he was experiencing with his son and family leadership. I could relate to his dilemma and said, "Don't you wish we could be as effective at home as we seem to be at work?" We both smiled and stared at each other. "Why not? Let's give it a try!" blurted out Ted. So we agreed to pray for each other and think about what it means to lead well in the home and share our thoughts later in the week. This pursuit went on for a couple months and significantly affected our growth as dads and husbands.

Building on this positive experience, we began discussing other areas of our lives in which we wished to see similar progress. In the process of seeking to grow together, we opened up more and found ourselves appreciating the effect we had on each other's life. A bond of friendship developed. Reflecting on this one day, I suggested we surface some of the expectations that we each had for our relationship. It became evident that there were some clear yet unspoken expectations such as openness, trust, honesty with one another, freedom to discuss most things with confidentiality, and commitment to help and pray for each other. Then Ted introduced the idea of a shared purpose for our lives. We agreed that to know and love Christ in a way that would glorify Him through our lives at home and work would be a worthy goal.

"What about when one sees the other

falling short? Do we hold each other accountable and have the right to ask questions and
challenge one another?" asked Ted. "Sure!" I
responded. "If we really mean business, let's
go all the way!" So we made a covenant to one
another before God in prayer.

Things went well and God taught us much
about Himself and what it means to follow His
Son. We also grew closer to one another and
were finding out what it meant to believe God
for each other. Then it happened.

I was in a full-time, parachurch ministry and carried a responsibility that required
traveling and supervising other staff. My son
Paul was the starting center for the local high
school, and their team was doing very well.
A big game was coming up on a Friday night,
which would determine the league leader,
and everyone was excited. Then I received
an unexpected call on Thursday concerning
a problem that seemed impossible to settle
over the phone. Reluctantly, I flew out on Friday morning and had to be gone the whole
weekend.

Ted arrived back in town from a business
trip on Friday afternoon and quickly ate dinner and went with his family over to the game.
He loved basketball and watching Paul play.
They got to the gym just in time, but could
not find me so just grabbed seats where they
could. It was a tight and well-played game.
Paul's play was outstanding, and he led his
team to an exciting victory. When the final

buzzer sounded, the crowd poured out onto the court and everyone was yelling, hugging, and dancing.

Ted worked his way to Paul and gave him a big hug and congratulated him. "Where's your dad?" he asked Paul. "Oh, he had to go somewhere suddenly," Paul responded with disappointment. "Boy, would he have loved this game!" Ted shot back. "Yeah, I guess," said Paul as he turned to get another hug.

I got back on Sunday afternoon and Tuesday morning met Ted for breakfast. I had heard all about the game and was very proud of my son. Ted filled me in on some of the details of the game, then looked at me and asked, "Did you really have to go on that trip this past weekend?" "I didn't want to, but I had no choice," I replied. There was a silence that I broke. "Do you think I should have not gone?" Ted thought for a moment and said, "I know you prayed about it and wanted to be at your son's game, but if you could have seen Paul's response when I asked him if you were there. . . ." Realizing this was a critical moment of accountability, I asked again, "But do *you* think I made the wrong decision?"

"Yes, I think you blew it, and I am really concerned about your traveling over all. If you don't watch it, you're going to lose what you've got with your kids!" Ted declared. Somewhat defensive, I came back, "You're concluding all this because I missed one important game? Paul didn't seem to mind . . . he said he understood." Ted took a deep breath and said, "Well, I know you're committed to your kids, but I wonder how your two teenagers feel about their priority right now. You don't seem to be involved with them the way you once were, and you've told me you aren't sure you know what is going on with Paul. I remember you said last week that you sensed a distance between you and him. I think you should talk to him and tell him you feel bad about not being at the game and that maybe you made the wrong decision to go. Ask him, if he were you, what he would have done. Let him know you want to reevaluate your travel and you want his input."

I agreed to do what Ted suggested. That night after supper, I took our two teenagers into the living room and let them know I was reevaluating my travel and wanted their input. "Let's start with this past weekend. Should I have gone on that sudden trip or stayed home to be at Paul's game? I am wondering if I blew it on that one." Paul immediately responded, "Dad, I told you it was okay. I understand." But his older sister broke in, "That's not what you told me. I think it really hurt you. And, Dad, I agree with you—you blew it!"

Paul finally confessed his hurt and went on to share how he felt I was just not tuned into him. "You seem to be on another frequency, Dad, and so busy that I don't want to bother you." My daughter added, "Dad, there are other things you've missed. Nothing big, but you used to always be there."

Needless to say, my schedule and priorities went through a real shakedown. My wife, kids, and Ted helped me set some new procedures in order to resolve the competing time demands and the tension between family schedules and sudden job responsibilities.

In this way, Ted and I passed through our first tough accountability challenge. If I had been continually defensive or passed it off with, "Thanks, buddy, I'll pray about it," and not pursued it, that may have been the last time Ted would have tried it. Ted's honest sharing not only made a big contribution to my life and family, but it set us up for more such interaction.

Dr. James Houston of Regent College had this to say about the importance of a close friend (buddy):

> Sin always tends to make us blind to our own faults. We need a friend to stop us from deceiving ourselves that what we are doing is not so bad after all. We need a friend to help us overcome our low-image, inflated self-importance, selfishness, pride, our deceitful nature, our dangerous fantasies, and so much else. (Jones 1991:43)

A close buddy is an answer to prayer . . . a gift, an opportunity, and a resource like no other. The place to start looking is among your "friends" and then begin spending some time together and talk. Talk about life, ministry, family, personal needs, and desires, and see where it goes. Have fun together! See if there is compatibility and response to one another.

Keep praying and be patient, but do not be afraid to share some of your desires for a meaningful peer relationship. And be willing to be vulnerable.

Peer Coaching

Melissa had taught middle school for eight years but still was not able to develop meaningful class participation. She tried various approaches suggested at teacher workshops such as student presentations, working in teams, and role playing but they failed to generate the class participation and interaction that she desired.

One day at lunch Melissa discussed her frustration with Jennifer and Jayne, colleagues in the same school. Jennifer expressed her desire to also strengthen her ability to develop class participation and related how her visit to Jayne's classroom in a combined classes situation had really helped her. Jayne built much of her instruction around class interaction and had been successful. Jayne modestly denied being good at it, but Melissa and Jennifer knew better.

After some discussion on stimulating student involvement, Jayne shifted the conversation to a need she faced with teaching mathematics to slower students when others in the class wanted to move faster. Jennifer had taken some classes in college that dealt with this problem and found real success in applying what she had learned.

Jayne stated the obvious, "Let's help each

other! We've got a lot we can share." Each of the three teachers identified one area they wanted to improve in their teaching and one personal development project. They met, shared these areas, and helped each other refine and focus their desires so they would be reachable in four to five months. Learning to use each other as resources was exciting and involved visiting each other's classrooms to learn and evaluate. Jennifer presented to her friends the principle she had learned and applied to help slower students in the context of more gifted students. Then Melissa and Jayne attended Jennifer's class to watch her work with that principle.

Over the five-month period, each prepared subjects for the other two and they all visited each other's classrooms several times. The information passed on was instructive and practical, but the feedback and evaluation on their teaching proved to be invaluable and an unexpected blessing.

They held each other accountable on their personal development projects simply by scheduling update times that served as an encouragement to keep going and share what each was learning. Melissa completed a night course she had been putting off for years. Jennifer read the two books she needed to evaluate for a course she was going to teach next year. And Jayne got her resource files organized and set up so she could make them work for her. Their teaching competence was strengthened and classroom participation moved to a new level.

Even Jayne's classes were stimulated with new
participation approaches by the three teachers.

Melissa, Jennifer, and Jayne experienced the
effects of *peer coaching*. Those familiar with ongoing
teacher development in our public schools are aware
of this co-mentoring program that has been developed over the last ten years across the country.

Co-mentoring is available wherever two or more
peers desire to develop ability in an area of mutual
interest. As a matter of fact, within any given group
someone always knows or has experienced something that would contribute to another's development. But unless someone takes the initiative, this
relational experience is never made.

We have observed co-mentoring taking place informally among young mothers, Boy Scout leaders, financial investors, Bible study leaders, Sunday school
teachers, and many professions or common-interest
groups. Excellent resources are available and waiting
for the learner.

EXTERNAL AND INTERNAL PEERS

Those in organizations or groups, no matter the size,
will seek to develop peer relationships within them.
This is quite natural, since a great deal of time is
spent with these peers in the context of work and
ministry. However, we have discovered a special need
in these situations. We call them *external* and *internal peers*.

Obviously, an internal peer is found within the
context of a group or organization and an external
peer is outside. We encourage a balance. Both are

important. Those who enjoy the relationships within their group and spend most of their time there find it easy to develop only internal peer relationships. Internal peers know the same things and provide a safe place for confidential sharing that only members of the same group can have. On the other hand, external peers provide an objective perspective that will check tendencies toward narrowness often held by a group. This need for internal and external peers applies to churches, fellowship groups, ministries, parachurch groups, and the workplace.

THREE INGREDIENTS FOR CO-MENTORING

From our overview of the Constellation Model we can summarize some important insights about peer co-mentoring. Peers should provide accountability and challenging perspectives. In order for empowerment to occur along lines of accountability and perspective, at least three kinds of relational ingredients are necessary for meaningful co-mentoring. There should be "a fit," enjoyment, and empowerment.

Fit . . .

First, *peers must accept and appreciate one another.* An attraction to each other should be apparent to both. There can be differences, of course, but each will feel a sense that *here is a person I like and want to get to know.* This reflects a clear compatibility. Now this match, this chemistry, may not be there at first. Sometimes first impressions do not generate such a sense of fit. But it must eventually develop if there is to be respect for one another's opinions. Without it, neither accountability nor empowerment can occur.

Fun . . .

In addition to that sense of fit, co-mentoring relationships should be fun. *Co-mentors should enjoy being with one another.* This can develop through some commonly shared hobby, interest, or discipline. In fact, this shared interest may provide the springboard to acceptance. If you enjoy being with your co-mentor then you will spend time together, which is necessary for building a relationship. Leisure time is just as important as serious time. In fact, each makes the other more effective. We suggest that in developing your peer relationships you enjoy meals together, participate in athletic endeavors, learn about each other's hobbies, and just hang around together—sometimes even without an agenda—something that is easy for friends to do yet tough for task-oriented people.

Empowerment . . .

A final ingredient necessary to the dynamics of co-mentoring centers around openness, trust, commitment, and confidentiality: Empowerment. This lies at the heart of an effective co-mentoring relationship. *Co-mentors must be willing to be transparent with each other on important issues or they will not experience empowerment.* Levels of transparency, of course, will develop as the relationship develops. In fact, *the depth of transparency or openness is one major indicator of the effectiveness of a co-mentoring relationship.* Openness hinges on the other two characteristics—trust and confidentiality. If you trust your peer and know that he or she will keep confidentiality, then you will be open. This openness allows you both to spot problems or potential problems and to intervene so as to empower. But still, you will not learn unless you are committed to do so.

So then, words like *acceptance, chemistry, fun, time together, openness, trust, confidentiality,* and *commitment* describe the ingredients of an effective relationship that co-mentors should seek.

Proximity and continuity are two underlying dynamics that will allow these ingredients to come alive. You must be available to each other and have regular, ongoing times together if the co-mentoring relationship is to work. Regularity will depend on your proximity and schedules. Ideally, you should have contact with your co-mentors (friends and close buddies) once or twice a week. If on a monthly basis, then you should meet for a more extended time. While distance mentoring is possible with upward mentoring relationships, it is less effective with co-mentors.

HOW TO ESTABLISH PEER RELATIONSHIPS
We believe that peer mentors are given by God. Occasionally, you will be able to identify a given need in your life and will seek a special person, perhaps a co-mentor, who can meet that need. But normally that function will be provided by an upward mentor. The nature of co-mentoring focuses on relationship, not on a need-centered function (as with other mentor types). Because that is so, you do not always even know what kind of person you need in a co-mentoring relationship. You must depend upon God, then, to provide you with people who will become co-mentors.

You can be alert. You can know that you need co-mentors. You can begin to move along the friendship-mentor continuum. But in the end it will be God who guides you to those who will become co-mentors. Our guidelines for entering into co-mentoring are common-sense notions based on this conviction.

Table 12-2. Five Steps Toward Establishing Co-Mentor Relationships

STEP GUIDELINE

1. *Pray and seek.* Actively trust God for needed relationships. Look for them in your spheres of involvement.

2. *Make contacts.* Explore chemistry. Have fun together. Do things that will be foundational to relationship building. Discover shared values and desires.

3. *Share desires* and set expectations for a co-mentoring relationship.

4. *Give time.* Prioritize your schedule and activities so you have adequate time to build a relationship that moves deeper toward empowerment. The more your spheres of involvement overlap, the greater the exposure and amount of time you can spend together, which are key to relational development.

PREVENTATIVE RATHER THAN CURATIVE

As we mentioned in the preface, our studies on how leaders develop over a lifetime indicate that *few leaders finish well.* There are numerous pivotal points in their lives where they can go astray. Five common pivotal points include:

- ◆ Sexual relationships
- ◆ Power
- ◆ Pride
- ◆ Family
- ◆ Attitude toward and use of money

You can correct tendencies toward failure in all of these areas, especially in the beginning stages. But this will require the special relationship that primarily peer mentoring can provide. Upward mentors help you develop in many ways, but they will not usually spend the time with you nor develop the intimate relationship that co-mentors will. Nor will mentorees in a downward relationship usually have the power or confrontive ability to bring about preventive action. Peer mentors will.

Leaders need peer mentors. One reason for much of the failure in Christian leadership stems from the lack of intimate friendships with peers. This ought not to be. Each leader should make choices to develop accountable peer relations—choices that give these relationships priority, time access, and mutual accountability.

SUMMARY

> See to it, brothers, that none of you has a sinful, unbelieving heart that turns away from the living God. But encourage one another daily, as long as it is called Today, so that none of you may be hardened by sin's deceitfulness. We have come to share in Christ if we hold firmly till the end the confidence we had at first. (Hebrews 3:12-14)

> Two are better than one,
>   because they have a good return for their
>   work:
> If one falls down,

his friend can help him up.
But pity the man who falls
and has no one to help him up!
(Ecclesiastes 4:9-10)

As iron sharpens iron,
so one man sharpens another.
(Proverbs 27:17)

Today's success-oriented, individualistic society discourages those close relationships that you need in order to grow. The higher a leader rises, often the harder it is to find co-mentoring. Yet the higher a leader rises, the greater the pitfalls and the more important it becomes to develop accountable relationships with peers.

Such friendships do not just happen. They are given by God and must be deliberately developed if you desire to reach the level of freedom and vulnerability you need to bring commitment to each other's best.

FOR FURTHER STUDY

1. Using the Types of Peer Relationships (figure 12-1, page 173), list the names of your peers in each category. Stick to the descriptions of each type in this chapter. Does fear or pride hold you back from going deeper with your peer relationships?

2. a. Using a concordance do a topical study on friends, looking for different aspects of an accountable friendship. Include the "one another" verses (page 175) with the verses you

found, and grade how you are doing in being a friend to those you have listed above.

b. What specific things can you do this week to apply these verses? (Example: What could you do to encourage a specific friend toward spiritual growth?)

3. Next, grade how receptive you are to others applying the "one anothers" to your life. Are you receptive to their encouragement and correction? Do you let them into your life so they can help carry your burdens?

4. In what ways has a friend or close buddy held you accountable? (If they haven't, maybe you have not allowed them to get as close as you thought.)

5. Consider: Do you allow friends to hold you accountable in some areas of your life more readily than in others? In which areas is it harder to receive correction? Which areas are just too close to allow others in? Why? Is it worth the struggle on your own?

6. Choose an area and friend. Tell that person this week that you *give* them the freedom and *ask* him or her to hold you accountable in that area. It's a start.

Chapter Thirteen

THE TEN COMMANDMENTS OF MENTORING

Not all mentoring relationships work out well. Sometimes you both expect more than what happens. Occasionally your relationship sags in the middle. Sometimes it drifts off and never finishes. The mentoring relationship can disappoint. You may not know what to do to repair it or improve it. Even so, you almost always gain some empowerment. Learning the hard way, you discover some practical guidelines that can help improve your mentoring.

We could list many important guidelines that would help you in specific mentoring relationships. In this chapter we will describe some common ones that we found helpful for Intensive and Occasional mentoring situations. May you will add new ones, but these are good for starters.

Table 13-1. The Ten Commandments of Mentoring

1. Establish the mentoring.
2. Jointly agree on the purpose of the relationship.
3. Determine the regularity of interaction.

4. Determine the type of accountability.
5. Set up communication mechanisms.
6. Clarify the level of confidentiality.
7. Set the life cycle of the relationship.
8. Evaluate the relationship from time to time.
9. Modify expectations to fit the real-life mentoring situation.
10. Bring closure to the mentoring relationship.

COMMANDMENT 1: RELATIONSHIP

The stronger the relationship, the greater the empowerment. In all dimensions of the Constellation Model—vertical and lateral—relationships are vital. Sometimes mentoring relationships just happen and develop in a natural way. Others take time and are more deliberate. Compatibility and chemistry are true advantages, especially for co-mentoring. Most relationships will not grow to an intimate level, and not all need to. But it is important to keep in mind that you need to continue to develop the relationship.

COMMANDMENT 2: PURPOSE

Sometimes mentoring proves disappointing. This disappointment can frequently be traced back to differing or unfulfilled expectations. We find that expectations should be expressed, negotiated, and agreed upon at the beginning of a mentoring relationship. Commandments two through eight all deal with important areas of expectations. Along with expectations, you need to discuss and mutually affirm the purpose or basic aims of the mentoring relationship.

COMMANDMENT 3: REGULARITY

Disappointments can arise from differing expectations as to regularity of meetings between the mentor and mentoree. Some mentors may have in mind less frequent times together, while growing mentorees may envision more time together. It is better to talk this over and set some ground rules both for regular meeting times and for impromptu interactions. Availability for impromptu times always facilitates the development of the relationship, but there could be conflict with competing time demands if the mentor is heavily engaged in other priorities. Clarify these issues early on in the relationship.

Intensive mentoring probably works best with at least once-a-week contact either face-to-face or by phone. Regularity may vary if the mentoree is a self-starter or a person with heavy responsibilities.

COMMANDMENT 4: ACCOUNTABILITY

Accountability or mutual responsibility is an important mentoring dynamic. Again, it usually does not just happen. You must plan for it. Agree together on how you will establish and monitor mentoring tasks. The heart of empowerment lies not only in what the mentor shares with the mentoree but also in the tasks the mentor gives to the mentoree. You must complete the tasks in order to benefit. Accountability is the prod to make sure this happens, because change is difficult and rarely takes place without it. It can occur many ways: written reports, scheduled phone calls, probing questions during meetings, or a planned evaluation time. What a mentor likes to see is a mentoree who takes responsibility to see that accountability takes place. The mentoree's self-initiative in accountability speeds and enhances empowerment.

Laying Out Expectations by Letter

Mentors differ in how they clarify purpose, regularity, and accountability. The heavy structure given in the following may not fit everyone. But it shows what the second, third, and fourth commandments of mentoring mean.

Dear Mark and Gayll,

You two have been my (Bobby's) top students over the past year. In every class you have shown a creative bent toward excellence. I believe God has great things in store for your leadership in the future. I am thankful for the input I have been able to give at such an important juncture in your life. And I feel I can contribute further if you are willing. So I am hoping that you will consider a mentoring relationship—for the next six months. I would like you to read my suggestions below and then respond to me.

From my standpoint, here are six things that a mentoring relationship with you would entail:

1. I would want each of you to design some *personal growth project*. It could be in the Word, prayer, skill-development, or something else of interest to you. I would simply help you with accountability for it and give advice as to how to go about it. The project, its scope, accountability measures, and closure would be your own. I would simply make sure you progress in it. I have found that personal

growth projects have been one of the great stimuli in my own life for maintaining a growth posture.

2. I would be *accessible anytime*. You can sign up on my office sheet for time, call me at home, or whatever. I will be available. In addition, I will pray especially for you two during this period of mentorship.

3. I would want you to work on some *spiritual disciplines* (maybe one per month or two).

4. We would have *regular accountability and sharing times*. I assume we would get together once or twice per month (depending on what your learning project is). Also, once during the six months we would probably get together for a potluck and sharing time with all the people I am mentoring. During our regular times together I want to share some of the following: what I have done in terms of my Word goals for a lifetime, my hermeneutical approach to the study of the Scriptures, my definition of spirituality, my identification of spiritual dynamics, my understanding of spiritual authority, my prayer life, approach, notebook, etc.

5. I would want you to be working on *two Word disciplines*. Particularly I want each of you to do two things: (1) use a balanced framework for systematic study of the Word during the six months; (2) work on what I call integrating perspectives, that is, learning the Bible as a whole, seeing books as a whole, and seeing books in the context of the

Bible as a whole.

6. I would like to occasionally *co-minister* with you in your ministry—that is, I would like to visit and observe what you do—see you in action, see some of your disciples in action. And vice versa, sometimes I would like for you to see me in action—maybe attend a special ministry time outside of my normal class time.

Mark and Gayll, I don't know whether this appeals to you or not, or whether this is the wrong time or you are facing too heavy a load. Feel perfectly free not to accept this offer or to modify it to fit your time pressures. I'll not think the less of you if you decide you can't do it at this time or if you want to change these ideas.

I hope you two will pray about this and let me know by the end of the first week in January. If it is a yes, we need to lay out some of the ministry tasks described above.

Adjusting the Expectations

Soon after we joined our church, Terry and I (Paul) got into a conversation about "making your life count." Terry responded to some of the things I said and wanted to get together again. I gave him a little ministry task about the five Great Commission verses and said, "Let's meet to discuss the conclusions when you finish. Give me a call."

A few days later Terry called and we met

and talked about the Great Commission and what it means for a disciple of Christ. Terry seemed to be eager to learn how to disciple others, so I invited him to consider meeting together for that purpose. He accepted, and we began.

At the first meeting we worked through a plan that fit his desires, the skills he would need, and the biblical foundation for discipling. We discussed our expectations and the need for accountability. We made a personal covenant to pursue Christ together, pray for one another, and be open and honest with each other. The plan shifted some after four months as Terry started discipling two other men. His needs and questions were different, and we adjusted accordingly. There is nothing more exciting than to coach someone who is discipling another.

COMMANDMENT 5:
COMMUNICATION MECHANISMS

Frequently mentors see something in a mentoree that needs correction or about which they feel concern. How and when to communicate this is important to clarify early in a mentor relationship. This is particularly important among peers, who are more apt to hold one another accountable in personal areas. As mentors, we have always asked our mentorees, "If I see or learn of an area of need or concern for you—and it may be negative—how and when do you want me to communicate it to you?" It is important to discover timing and procedure so that when the opportunity comes for correction and challenge (and it will!), we are ready for it and can anticipate a mature response. When peers commit to each other, this is important for them to discuss when they make a covenant. A mentoree can also initiate this as he or she is in a place to learn, grow, and respond to challenge by the mentor.

COMMANDMENT 6: CONFIDENTIALITY
Commandments five and six have to do with communication. Five concerns communication between mentor and mentoree, and six concerns communication *outside* the mentoring relationship. The mentoring relationship, if it deepens, may involve a sharing of personal matters between mentor and mentoree. It may be that one or both of them do not want these things conveyed to those outside the relationship.

Several factors influence the level of confidentiality. One factor involves the personalities of both mentor and mentoree. Some people are more vulnerable, and others are less vulnerable. Some are not concerned that others know the deeper issues of their lives, while others feel threatened by the thought that someone may find out about their personal concerns. They may not even want their age known.

A mentoring relationship must honor the participants' personalities and feelings about confidentiality. You will have to explore this with each individual mentoring relationship you set up. In counseling, you should consider all things confidential and not to be shared with others without permission. For other mentoring relationships, you both need to make it clear when something you share should be treated as confidential. Such a simple statement to each other will free you to speak openly and may save much grief later on.

COMMANDMENT 7: LIFE CYCLES OF MENTORING
Periods of mentoring vary in length of time for empowerment to happen. You should realize this and set reasonable time lengths for the type of mentoring you are involved in. *Avoid open-ended mentorships.* When you enter a mentoring relationship, do not expect it to last forever. In fact, we prefer breaking up potentially long mentoring experiences into obvious or logical segments, so that at each juncture closure can be made if desired. If you assume that the given purposes and accountability measures will take six months, set up a smaller goal of three months with evaluation. Then both of you can back out without losing face if the mentoring relationship does not meet your expectations. On the other hand, if it goes well you can continue the relationship and set up a new evaluation point. Better to have short periods, evaluation, and closure points with the possibility of reentry than have a sour relationship for a long time that each fears terminating.

In summary, here are the basic guidelines: Set realistic time limits. Have exit points where both parties can leave without bad relations. Have open doors where the invitation to continue can be open. Recognize the necessity of a time limit in any mentoring situation.

COMMANDMENT 8: EVALUATION

No mentoring relationship is ideal. Expectations are seldom totally realized. From time to time the mentoring relationship should be evaluated. Wise mentors will use the three dynamic factors (attraction, responsiveness, accountability) and empowerment to help them evaluate the ongoing state of the mentoring venture. This allows for mid-course corrections. Evaluation is dominantly a mentor function. Mentorees will sense growth but will not have the perspective to effectively evaluate; therefore, a joint evaluation is best.

In fact, in preparing for mentoring sessions it is a good idea for the mentor to review the whole process and see where progress has been made, where there are problems, and what should be done at the present juncture to improve the mentoring.

The following is an example of the evaluation steps we suggest:

Step 1: Mentor evaluates first, on his own.
- ◆ Lacks attention
- ◆ Little prayer
- ◆ Assignments not really on target
- ◆ Interest is flagging
- ◆ Ready to go on
- ◆ Need to redefine

Step 2: Mentor initiates appropriate self-correction.

Step 3: Evaluate and discuss—mentor and mentoree.

Step 4: Mutual agreement to redefine or modify expectations.

COMMANDMENT 9: EXPECTATIONS

Commandments eight and nine are two sides of the same coin. While evaluation, commandment eight, is mainly the responsibility of the mentor, expectation, commandment nine, is mainly the responsibility of the mentoree.

Expectations are the root of most disappointing mentoring experiences. The basic rule that can offset missed expectations is a simple one: Use evaluation and feedback to modify your expectations so that they fit your real-life mentoring situation. Recognize that you will seldom reach ideal expectations, because real-life situations have complexities you cannot always anticipate. But you will probably reach realistic expectations. After a time of mentoring, modify what you ideally hoped for down to what is most likely going to happen. Recognize that there will be empowerment and rejoice in that. Lack of meeting ideal expectations does not have to be the source of dissatisfaction in mentoring.

COMMANDMENT 10: CLOSURE

A basic rule in planning passed around more and more is, "Begin with the end in mind." All mentoring should follow this basic notion. Closure has to do with bringing a satisfactory end to a mentoring experience. Vertical mentoring that has no clear end in mind will usually dwindle to nothing with uneasy feelings on the part of both people. Vertical mentoring is not intended to be an ongoing experience. A happy ending for a mentoring experience involves closure, in which both parties evaluate, recognize how and where empowerment has occurred, and mutually end the mentoring relationship. What frequently happens in successfully closed mentoring is an ongoing friendship that allows for occasional mentoring and future interweaving of lives as needed. So then, don't forget this final commandment: "Bring closure to the mentoring relationship." This is probably the most violated of all the commandments, and the most detrimental. Even unsuccessful mentoring experiences should have closure.

BEYOND INDIVIDUAL MENTORING

Alternative forms of mentoring can broaden our understanding and suggest even greater usefulness. We have talked about mentoring as if it were only individualistic. And in essence it is. But mentoring can be done not only via individual relationships but in various kinds of focused small-group situations.

Small-Group Mentoring

Effective discipling can be done in group contexts in which a Discipler takes a small group of mentorees through a well-designed training program. Two weaknesses must be guarded against in such group programs. One of the strengths of individual discipling is the experiential component. The Discipler shows the mentoree how to do many of the skills in a live context. This shared experience moves the will and changes the values of a mentoree. Group contexts often miss out on the individual contact that may accomplish the experiential component of discipling. A second weakness involves conformity to the program. Group discipleship programs usually require everybody to do all the same things on the same time schedule, when in fact people differ in their motivation and ability to process information and learn skills. Every group member does not need all that the programs provide, nor is every member able to take it at the same rate. But this is offset somewhat by the group-supported momentum that encourages growth and completion.

Peer Group Accountability

A hybrid form of mentoring occurs in groups made up of peers who meet on a regular basis for fellowship, stimulation for growth, and accountability. Accountability groups made up largely of peers are a form of lateral mentoring. Such groups usually commit themselves to each other for a long period of time. They develop in-depth relationships and a high level of transparency in the meetings. The focus of the meetings may differ—Bible study, prayer, sharing, or whatever—but the major accomplishment is a responsibility for each other. And the openness with which each person shares also allows for stimulation through diverse perspectives. The major functions of lateral mentoring, those of perspective and accountability, can happen effectively in these kinds of accountability groups.

Master/Apprenticeship Groups

Another hybrid form of mentoring occurs in groups made up of peers headed by one who mentors the entire group in some specialty. An example of this is the cluster-group church growth consulting done by Dr. Dan Reeves under the auspices of Church Growth Consultants. Reeves meets with a cluster of ten to fifteen pastors on a face-to-face basis one day per quarter. In between these meetings, pastors do monthly assignments that involve lateral mentoring with each other and downward mentoring in their churches. This powerful and structured format combines expert downward mentoring by a church growth consultant and co-mentoring by peers.

Distance Mentoring

Distance mentoring requires a certain level of maturity on the part of mentorees. They must be self-starters who can assume responsibility and faithfully carry out a task without someone directly looking over their shoulders. Within these parameters, effective mentoring can take place.

In our illustration in chapter five (page 76), we didn't mention that Diane moved to another city before Pat could complete the goals of their mentoring relationship. However, since they were only an hour apart they agreed to keep going. They met every three months for a day and spoke on the phone every two weeks. At each meeting they evaluated their progress and reset their goals and expectations, and Pat gave Diane several ministry and growth tasks to do during the next three months. This went on for a year until they reached their goals. The mentoring has been concluded, but a strong friendship continues.

Some church growth consultants use a modified form of face-to-face mentoring in group contexts on a quarterly basis, but follow up with mail assignments. One sets up a telephone appointment to discuss the assignments. The telephone sessions are effective because their agenda is part of the assignment in the mail. Distance mentoring can be effective if there are good assignments and responsible mentorees.

LEARNING FROM OUR MISTAKES
Both of us have become increasingly involved in mentoring over the past years. Perhaps you can profit from some of our mistakes. We certainly have! Here are five mistakes to avoid.

1. Don't be too dominant in establishing the purpose of the mentoring relationship. Draw the mentoree into it for his or her motivation, ownership, and appropriate focus.
2. Do not give out too many tasks too early. Let the mentoree set the pace.
3. Watch out for midway relational "sag." The mentoring relationship tends to lose its original zest at about the midpoint. Ensure that the mentoree makes bite-size progress, and keep frequent contact.
4. Assess and select mentorees carefully. Check motivation, responsiveness, and right timing.
5. Be careful of "weak closure" and sloppy accountability. Be faithful to the mentoree during the mentoring experience, and end well.

SUMMARY
Following our "Ten Commandments of Mentoring" from the outset of a mentoring relationship can save

a lot of disappointment and misunderstanding later on. We came up with these ten points from years of experience . . . and mistakes. The key is good communication and spelling out the expectations from both sides. We are still learning as we go. Our experiences have not always gone the way we hoped. But when you experience that successful mentoring relationship, there is nothing like it . . . it's exciting!

FOR FURTHER STUDY (CHAPTER 13)

1. Arrange to meet with someone who has done some mentoring. Take along a list of the commandments of mentoring. Ask that mentor to comment on his or her experience along the lines of confirming, modifying, or adding to the commandments.

2. What does the concept of distance mentoring do to the availability of mentors? Are mentors available to you at a distance? What would you need to make mentoring at a distance work for you?

3. What advantages do you see in the "group mentoring" ideas?

4. Examine the commandments carefully in terms of a past mentoring situation in which you were involved. Which commandments could have aided that relationship?

Chapter Fourteen
FINISHING WELL

"Congratulations, you're halfway there!" read the handwriting across the top of a birthday card sent to me (Paul) on my thirty-fifth birthday (fifteen years ago!). I smiled as I assumed my friend referred to the psalmist's "three score and ten." I remember reflecting that thirty-five was on the short end today as people are living much longer. But then the next sentence on the card stirred my thinking: "May your second half be greater than your first."

The next day I thought further about my friend's birthday wish. Certainly that should be true for everyone at mid-life. Knowing what we know at age thirty-five and having a degree of maturity, some experience, and lots of energy . . . the next thirty-five years should be greater, more productive, meaningful, and highly contributive years. But how could I be sure to make it? There are so few who finish well!

The concern for finishing well launched me into an ongoing study of the subject. What does it mean to finish well? Who did? Who did not? Why? Since Bobby and I joined forces our studies have taken us through the Bible, across history and into biographies. We have observed contemporary leaders. These studies have been highly instructive, personally challenging, and sobering. We continue to be amazed by the large number of those who start following Christ, serving Him in many fields, intent on faithfulness and fruitfulness, and yet do not finish well. Something caused a loss of zeal, resolve, and love of Christ. For some it was a clear point of decision or an experience that became a fork in the road . . . and they did or did not choose the correct fork. For others it was an accumulation of little choices that moved them closer or further away from being Christ's disciple.

The Apostle Paul was obsessed with finishing well. He saw life as a race. When meeting with his beloved Ephesian elders for the last time, he said, "I consider my life worth nothing to me, if only I may finish the race and complete the task the Lord Jesus has given me—the task of testifying to the gospel of God's grace" (Acts 20:24). Paul was so motivated to finish well that he challenged the Corinthian believers to "Run [the race] in such a way as to get the prize. . . . Not . . . running aimlessly" (1 Corinthians 9:24-26). He disciplined his body to make it do what it must, not what it wanted to, so that "[having] preached to others, I myself will not be disqualified for the prize" (verse 27). What joy filled his heart as he testified at the end of his life: "I have fought the good fight, I have finished the race, I have kept the faith" (2 Timothy 4:7).

What moved the Apostle Paul to press on, go all

the way? It must have been the same thing that caused Daniel and his three buddies, Shadrach, Meshach, and Abednego, to fix their eyes on God and be His all the way to the end, no matter what. Or David, Joseph, the apostles, Barnabas, George Mueller, Billy Graham, and thousands of followers of Christ whose names will be known by few, but who have affected those who knew them.

To finish well does not mean to reach perfection, but, like Paul, to keep pressing on toward it. So when your time comes to an end, you are still growing in your love for Christ and intimacy with Him, still pressing on to make Him known, still living as His disciple and loving the people God places in your life, and relentlessly seeking to know and do God's will.

We have compared notes on the many leaders we have studied—those who have and have not finished well. Those who finished well seemed to share some common characteristics. Those who did not finish well were missing the same characteristics.

Table 14-1. Characteristics of Those Who Finish Well

1. They had perspective which enabled them to focus.
2. They enjoyed intimacy with Christ and experienced repeated times of inner renewal.
3. They were disciplined in important areas of life.
4. They maintained a positive learning attitude all their lives.
5. They had a network of meaningful relationships and several important mentors during their lifetime.

Perspective stands out as a characteristic of every good leader and finisher. It involves seeing the broader context of the present circumstance or relating what is happening to a long-range view. With clear and proper perspective, you can focus on the important or priority matters . . . without it you can lose focus.

A friend of mine in college used to buy jigsaw puzzles and organize team competitions in the dormitory to see who could put the puzzles together the fastest. They got to a point where the teams became quite good. One day they poured the puzzle pieces out on the floor but did not let the teams see the picture on the box. They were completely confused without an overall scheme to help them organize the pieces. It took hours instead of minutes.

Perspective is like the picture on the puzzle box. Without a clear focus for our lives and contributions, we will be prone to scatter our energies and slide into mediocrity . . . doing a little in a lot of areas but not having much effect in any. People who influence their world are people who can focus in appropriate areas and sustain that focus.

The Apostle Paul demonstrates the mutual effect that perspective and focus have on one another. In Philippians 1:12-19, Paul learned that some people who knew of his imprisonment were preaching about Christ with motives of rivalry, evil, and ambition. He could have become angry and urged the Christians to stop them, but his focus for ministry was to bring Christ to the Gentiles (Colossians 1:27, Galatians 2:7).

His perspective reminded him that God's salvation comes through the name of Jesus Christ, not through a presentation or the motive of the presenter . . . and God was using his difficult circumstances (jail, among others) to spread the gospel to the Gentile communities—his focus.

You develop perspective as you gain experience and reflect on that experience in the presence of God. Asaph, the writer of Psalm 73, was discouraged as he observed the wicked prosper and his own efforts to keep pure seemingly unrewarded. "When I tried to understand all this, it was oppressive to me till I entered the sanctuary of God; then I understood their final destiny" (verses 16-17). True perspective comes from God's Word and presence.

Focus develops as you begin to understand the priorities of Christ and personalize them. There is no shortcut to this. It simply demands time and investment into knowing Christ and His Word—allowing His mind to invade your mind. A mentor or peer who reflects this in his or her own life is a tremendous asset in this pursuit.

Intimacy with Christ forms the core of your inner being. Solomon, the King of Israel, wrote in Proverbs, "Above all else, guard your heart, for it is the wellspring of life" (4:23). *The power to lead and minister comes from the inner life.* This was the focus area of the Apostle Paul's life: to know Christ intimately (Philippians 3:10). He saw this as a lifelong pursuit that needed multiple inputs.

The promise of Christ in John 14:21 assures you that if you obey the commands of God, both the Father and Christ will love you and reveal more of themselves to you. Matthew 11:28-30 invites you to yoke up with Christ—to obey Him and co-labor with Him and, thereby, learn from Him. On one occasion as a boy I worked all day with my dad on a tough repair job. It was just the two of us—thinking, digging, grunting, sweating, talking—to repair a water pipe and valve. I learned more about him through that experience than at any other time. We "yoked up" together.

Spending time with Christ, seeking to obey Him, and joining Him as He ministers to His sheep (John 21:15-17, Matthew 25:40) will develop an intimacy with Christ that will affect every area of your life. Integrity and Christlike character will become part of you as the Holy Spirit possesses more of you and you experience close fellowship with Christ over a period of time.

When you see a breach of integrity in the outer life, it is a clear symptom of lack of integrity in the inner life that no one sees. And when there is a lack of integrity, there is no spiritual power, confidence, freedom, or transparency. The secret to inner integrity is intimacy with Christ.

Almost every leader we studied who did not finish well failed in the inner life. Their integrity broke down, and they made bad choices. Because they were aware of the growing gap between truth and life in the inner self and feared others discovering it, they drew away from the very fellowship they needed . . . and soon from fellowship with Christ.

Several years ago, I met an older brother who experienced intimacy with Christ by his demonstrated integrity, fruit of the Spirit (Galatians 5:22-23), and passion for Christ's glory. As I prayed with him, my heart became aware of the presence of Christ and the familiarity he had of the Master. I asked him about his relationship with the Lord Jesus and how it had developed. "It all began to change when I committed myself to Matthew 22:37-39: "'Love the Lord your God with all your heart and with all your soul and with all your mind.' This is the first and greatest commandment. And the second is like it: 'Love your neighbor as yourself.'"

His challenge moved my pursuit of intimacy to a deeper level. Have you ever tried to fulfill that command? Jesus did in His love for God the Father. Take a look at His life:

- ◆ *"Yet not my will, but yours be done."* (Luke 22:42)
- ◆ *"For I always do what pleases him."* (John 8:29)
- ◆ *"I do know him and keep his word."* (John 8:55)
- ◆ *"Now my heart is troubled, and what shall I say? 'Father, save me from this hour'? No, it was for this very reason I came to this hour. Father, glorify your name!"* (John 12:27-28)
- ◆ *"For I did not speak of my own accord, but the Father who sent me commanded me what to say and how to say it."* (John 12:49)
- ◆ *"I have brought you [the Father] glory on earth by completing the work you gave me to do."* (John 17:4)
- ◆ *"Put your sword away! Shall I not drink the cup the Father has given me?"* (John 18:11)

These verses reveal a surrendered spirit and will, a drive to please His father, a trust in all things . . . a passion for God's glory. Jesus was in harmony with

Him because He knew Him, brought all things to Him and spent time with Him. You can say, "That's Jesus; I could never do that!" Or you can begin to try . . . and God will meet you and empower your efforts. We can testify to that.

Discipline was not demonstrated in all areas by those who finished well, but definitely in the important ones—and even this varied. For instance, some were disciplined in their prayer and Bible study, but not in their diet. Some were disciplined in their schedules, but not in organization. And so it went on . . . but each had established discipline in the important areas.

Webster (1957) defines discipline as "training that develops self-control, character or orderliness and efficiency." In order to finish well you must be self-controlled and channel your energy in a specific direction. Nancy Moyer, an expert in working with talented and gifted children, told us, "There is nothing more disappointing than to watch talented children squander their God-given assets. Very few gifted children (or even adults) reach their potential for one simple reason: discipline."

In order to develop your gifts, abilities, and skills so that they become true assets and resources to your pursuit of life goals, discipline is required. In what areas? Those areas that are critical to one's finishing well.

When missionaries go to another culture or even to another kind of people to reach the lost, they commonly go into 1 Corinthians 9:19-23 to find instructions on adjusting their lifestyle to fit those they are trying to reach. In this passage Paul emphasized that the goal is "to win as many as possible." So he became "all things to all men"—the legalists, secularized, weak, strong—whoever. He did "all this for the sake of the gospel."

As a supervisor of missionaries I noticed that many struggled with lifestyle, for they fell into some of the abuses of the culture they were in or were greatly tempted. One fruitful missionary who seemed to be quite free and spiritually strong in the midst of those living contrary to the gospel shared his secret: "You've got to apply the last four verses [1 Corinthians 9]."

As we mentioned previously, in 1 Corinthians 9:24-27 Paul stresses the importance of perseverance and focus . . . with discipline! Verses 25 and 27 capture it: "To win the contest [race] you must deny yourself many things that would keep you from doing your best. . . . Like an athlete I punish my body, treating it roughly, training it to do what it should, not what it wants to" (TLB). Paul is talking about discipline and self-control. If you loosen up in your lifestyle, you must be disciplined in the areas that sustain your inner life or you may "be declared unfit and ordered to stand aside" or not finish the race.

What are the areas you see as crucial to your inner life or spiritual-life growth? What feeds your intimacy with Christ? Perhaps you need to bring discipline to these areas. Not discipline for discipline's sake, for that will soon turn to legalism and hardness. Rather, discipline for intimacy's sake . . . for growth's sake . . . for ministry's sake . . . for Christ's sake. Discipline in the right areas for the right reasons will sustain growth and set you up to respond to God's grace and His Spirit more completely.

We have observed that most people cease learning by the age of forty. By that we mean they no longer actively pursue knowledge, understanding, and experience that will enhance their capacity to grow and contribute to others. Most simply rest on what they already know. But those who finish well maintain a *positive learning attitude* all their lives.

Many people, particularly leaders, plateau. They become satisfied with where they are and with what they know. This often occurs after they attain enough to be comfortable or can maintain a relatively secure and predictable future. But this contradicts the biblical principle of stewardship.

We observed that God will often providentially challenge a believer to eventually take steps to develop and use his or her capacity for God's purposes and glory. Many are unaware of this capacity until God brings unusual guidance through people or events to stimulate growth. We all have a stewardship responsibility to continue to develop what God has given us.

Keeping a clear perspective will help you identify what you need to learn to keep growing and pursuing your focus point. Keeping in the company of those who value learning and growing is also helpful. Placing yourself into new or changing situations will stimulate your learning need.

My (Paul's) mother is eighty-five and is always reading a book, learning more about nutrition (her hobby), and talking to people about what is going on in their lives. When invited to attend a senior citizens' Bible study, she went once. Later she joined a Bible study with young women that required advanced preparation each week. I asked her why she didn't stay with the senior citizens' group. She replied, "Oh, they were sweet, but they just wanted to talk about the same things. I want to learn new things." And so she does, and she will finish well.

Every leader that we studied had a *network of meaningful relationships* and several important *mentors* during their lifetime. Since we discussed this network of relationships in the previous chapters, we will not repeat ourselves. But it is important to recognize that a few mentors and close peers in your life will help and encourage you in the other four aspects of finishing well. For instance:

◆ Mentors give perspective at crucial times in your development.
◆ Mentors are often aware of the need for renewal experiences and can help you interpret them.
◆ Mentors can detect and warn against negative patterns and the shying away from opportunity or abuse of power and authority in your life.
◆ Peers and mentors can stimulate and provide accountability for your personal life, growth, and intimacy with Christ.
◆ Peers and mentors can encourage you to develop the right disciplines and new perspectives.
◆ Peers and mentors can model values and a positive learning attitude.
◆ Mentors can spot signs of plateauing and stimulate learning.

You have observed by now that the "Character-istics of Those Who Finish Well" listed in table 14-1 serve to complement one another. We suggest that you begin to develop (or continue developing) one characteristic with a friend to mutually strengthen the efforts. You can develop these characteristics over a lifetime, and the earlier you start the greater chance you have of finishing your life well. Remember, your goal is not just to finish the race, but to finish *well*. And not just at the end of your life, but at the end of each day, month, and year. Make finishing well a habit and an attitude.

If we would add a sixth characteristic of those who finish well, it would be that *they help others be finishers*. To encourage this, we would like to close with a favorite poem. We have found it a real inspi-ration. Take time to read and think about it.

THE RACE
by D. H. Groberg[1]

I.

"Quit! Give up! You're beaten!"
They shout at me and plead.
"There's just too much against you now.
This time you can't succeed!"

And as I start to hang my head
In front of failure's face,
My downward fall is broken by
The memory of a race.

And hope refills my weakened will
As I recall that scene;
For just the thought of that short race
Rejuvenates my being.

II.

A children's race—young boys, young men
How I remember well.
Excitement, sure! But also fear;
It wasn't hard to tell.

They all lined up so full of hope;
Each thought to win that race.
Or tie for first, or if not that,
At least take second place.

And fathers watched from off the side,
Each cheering for his son.
And each boy hoped to show his dad
That he would be the one.

The whistle blew and off they went!
Young hearts and hopes afire.
To win and be the hero there
Was each young boy's desire.

And one boy in particular
Whose dad was in the crowd,
Was running near the lead and thought,
"My dad will be so proud!"

But as they speeded down the field
Across a shallow dip,
The little boy who thought to win
Lost his step and slipped.

Trying hard to catch himself
His hands flew out to brace,
And mid the laughter of the crowd
He fell flat on his face.

So down he fell and with him hope
He couldn't win it now—
Embarrassed, sad, he only wished
To disappear somehow.

But as he fell his dad stood up
And showed his anxious face,
Which to the boy so clearly said:
"Get up and win the race."

He quickly rose, no damage done.
Behind a bit, that's all—
And ran with all his mind and might
To make up for his fall.

So anxious to restore himself
To catch up and to win—
His mind went faster than his legs;
He slipped and fell again!

He wished then he had quit before
With only one disgrace.

"I'm hopeless as a runner now;
I shouldn't try to race."

But in the laughing crowd he searched
And found his father's face.
That steady look which said again:
"Get up and win the race!"

So up he jumped to try again
Ten yards behind the last—
"If I'm to gain those yards," he thought,
"I've got to move real fast."

Exerting everything he had
He gained eight or ten
But trying so hard to catch the lead
He slipped and fell again!

Defeat! He lay there silently
A tear dropped from his eye—
"There's no sense running any more;
Three strikes: I'm out! Why try?"

The will to rise had disappeared
All hope had fled away;
So far behind, so error prone;
A loser all the way.

"I've lost, so what's the use," he thought.
"I'll live with my disgrace."
But then he thought about his dad
Who soon he'd have to face.

"Get up," an echo sounded low.
"Get up and take your place;
You were not meant for failure here.
Get up and win the race."

"With borrowed will, get up," it said,
"You haven't lost at all,
For winning is no more than this:
To rise each time you fall."

So up he rose to run once more,
And with a new commit
He resolved that win or lose
At least he wouldn't quit.

So far behind the others now,
The most he'd ever been —
Still he gave it all he had
And ran as though to win.

Three times he'd fallen, stumbling;
Three times he rose again;
Too far behind to hope to win
He still ran to the end.

They cheered the winning runner
As he crossed the line first place,
Head high, and proud, and happy;
No falling, no disgrace.

But when the fallen youngster
Crossed the line last place,

The crowd gave him the greater cheer
For finishing the race.

And even though he came in last
With head bowed low, unproud,
You would have thought he'd won the
Race to listen to the crowd.

And to his dad he sadly said,
"I didn't do so well."
"To me, you won," his father said.
"You rose each time you fell."

III.

And now when things seem dark and hard
And difficult to face,
The memory of that little boy
Helps me in my own race.

For all of life is like that race,
With ups and downs and all.
And all you have to do to win,
Is rise each time you fall.

"Quit! Give up! You're beaten!"
They still shout in my face.
But another voice within me says:
"GET UP AND WIN THE RACE!"

APPENDIX:
HOW ADULTS LEARN–
FOUR GUIDING PRINCIPLES

Malcolm Knowles (1980:43-44) identifies four principles unique to adult learning that we have applied to the mentoring situation.

1. *Adults generally have a deep need for self-directed learning, even if that need varies between adults.*

    Implication: The mentor needs to understand this principle and capitalize on it as learning and growth are pursued. The mentoree should participate in designing his or her own development tasks. The mentor helps focus the learning/growth goal(s) and provides the resources, ideas, and feedback necessary for a sense of progress.

2. *Adults increasingly appreciate learning that takes place through experience.*

    Implication: For adult mentorees, experience is always a great teacher, as it draws upon their relevant knowledge and experience and stimulates the learning process. The alert mentor will use tasks and methods that are experience-based and/or include self-discovery experiences. Case studies, observation and design, discussion, experiment, simulation, field participation (activities that require application of concepts being learned), and evaluation are experience-based learning approaches.

3. *The learning readiness of adults arises primarily from the need to accomplish tasks and solve problems that real life creates.*

    Implication: Real-life situations create the questions and challenges that motivate mentorees to learn and grow in order to successfully deal with them. The wise mentor will take advantage of this motivation by helping the mentoree identify the appropriate solution (learning, personal growth, skill development, etc.) to his or her real-life need(s).

4. *Adults see learning as a process through which they can raise their competence in order to reach full potential in their lives. They want to apply tomorrow what they learn today.*

    Implication: Adults are motivated in the learning process by the results they perceive will benefit them personally. Therefore, the mentoree must perceive that there is significant personal growth in valued areas ahead and appropriate applications to present situations, otherwise he or she will abandon the process. The mentor needs to ensure that the connection between the mentoree's desires for growth and anticipated results is clear, personal, and realistic; then the mentor can facilitate such growth. Adults are goal-oriented in their learning.

NOTES

CHAPTER TWO — UNDERSTANDING MENTORING

1. Mentoring has become quite a focus for research. Dr. William A. Gray and Marilynne Miles Gray have trained over five thousand mentors and proteges in a variety of settings, such as major corporations, universities, government agencies, and school systems. They have formed Mentoring Institute Inc. for the purpose of training and promoting research in mentoring. A related enterprise, International Centre for Mentoring, publishes and distributes written materials on mentoring and coaching. *Mentoring International* is the journal.

2. Robert Bellah, et al., *Habits of the Heart* (University of California Press, 1985). Dealing with individualism and commitment in American life.

3. Our findings are derived from the comparative studies of six hundred leaders in many fields over a period of eight years.

4. Spiritual gifts that seem to work hand in hand with mentoring include mercy, giving, exhortation, teaching, faith, word of wisdom. These gifts all offer encouragement.

CHAPTER SIX—OCCASIONAL MENTORING:
THE COUNSELOR
1. From discussions with many professional counselors and
   our own observations, *accountability* is the missing and
   desperately needed factor in bringing about necessary
   change in a counselee's life (inner and behavioral). In certain cases the Counselor may not be in the best position
   to provide the accountability necessary for change. In such
   situations another mentor or peer can be very important to
   the change and development process.

CHAPTER SEVEN—OCCASIONAL MENTORING:
THE TEACHER
1. Walk Thru the Bible Ministries of Atlanta has excellent
   seminars and self-study videos on Gregory's laws and the
   "Seven Laws of the Learner."

CHAPTER EIGHT—OCCASIONAL MENTORING:
THE SPONSOR
1. We shall elaborate on this responsibility in depth in the
   chapter on downward mentoring when we talk about
   supervisory mentoring—that is, deliberately mentoring
   people who are under your line of authority.
2. Paul developed beyond Barnabas. Barnabas stepped down
   (switched roles with Paul), allowing Paul to further develop
   toward his potential as a leader. See Acts 13, where Paul
   takes charge.

CHAPTER NINE—PASSIVE MENTORING:
THE CONTEMPORARY MODEL
1. We have provided an annotated bibliography at the end of
   the book that will further serve as a resource for historical
   models.
2. In 1 Peter 5:3, Peter advocates modeling as a major leadership style by which pastors should influence their
   churches. Both Peter (1 Peter 2:21) and John (1 John 2:6)
   stress Christ's role as a Model for all followers of Christ, as
   does the author of Hebrews (Hebrews 12:1-3).
3. Goodwin in his booklet *The Effective Leader* (1981:41)
   identified this social dynamic. It has long been known
   in secular leadership circles. See Bass (1981). We have
   adapted Goodwin's wording, which is, "People have a

tendency to try to live up to the genuine expectations of persons whom they admire and respect."

CHAPTER TEN — PASSIVE MENTORING:
THE HISTORICAL MODEL
1. For seven years Bobby has surveyed leaders in his classes concerning how many biographies they have read. He looks for total read, the number that have impacted their lives, and the number that have been reread. The overwhelming majority of leaders have read five or less biographies. Almost everyone has been helped in some way by at least one biography. But most have not seen it as an ongoing means of development in their lives nor ever reread a biography.

CHAPTER ELEVEN — THE CONSTELLATION MODEL:
A RANGE OF NEEDED MENTORING
1. Because mentoring deals primarily with adults, it is important to review the motivations and uniqueness of adult learning. The appendix elaborates on Malcolm Knowles' (1980: 43-44) four principles to keep in mind.

CHAPTER FOURTEEN — FINISHING WELL
1. This poem has been in our files for several years, and we have not been able to discover the source.

REFERENCES CITED IN THIS BOOK

Allen, Ronald B.
1988   "Accountability in Leadership" in *Worship Times*, vol.
          2, no. 4.
Bass, Bernard M.
1981   *Stogdill's Handbook of Leadership: A Survey of
          Theory and Research.* New York: The Free Press.
Bellah, Robert, et al.
1985   *Habits of the Heart.* Berkeley, CA: University of
          California Press.
Boynton, Robert S.
1989   "Doctor Success" in *Manhattan, Inc.* August, pages
          52-59.
Clinton, J. Robert
1985   *Spiritual Gifts.* Alberta, Canada: Horizon House.
1989   *Leadership Emergence Theory.* Altadena, CA: Barna-
          bas Resources.
Covey, Stephen
1989   *The Seven Habits of Highly Effective People.* New
          York: Simon and Schuster.
Emenhiser, David L.
1989   Cassette tape on "Power Structures in Indianapolis."
          Hoke Communications.
Goodwin, Bennie E., II
1981   *The Effective Leader: A Basic Guide to Christian*

Leadership. Downers Grove, IL: InterVarsity Press.

Greenleaf, Robert
1983   *The Servant as Religious Leader.* Peterborough, NH:
        Center for Applied Studies.

Gregory, John Milton
1954   *The Seven Laws of Teaching.* Grand Rapids, MI:
        Baker Book House.

Hall, Clarence
1933   *Samuel Logan Brengle: Portrait of a Prophet.* New
        York: Salvation Army.

Jones, Timothy K.
1991   "Believer's Apprentice" in *Christianity Today.* March
        11, pages 42-44.

Knowles, Malcolm
1980   *Modern Practice of Adult Education, From Pedagogy
        to Andagogy.* Chicago: Follet Publishing.

Maxwell, L.E.
1945   *Born Crucified.* Chicago: Moody Press.

Pierson, Arthur T.
1899   *George Muller of Bristol.* Old Tappan, NJ: Fleming
        H. Revell.

Taylor, Dr. and Mrs. Howard
1935   *Hudson Taylor's Spiritual Secret.* Chicago: Moody.
1957   *Webster's New World Dictionary of the American Lan-
        guage.* New York: World Publishing.

ANNOTATED BIBLIOGRAPHY

GENERAL
Engstrom, Ted, and Norman B. Rohrer
1989   *The Fine Art of Mentoring.* Brentwood, TN: Wolge-
         muth and Hyatt Publishers.
             One of the first Christian books on mentoring.

HELPS FOR THE DISCIPLER
Bruce, Alexander B.
1971   *Training of the Twelve.* Grand Rapids, MI: Kregel
         Publications.
             A classic that explores Christ's discipleship
         model in detail.
Hull, Bill
1988   *The Disciple Making Pastor.* Old Tappan, NJ: Fleming
         H. Revell.
             An application of discipleship to the local
         church setting.
no name
1974   *The 2:7 Series — Navigator Discipleship Training
         for Laymen Courses 1–3.* Colorado Springs, CO:
         NavPress.
             The Navigator books used in small-group train-
         ing within a church setting. These are workbooks

with questions and exercises that seek to instill the basic discipleship habits over a protracted length of time. People must commit themselves to regular meetings.

Morley, Patrick
1989   *The Man in the Mirror: Solving the 24 Problems Men Fear.* Brentwood, TN: Wolgemuth and Hyatt.
     A real challenge in discipleship from a man with a clear vision for people.

Watson, David
1982   *Called and Committed.* Wheaton, IL: Harold Shaw Publishers.
     An overview of discipleship in the broadest sense. Not a book on techniques but of philosophy underlying discipleship.

Wilson, Carl
1976   *With Christ in the School of Disciple Building.* Grand Rapids, MI: Zondervan.
     This study on Christ's methods of building disciples discusses seven steps and seven important principles of discipling.

HELPS FOR THE SPIRITUAL GUIDE

Brother Lawrence
n.d.   *Practicing His Presence.* Philadelphia: The Judson Press.
     A classic focusing on a combination of the inner life and Spirit sensitivity.

Coombs, Maria Theresa, and Francis Kelly Nemeck
1986   *The Way of Spiritual Direction.* Wilmington, DE: Glazier.
     A Catholic book for use in training of Spiritual Guides. Stresses a focus on listening for what God is doing in the mentoree and working with that issue for development.

Guyon, Jeanne
1975   *Experiencing the Depths of Jesus Christ.* Goleta, CA: Christian Books.
     This French Catholic mystic has helped many to sense the Spirit of Christ in their lives. This translation concentrates on putting simply this Spiritual

Guide's secret to in-depth communion with God.
Also redone by Christian Books of Auburn, Maine.
MacDonald, Gordon
1988   *Rebuilding Your Broken World.* Nashville, TN: Thomas
        Nelson.
            There are consequences we must pay when we
        sin, but we serve a God of grace (and the "second
        chance") who is concerned about how we respond to
        His correction and grow and develop from it.
Maxwell, L. E.
1945   *Born Crucified.* Chicago: Moody Press.
            For those wanting to go deeper into discipleship.
        Good book to discuss one-on-one.
Molinos, Michael
1987   *The Spiritual Guide.* Auburn, ME: Christian Books.
            Deals with the contemplative life. Molinos, an
        Italian Catholic mystic who was imprisoned because
        of his emphasis on a personal relationship with God
        through Christ, gives a series of very short essays on
        various aspects of the inner life.
Nouwen, Henri J. M.
1972   *The Wounded Healer: Ministry in Contemporary Soci-
        ety.* New York: Doubleday.
1981   *The Way of the Heart.* New York: The Seabury Press.
            A seeker after a deeper spiritual walk shares
        findings from his own pilgrimage.
1989   *In the Name of Jesus — Reflections on Christian Lead-
        ership.* New York: Crossroads.
            Nouwen's books provide a source for lots of
        interaction for those who want to think about
        leadership and ministry from a very different per-
        spective. Emphasizes downward mobility.
Willard, Dallas
1989   *The Spirit of the Disciplines.* San Francisco: Harper
        and Row.
            This Protestant writer gives insights into spir-
        itual disciplines and shows why they are important
        for today.

HELPS FOR COUNSELORS
Augsburger, David W.
1986   *Pastoral Counseling Across Cultures.* Philadelphia:

The Westminster Press.

> One of the few counseling books that looks at the difference in counseling that originate due to differing cultures.

Crabb, Larry J.
1977   *Effective Biblical Counseling.* Grand Rapids, MI: Zondervan.

> Crabb took a year off to integrate psychology with biblical approaches to counseling. He did this sabbatical study in a church context. Probably the foremost book on counseling using a biblically based approach.

1989   *Inside Out.* Colorado Springs, CO: NavPress.

> This is practical help for lay and full-time Christian workers who are involved in serious counseling.

Egan, Gerald
1990   *Exercises in Helping Skills.* Pacific Grove, CA: Brooks/Cole Publishing Co.

> Companion book for his text *The Skilled Helper.*

1990   *The Skilled Helper.* 4th ed. Pacific Grove, CA: Brooks/Cole Publishing Co.

> This is one of the best-selling books on training anyone in counseling. Used as a text in many formal counseling courses.

Linn, Dennis, and Matthew Linn
1978   *Healing Life's Hurts.* New York: Paulist Press.

> These Catholic priests have a ministry in inner healing. This book, along with Sandford's, is considered a basic text for inner healing. They have an interesting thesis. Forgiveness is a major issue in all inner healing. They take the five steps in death and dying and apply them function-wise to the process of forgiveness.

Sandford, John, and Paula Sandford
1982   *The Transformation of the Inner Man.* South Plainfield, NJ: Bridge.

> The most comprehensive book on inner healing. Any person in momentary counseling dealing with inner healing should have this book in his or her library.

Seamands, David
1981   *Healing for Damaged Emotions.* Wheaton, IL: Victor.

1985   *Healing of Memories.* Wheaton, IL: Victor.
        Both of Seamands' books have a well-balanced
        approach to counseling and inner healing.
Smalley, Gary, and John Trent
1986   *The Blessing.* Nashville, TN: Thomas Nelson.

HELPS FOR TEACHERS
Gregory, John Milton
1954   *The Seven Laws of Teaching.* Grand Rapids, MI:
        Baker Book House.
        Gregory, a Christian and foremost educator
        in the nineteenth century, identified the dynamics
        of good teaching. Focuses on the teaching side of
        the teacher/learner combination. This is a classic
        that will help anyone who wants to communicate
        to others.
Hendriks, Howard G.
1987   *Teaching to Change Lives.* Portland, OR: Multnomah
        Press and Walk Thru the Bible Ministries.
        A professor who is a powerful Teacher-mentor
        gives insights into this form of mentoring. He has
        consistently applied Gregory's seven laws in his min-
        istry in creative ways.
Shafer, Carl
1985   *Excellence in Teaching with the Seven Laws.* Grand
        Rapids, MI: Baker Book House.
        A modern explanation of Gregory's seven laws.

HELPS FOR COACHES
Blanchard, Kenneth, and Spencer Johnson
1981   *The One Minute Manager.* New York: William Morrow.
        Excellent primer in helping those who are begin-
        ning to lead others.
Clinton, J. Robert
1984   *Reading on the Run.* Altadena, CA: Barnabas
        Resources.
        This self-instructional booklet coaches one in
        effective reading techniques. Its basic thesis is that
        different books must be read at different levels:
        scanned, ransacked, browsed, and in-depth. Each
        type of reading has certain procedures that can be
        followed. One can learn very effectively by reading

selectively with a purpose and without reading
every word.

1988   *Making of a Leader.* Colorado Springs, CO: NavPress.
Especially for those thirty and older who want
to develop further in their life and not plateau. God
is the one who develops His leaders by allowing circumstances and people to come into their lives. How
they process and respond to them is key.

Covey, Stephen

1989   *The Seven Habits of Highly Effective People.* New
York: Simon and Schuster.
This book coaches one on how to bring focus
to a life.

DePree, Max

1989   *Leadership Is an Art.* New York: Doubleday.
Contains many nuggets of wisdom profitable for
discussion with other leaders.

Griffen, Em

1982   *Getting Together: A Guide for Good Groups.* Downers
Grove, IL: Intervarsity Press.
Coaching on how to handle small groups. There
are now hundreds of books out on small groups that
can effectively help in this special and needed function in church life.

Morley, Patrick

1989   *The Man in the Mirror: Solving the 24 Problems Men
Face.* Brentwood, TN: Wolgemuth and Hyatt.
Good to use in a support group as basis for
accountability issues.

Wagner, C. Peter

1988   *How to Have a Healing Ministry without Making Your
Church Sick!* Ventura, CA: Regal.
Coaching on the change dynamics of starting
a healing ministry so as to gain its benefits with
a minimum loss in a local church setting. Shows
the benefits of this kind of ministry for a local
church setting.

HELPS FOR SPONSORS
Bagnal, Charles W., Earl C. Pence, and Thomas N.
Meriwhether

1985   "Leaders as Mentors" in *Military Review*, July.

In 1985, the secretary of the Army and the chief
of staff established leadership as the Army theme.
This article is important because it shows that the
military view mentoring as an important means of
instilling leadership.

Kram, Kathy E.
1985   *Mentoring at Work—Developmental Relationships in
Organizational Life.* Glenview, IL: Scott, Foresman,
and Co.
A very good treatment of mentoring in the secular world. It identifies four phases in a sponsorship
mentoring situation, talks about lateral mentoring,
gives much practical advice.

Zey, Michael G.
1984   *The Mentor Connection.* Homewood, IL: Dow Jones-
Irwin.
Deals with the Sponsor-mentor and mentoree.
Gives some good warnings in a chapter entitled the
Negative Side of Mentoring.

HISTORICAL MODELS—BIOGRAPHIES
Aldridge, Alfred
1964   *Jonathan Edwards.* New York: Washington Square
Press.
He illustrates the power of a pastor/teacher/
educator in a lifetime of ministry. He was used by
God to begin one of the major revivals in American
history. Values: spiritual guidance, teacher, contemporary model of his time, a pastoral/educator type
of hero.

Allen, Catherine
1980   *The New Lottie Moon Story.* Nashville, TN: Broadman.
A Southern Baptist missionary in China. A cru-
sader and missionary heroine.

Anderson, Courtney
1972   *To the Golden Shore: The Life of Adoniram Judson.*
Grand Rapids, MI: Zondervan.
The major pioneer in American mission history.
A missionary hero.

Athanasius
1980   *The Life of Anthony.* New York: Paulist Press.
Deep spiritual life. Anthony was a monk who

lived in the fourth century. He was driven into the desert in a search for God. His life and example attracted many others who were seeking God. He operated in his last years as a Spiritual Guide and a Counselor.

Ayling, Stanley
1979   *John Wesley.* Cleveland, OH: Collins.
        Illustrates Coach and Teacher types. A church/ innovator hero.

Beets, Henry
1937   *Johanna of Nigeria: Life and Labors of Johanna Veenstra.* Grand Rapids, MI: Grand Rapids Printing Company.
        A missionary heroine.

Bentley-Taylor, David
1975   *My Love Must Wait: The Story of Henry Martyn.* Downers Grove, IL: InterVarsity Press.
        Martin was a mentoree of Charles Simeon. A missionary hero who has inspired many concerning Islamic work.

Bishop, Morris
1974   *Saint Francis of Assisi.* Boston: Little, Brown.
        A model of deep spiritual life in practical terms.

Bobe, Louis
1952   *Hans Egede: Colonizer and Missionary of Greenland.* Copenhagen, Denmark: Rosenkilde and Bagger.
        A missionary hero.

Broderick, James
1952   *Saint Francis Xavier.* New York: Wicklow.
        A missionary hero in the far east.

Broomhall, Marshall
1924   *Robert Morrison: A Master-builder.* New York: Doran.
        A missionary hero to China.

Carlson, Lois
1966   *Monganga Paul: The Congo Ministry and Martyrdom of Paul Carlson, M.D.* New York: Harper and Row.
        A missionary hero to Africa.

Christian, Carol, and Gladys Plummer
1970   *God and One Red Head: Mary Slessor of Calabar.* Grand Rapids, MI: Zondervan.
        A missionary heroine.

Conwell, Russell H.
1892   *Life of Charles Haddon Spurgeon.* New Haven, CT:
         Edgewood Publishing.
            An evangelist and pastor hero who also founded
         numerous Christian organizations—including his
         children's homes.

Crossman, Eileen
1982   *Mountain Rain.* Singapore: OMF Books.
            A missionary hero to tribes in southwest China.
         Shows the power of prayer in a ministry.

Dallimore, Arnold
1970   *George Whitefield: The Life and Time of the Great*
         Evangelist. London: Banner of Truth Trust.
            Evangelist who was instrumental in the Great
         Awakening in Britain and the United States in the
         eighteenth century.

Donze, Mary Terese
1982   *Teresa of Avila.* New York: Paulist Press.
            A Catholic feminine model of deep spiritual life.

Drewery, Mary
1979   *William Carey: A Biography.* Grand Rapids, MI:
         Zondervan.
            The missionary pioneer who inspired Protestant
         missionary work in the late eighteenth century. A
         real missionary hero.

DuPlessie, Johanes
1920   *The Life of Andrew Murray of South Africa.* London:
         Marshall Brothers.
            Murray lived and taught the "deeper life"
         message.

Edwards, Jonathan
1949   *Life and Diary of David Brainerd.* Chicago: Moody.
            Brainerd was an early American missionary to
         Indians in colonial America. His diary gives insights
         about the struggle of the inner life.

Elliot, Elisabeth
1950   *Shadow of the Almighty.* New York: Harper & Brothers.
            The story of Jim Elliot, missionary martyred by
         Auca Indians in Ecuador.
1968   *Who Shall Ascend: The Life of R. Kenneth Strachan of*
         Costa Rica. New York: Harper and Row.
            An important work for at least two reasons. Sets

a new tone in Christian biographical genre. Gives the life of an innovative "missionary kid" who maintained a learning posture all his life. A missionary hero in Latin America who fostered several movements including indigenous leadership in missions and country-wide evangelism.

Fox, George

1901   *Journal of George Fox; Being an Historical Account of His Life, Travels, Sufferings, Christian Experience.* London: Friends' Tract Association.

        The founder of the Friends (Quaker Movement). A church hero.

Francis, Convers

1969   *Life of John Eliot, the Apostle to the Indians.* New York: Garett.

        A missionary hero.

Fullerton, W. Y.

n.d.   *F. B. Meyer: A Biography.* London: Marshall, Morgan & Scott.

        A church hero from England.

Goforth, Rosalind

1937   *Goforth of China.* Grand Rapids, MI: Zondervan.

        A missionary hero to China. This Canadian Presbyterian was a flexible leader who was able to learn and adapt all his life. An inspirational model for knowing and using one's Bible.

Green, Melody, and David Hazard

1989   *No Compromise: The Life Story of Keith Green.* Chatsworth, CA: Sparrow Press.

        Keith Green was a musician in the late 1960s through the early 1980s who was used by God to challenge his generation through his passionate music and message.

Greenway, George William

1955   *Saint Boniface.* London: Adam and Charles Black.

        A Catholic example of deep inner life.

Grubb, Norman P.

1969   *Once Caught, No Escape: My Life Story.* Fort Washington, PA: Christian Literature Crusade.

        A proponent of Union Life.

1972   *C. T. Studd: Cricketer and Pioneer.* Fort Washington, PA: Christian Literature Crusade.

A missionary hero to Africa who had a strong task orientation.

1973   *Rees Howells Intercessor.* London: Lutterworth Press. Models a spiritual life which focuses on intercession.

Hall, Clarence

1933   *Samuel Logan Brengle; Portrait of a Prophet.* New York: Salvation Army.
A Protestant model of deep spiritual life.

Hefley, James, and Marti Hefley

1974   *Uncle Cam: The Story of William Cameron Townsend, Founder of the Wycliffe Bible Translators and the Summer Institute of Linguistics.* Waco, TX: Word.
A missionary statesman with big vision.

Hitt, Russell T.

1973   *Jungle Pilot: The Life and Witness of Nate Saint.* Grand Rapids, MI: Zondervan.
A "helps" oriented missionary who was martyred by the Auca Indians of South America. Practical piety.

Hopkins, C. Howard

1979   *John R. Mott, 1865–1955: A Biography.* Grand Rapids, MI: Eerdmans.
A missionary statesman with wide sphere of influence.

Hopkins, Hugh Alexander

1977   *Charles Simeon of Cambridge.* London: Hodder and Stoughton.
Simeon was a mentor with wide influence. His ministry philosophy shows the importance of focus. A pastor hero in England.

Horst, Irvin

n.d.   *A Biography of Menno Simons.* Nieuwpoort: B. Le Groat.
He was an early leader of the Dutch Anabaptists who, because of his preaching influence, changed their names to "Mennonites." A church hero.

Houghton, Frank

1954   *Amy Carmichael of Dohnavur.* London: Society for the Propagation of Christian Knowledge.
A missionary heroine to India. An excellent example of someone who was mentored and in turn

went on to mentor others.

Howard, Philip Eugene
1944   *Charles Galaudet Trumball: Apostle of the Victorious
        Life.* Philadelphia: Sunday School Times.
            A Protestant model of victorious Christian
        life.

Hunter, J. H.
1961   *A Flame of Fire: The Life and Work of R. V. Bingham.*
        Scarborough, Ontario, Canada: Sudan Interior
        Mission.
            A missionary hero.

Kinnear, Angus
1973   *Against the Tide.* Wheaton, IL: Tyndale House
        Publishers.
            The story of Watchman Nee—Chinese pastor
        and head of mission.

Lennox, Cuthbert
1902   *James Chalmers of New Guinea.* London: Melrose.
            A missionary hero.

Livingstone, W. P.
1915   *Mary Slessor of Calabar: Pioneer Missionary.* London:
        Hodder and Stoughton.
            A missionary heroine.

Mackie, Robert
1965   *Laymen Extraordinary: John R. Mott, 1865–1955.*
        New York: Association.
            A missionary statesman.

McQuilkin, Marguerite
1956   *Always in Triumph.* Columbia, SC: Bible College
        Bookstore.
            Founder of Columbia Bible College.

Miller, Basil
1943   *Praying Hyde.* Grand Rapids, MI: Zondervan.
            A missionary in India who found the power of
        prayer and intercession.
1948   *Wildred Grenfell, Labrador's Dogsled Doctor.* Grand
        Rapids, MI: Zondervan.
            A missionary hero.

Moody, William R.
1900   *The Life of Dwight L. Moody.* New York: Fleming
        H. Revell.
            The American pastor and evangelist.

Neely, Lois
1980   *Come Up to This Mountain: The Miracle of Clarence W. Jones and HCJB.* Wheaton, IL: Tyndale House Publishers.
        The founder of an important Christian radio station in Ecuador.
Northcott, Cecil
1973   *David Livingstone: His Triumph, Decline, and the Fall.* Philadelphia: Westminster.
        A missionary pioneer.
1973   *Robert Moffat: Pioneer in Africa, 1817-1870.* London: Lutterworth Press.
        A missionary hero.
Palau, Luis (as told to Jerry B. Jenkins)
1980   *The Luis Palau Story.* Old Tappan, NJ: Fleming H. Revell.
        Latin American evangelist with widespead ministry around the world.
Paton, William
1922   *Alexander Duff: Pioneer of Missionary Education.* New York: Doran.
        A missionary hero.
Peterson, William J.
1967   *Another Hand on Mine: The Story of Dr. Carl K. Becker of Africa Inland Mission.* New York: McGraw-Hill.
        A missionary hero.
Pierson, A.T.
1972   *George Mueller of Bristol.* London: Pickering and Inglis.
        Early Christian worker with Brethren movement and founder of huge orphanage. An inspiration in terms of trusting God.
Pike, Eunice V.
1981   *Ken Pike: Scholar and Christian.* Dallas: Summer Institute of Linguistics.
        Wycliffe Bible Translator and Summer Institute of Linguistics stalwart.
Pollock, J. C.
1976   *Hudson Taylor and Maria: Pioneers in China.* Grand Rapids, MI: Zondervan.
        Missionary innovator.

Ransford, Oliver
1978   *David Livingstone: The Dark Interior.* New York: St.
         Martins.
             Pioneer missionary hero.
Richards, Thomas Cole
1906   *Samuel J. Mills, Missionary Pathfinder, Pioneer and
         Promotor.* Boston: The Pilgrim Press.
             A founder of many Christian organizations or
         movements.
Rohrer, Norman B., and Peter Deyneka, Jr.
1975   *Peter Dynamite: The Story of Peter Deyneka—
         Missionary to the Russian World.* Grand Rapids,
         MI: Baker.
             Founder of mission organization, The Slavic
         Gospel Association.
Schaeffer, Edith
1981   *The Tapestry: The Life and Times of Francis and
         Edith Schaeffer.* Waco, TX: Word.
             Leaders in Christian apologetics and founders
         of L'Abri.
Spink, Kathryn
1982   *The Miracle of Love: Mother Teresa of Calcutta.* New
         York: Harper and Row.
             A contemporary Catholic model of Christ's
         values put into action.
Steer, Roger
1975   *George Mueller—Delighted in God.* London: Hodder
         and Stoughton.
             Founder of orphanage in England. He lived
         by the principle of letting his needs be known
         only to God.
Taylor, Dr. and Mrs. Howard
1935   *Hudson Taylor's Spiritual Secret.* Chicago: Moody.
             A missionary testimony of making God his
         resource, which often led him to leave the main-
         stream and standard ways of ministry of his day.
Taylor, Mrs. Howard
1960   *The Triumph of John and Betty Stam.* Philadelphia:
         China Inland Mission.
             Missionaries martyred in China.
Thompson, A. E.
1920   *The Life of A. B. Simpson.* New York: Christian

Alliance Publishing.
Founder of the Christian and Missionary Alliance.

Upham, T. C.
1984   *The Story of Madame Guyon's Life.* Augusta, GA: Christian Books.
Madame Guyon lived in France during the late 1600s and early 1700s. She was a Spiritual Guide and Counselor to many.

Weinlick, John R.
1956   *Count Zinzendorf.* Nashville, TN: Abingdon.
Involved in one of the great Christian movements. A model of piety.

Wessel, Helen, ed.
1977   *The Autobiography of Charles G. Finney.* Minneapolis, MN: Bethany Fellowship.
Evangelist/educator with powerful impact in the mid-1800s.

Whitney, Janet
1972   *Elizabeth Fry, Quaker Heroine.* New York: B. Blom.
A heroine who confronted social problems of the day—prisons/crime.

Wilson, J. Christy
1970   *Flaming Prophet: The Story of Samuel Zwemer.* New York: Friendship.
Inspiring missionary hero.